WITHDRAWN

Winter's Tales 26

Winter's Tales 26

Edited by
A. D. Maclean

St. Martin's Press
New York

Library of Congress Catalog Card No. 80-52132

First published in the United States of America in 1980.

Printed in Great Britain

ISBN 0-312-88414-1

Contents

Acknowledgements

The stories are copyright respectively

© 1980 Brian Aldiss
© 1979 and 1980 Beryl Bainbridge
© 1962 and 1980 Christopher Burney
© 1980 Douglas Dunn
© 1979 Nadine Gordimer
© 1979 Angela Huth
© 1980 Francis King
© 1979 Edna O'Brien
© 1980 Julia O'Faolain
© 1980 William Trevor
© 1980 Tobias Wolff

Nadine Gordimer's 'Rags and Bones' appeared in *Harpers*; 'Ladies' Race' has not been published in the United Kingdom but was included in Angela Huth's collection of stories *Infidelities* published in the United States by Clarkson Potter; Edna O'Brien's 'Kin' has appeared under the title 'My Mother's Mother' in *The New Yorker* and the *Irish Press*; and William Trevor's 'Autumn Sunshine' in *The New Yorker*.

A much longer version of Christopher Burney's 'Descent from Ararat' was published by Macmillan in 1962.

A slightly different version of Beryl Bainbridge's 'Beggars Would Ride' appeared in *The Listener* under the title 'Love and Best Wishes'.

Editor's Note

OF THE eleven contributors to *Winter's Tales 26*, six have had stories in earlier volumes and five — Beryl Bainbridge, Douglas Dunn, Angela Huth, Christopher Burney and Tobias Wolff — are very welcome newcomers to the series.

I should perhaps add something about Christopher Burney's 'Descent from Ararat' because a longer version of the story was published on its own in book form in 1962. Christopher Burney has already written two classic books (to be reissued together next year), *The Dungeon Democracy* and *Solitary Confinement*, about the three years he spent as a prisoner of the Nazis first in Fresnes prison in Paris and later in Buchenwald. Fifteen years after his liberation he was moved to write again, partly perhaps to try to illuminate the darkness which lay over the years following the end of the War. He has now cut the original, and I believe it to be both interesting and valuable as well as a successful story in its own right.

A.D. MACLEAN

Autumn Sunshine

William Trevor

THE RECTORY was in County Wexford, eight miles from Enniscorthy. It was a handsome eighteenth-century house, with Virginia creeper covering three sides and a tangled garden full of buddleia and struggling japonica which had always been too much for its incumbents. It stood alone, seeming lonely even, approximately at the centre of the country parish it served. Its church — St Michael's Church of Ireland — was two miles away, in the village of Boharbawn.

For twenty-six years the Morans had lived there, not wishing to live anywhere else. Canon Moran had never been an ambitious man; his wife, Frances, had found contentment easy to attain in her lifetime. Their four girls had been born in the rectory, and had become a happy family there. They were grown up now, Frances's death was still recent: like the rectory itself, its remaining occupant was alone in the countryside. The death had occurred in the spring of the year, and the summer had somehow been bearable. The clergyman's eldest daughter had spent May and part of June at the rectory with her children. Another one had brought her family for most of August, and a third was to bring her newly married husband in the winter. At Christmas nearly all of them would gather at the rectory and some would come at Easter. But that September, as the days drew in, the season was melancholy.

Then, one Tuesday morning, Slattery brought a letter from Canon Moran's youngest daughter. There were two other letters as well, in unsealed buff envelopes which meant that they were either bills or receipts. Frail and grey-haired in his elderliness, Canon Moran had been wondering if he should give the lawn in front of the house a last cut when he heard the approach of Slattery's van. The lawnmower was the kind that had to be pushed, and in the spring the job was always easier if the grass had been cropped close at the end of the previous summer.

'Isn't that a great bit of weather, Canon?' Slattery remarked, winding down the window of the van and passing out the three envelopes. 'We're set for a while, would you say?'

'I hope so, certainly.'

'Ah, we surely are, sir.'

The conversation continued for a few moments longer, as it did whenever Slattery came to the rectory. The postman was young and easy-going, not long the successor to old Mr O'Brien, who'd been making the round on a bicycle when the Morans first came to the rectory in 1952. Mr O'Brien used to talk about his garden; Slattery talked about fishing, and often brought a share of his catch to the rectory.

'It's a great time of year for it,' he said now, 'except for the darkness coming in.'

Canon Moran smiled and nodded; the van turned round on the gravel, dust rising behind it as it moved swiftly down the avenue to the road. Everyone said Slattery drove too fast.

He carried the letters to a wooden seat on the edge of the lawn he'd been wondering about cutting. Deirdre's handwriting hadn't changed since she'd been a child; it was round and neat, not at all a reflection of the girl she was. The blue English stamp, the Queen in profile blotched a bit by the London postmark, wasn't on its side or half upside down, as you might possibly expect with Deirdre. Of all the Moran children, she'd grown up to be the only difficult one. She hadn't come to the funeral and hadn't written about her mother's death. She hadn't been to the rectory for three years.

'I'm sorry,' she wrote now. *'I couldn't stop crying actually. I've never known anyone as nice or as generous as she was. For ages I didn't even want to believe she was dead. I went on imagining her in the rectory and doing the flowers in church and shopping in Enniscorthy.'*

Deirdre was twenty-one now. He and Frances had hoped she'd go to Trinity and settle down, but although at school she'd seemed to be the cleverest of their children she'd had no desire to become a student. She'd taken the Rosslare boat to Fishguard one night, having said she was going to spend a week with her friend Maeve Coles in Cork. They hadn't known she'd gone to England until they received a picture postcard from London telling them not to worry, saying she'd found work in an egg-packing factory.

'Well, I'm coming back for a little while now,' she wrote, *'if you could put up with me and if you wouldn't find it too much. I'll cross over to Rosslare on the twenty-ninth, the morning crossing, and then I'll come on to Enniscorthy on the bus. I don't know what time it will be but there's a pub just by where the bus drops you so could we meet in the small bar there at six o'clock and then I won't have to lug my cases too far? I hope you won't mind going into such a place. If you can't make it, or don't want to see me, it's understandable, so if you don't turn up by half six I'll see if I can get a bus on up to Dublin. Only I need to get back to Ireland for a while.'*

It was, as he and Slattery had agreed, a lovely autumn. Gentle sunshine mellowed the old garden, casting an extra sheen of gold on leaves that were gold already. Roses that had been ebullient in June and July bloomed modestly now. Michaelmas daisies were just beginning to bud. Already the crab-apples were falling, hydrangeas had a forgotten look. Canon Moran carried the letter from his daughter into the walled vegetable-garden and leaned against the side of a greenhouse, half sitting on a protruding ledge, reading the letter again. Panes of glass were broken in the greenhouse, white paint and putty needed to be renewed, but inside a vine still thrived, and was heavy now with black ripe fruit. Later that morning he would pick some and drive into Enniscorthy, to sell the grapes to Mrs Roche in Slaney Street.

'Love, Deirdre': the letter was marvellous. Beyond the rectory the fields of wheat had been harvested, and the remaining stubble had the same tinge of gold in the autumn light; the beech-trees and the chestnuts were triumphantly magnificent. But decay and rotting were only weeks away, and the letter from Deirdre was full of life. *'Love, Deirdre'* were words more beautiful than all the seasons's glories. He prayed as he leaned against the sunny greenhouse, thanking God for this salvation.

For all the years of their marriage Frances had been a help. As a younger man, Canon Moran hadn't known quite what to do. He'd been at a loss among his parishioners, hesitating in the face of this weakness or that: the pregnancy of Alice Pratt in 1954, the argument about grazing rights between Mr Willoughby and Eugene Ryan in 1960, the theft of an altar cloth from St Michael's and reports that Mrs Tobin had been seen wearing it as a skirt. Alice Pratt had been going out with a Catholic boy, one of Father Hayes's flock, which made the matter more difficult than ever. Eugene Ryan was one of Father Hayes's also, and so was Mrs Tobin.

'Father Hayes and I had a chat,' Frances had said, and she'd had a chat as well with Alice Pratt's mother. A month later Alice Pratt married the Catholic boy, but to this day attended St Michael's every Sunday, the children going to Father Hayes. Mrs Tobin was given Hail Marys to say by the priest; Mr Willoughby agreed that his father had years ago granted Eugene Ryan the grazing rights. Everything, in these cases and in many others, had come out all right in the end: order emerged from the confusion that Canon Moran so disliked, and it was Frances who had always begun the process, though no one ever said in the rectory that she understood the mystery of people as well as he understood the teachings of the New Testament. She'd been a freckle-faced girl when he'd married her, pretty in her way. He was the one with the brains.

Frances had seen human frailty everywhere: it was weakness in people, she said, that made them what they were as much as strength did. And she herself had her own share of such frailty, falling short in all sorts of ways of the God's image her husband preached about. With the small amount of housekeeping money she could be allowed she was a spendthrift, and she said she was lazy. She loved clothes and often overreached herself on visits to Dublin; she sat in the sun while the rectory gathered dust and the garden became rank; it was only where people were concerned that she was practical. But for what she was her husband had loved her with unobtrusive passion for fifty years, appreciating her conversation and the help she'd given him because she could so easily sense the truth. When he'd found her dead in the garden one morning he'd felt he had lost some part of himself.

Though many months had passed since then, the trouble was

that Frances hadn't yet become a ghost. Her being alive was still too recent, the shock of her death too raw. He couldn't distance himself; the past refused to be the past. Often he thought that her fingerprints were still in the rectory, and when he picked the grapes or cut the grass of the lawn it was impossible not to pause and remember other years. Autumn had been her favourite time.

'Of course I'd come,' he said. 'Of course, dear. Of course.'

'I haven't treated you very well.'

'It's over and done with, Deirdre.'

She smiled, and it was nice to see her smile again, although it was strange to be sitting in the back bar of a public house in Enniscorthy. He saw her looking at him, her eyes passing over his clerical collar and black clothes, and his thin quiet face. He could feel her thinking that he had aged, and putting it down to the death of the wife he'd been so fond of.

'I'm sorry I didn't write,' she said.

'You explained in your letter, Deirdre.'

'It was ages before I knew about it. That was an old address you wrote to.'

'I guessed.'

In turn he examined her. Years ago she'd had her long hair cut. It was short now, like a neat black cap on her head. And her face had lost its chubbiness, hollows where her cheeks had been, making her eyes more dominant, pools of seaweed green. He remembered her child's stocky body, and the uneasy adolescence that had spoilt the family's serenity. Her voice had lost its Irish intonation.

'I'd have met you off the boat, you know.'

'I didn't want to bother you with that.'

'Oh, now, it isn't far, Deirdre.'

She drank Irish whiskey, and smoked a brand of cigarettes called Three Castles. He'd asked for a mineral himself, and the woman serving them had brought him a bottle of something that looked like water but which fizzed up when she'd poured it. A kind of lemonade he imagined it was, and didn't much care for it.

'I have grapes for Mrs Roche,' he said.

'Who's that?'

'She has a shop in Slaney Street. We always sold her the grapes. You remember?'

She didn't, and he reminded her of the vine in the greenhouse. A shop surely wouldn't be open at this hour of the evening, she said, forgetting that in a country town of course it would be. She asked if the cinema was still the same in Enniscorthy, a cement building halfway up a hill. She said she remembered bicycling home from it at night with her sisters, not being able to keep up with them. She asked after her sisters and he told her about the two marriages that had taken place since she'd left: she had in-laws she'd never met, and nephews and a niece.

They left the bar and he drove his dusty black Vauxhall straight to the small shop he'd spoken of. She remained in the car while he carried into the shop two large chip-baskets full of grapes. Afterwards Mrs Roche came to the door with him.

'Well, is that Deirdre?' she said as Deirdre wound down the window of the car. 'I'd never know you, Deirdre.'

'She's come back for a little while,' Canon Moran explained, raising his voice a little because he was walking round the car to the driver's seat as he spoke.

'Well, isn't that grand?' said Mrs Roche.

Everyone in Enniscorthy knew Deirdre had just gone off, but it didn't matter now. Mrs Roche's husband, who was a red-cheeked man with a cap, much smaller than his wife, appeared beside her in the shop doorway. He inclined his head in greeting, and Deirdre smiled and waved at both of them. Canon Moran thought it was pleasant when she went on waving while he drove off.

In the rectory he lay wakeful that night, his mind excited by Deirdre's presence. He would have loved Frances to know, and guessed that she probably did. He fell asleep at half-past two and dreamed that he and Frances were young again, that Deirdre was still a baby. The freckles on Frances's face were out in profusion, for they were sitting in the sunshine in the garden, tea things spread about them, the children playing some game among the shrubs. It was autumn then also, the last of the September heat. But because he was younger in his dream he didn't feel part of the season himself, nor sense its melancholy.

A week went by. The time passed slowly because a lot was happening, or so it seemed. Deirdre insisted on cooking all the meals and on doing the shopping in Boharbawn's single shop or in Enniscorthy. She still smoked her endless cigarettes, but the peakiness there had been in her face when she'd first arrived wasn't quite so pronounced — or perhaps, he thought, he'd become used to it. She told him about the different jobs she'd had in London and the different places she'd lived in, because on the postcards she'd occasionally sent there hadn't been room to go into detail. In the rectory they had always hoped she'd managed to get a training of some sort, though guessing she hadn't. In fact, her jobs had been of the most rudimentary kind: as well as her spell in the egg-packing factory, there'd been a factory that made plastic earphones, a cleaning job in a hotel near Euston, and a year working for the Use-Us Office Cleansing Service. 'But you can't have liked any of that work, Deirdre?' he suggested, and she agreed she hadn't.

From the way she spoke he felt that that period of her life was over: adolescence was done with; she had steadied and taken stock. He didn't suggest to her that any of this might be so, not wishing to seem either too anxious or too pleased, but he felt she had returned to the rectory in a very different frame of mind from the one in which she'd left it. He imagined she would remain for quite a while, still taking stock, and in a sense occupying her mother's place. He thought he recognised in her a loneliness that matched his own, and he wondered if it was a feeling that their loneliness might be shared which had brought her back at this particular time. Sitting in the drawing-room while she cooked or washed up, or gathering grapes in the greenhouse while she did the shopping, he warmed delightedly to this theme. It seemed like an act of God that their circumstances should interlace this autumn. By Christmas she would know what she wanted to do with her life and in the spring that followed she would perhaps be ready to set forth again. A year would have passed since the death of Frances.

'I have a friend,' Deirdre said when they were having a cup of coffee together in the middle of one morning. 'Someone who's been good to me.'

She had carried a tray to where he was composing next week's sermon, sitting on the wooden seat by the lawn at the front of the house. He laid aside his exercise book, and a pencil and a rubber. 'Who's that?' he inquired.

'Someone called Harold.'

He nodded, stirring sugar into his coffee.

'I want to tell you about Harold, Father. I want you to meet him.'

'Yes, of course.'

She lit a cigarette. She said: 'We have a lot in common. I mean, he's the only person. . . .'

She faltered and then hesitated. She lifted her cigarette to her lips and drew on it.

He said: 'Are you fond of him, Deirdre?'

'Yes, I am.'

Another silence gathered. She smoked and drank her coffee. He added more sugar to his.

'Of course I'd like to meet him,' he said.

'Could he come to stay with us, Father? Would you mind? Would it be all right?'

'Of course I wouldn't mind. I'd be delighted.'

Harold was summoned and arrived at Rosslare a few days later. In the meantime Deirdre had explained to her father that her friend was an electrician by trade and had let it fall that he was an intellectual kind of person. She borrowed the old Vauxhall and drove it to Rosslare to meet him, returning to the rectory in the early evening.

'How d'you do?' Canon Moran said, stretching out a hand in the direction of an excessively thin youth with a birthmark on his face. His mouse-coloured hair was cut very short, cropped almost. He was wearing a black leather jacket.

'I'm fine,' Harold said.

'You've had a good journey?'

'Lousy, 'smatter of fact, Mr Moran.'

Harold's voice was strongly Cockney, and Canon Moran wondered if Deirdre had perhaps picked up some of her English vowel sounds from it. But then he realised that most people in

London would speak like that, as people did on the television and the wireless. It was just a little surprising that Harold and Deirdre should have so much in common, as they clearly had from the affectionate way they held one another's hand. None of the other Moran girls had gone in so much for holding hands in front of the family.

He was to sit in the drawing-room, they insisted, while they made supper in the kitchen, so he picked up the *Irish Times* and did as he was bidden. Half an hour later Harold appeared and said that the meal was ready: fried eggs and sausages and bacon, and some tinned beans. Canon Moran said Grace.

Having stated that County Wexford looked great, Harold didn't say much else. He didn't smile much, either. His afflicted face bore an edgy look, as if he'd never become wholly reconciled to his birthmark. It was like a scarlet map on his left cheek, a shape that reminded Canon Moran of the toe of Italy. Poor fellow, he thought. And yet a birthmark was so much less to bear than other afflictions there could be.

'Harold's fascinated actually', Deirdre said, 'by Ireland.'

Her friend didn't add anything to that remark for a moment, even though Canon Moran smiled and nodded interestedly. Eventually Harold said: 'The struggle of the Irish people.'

'I didn't know a thing about Irish history,' Dierdre said. 'I mean, not anything that made sense.'

The conversation lapsed at this point, leaving Canon Moran greatly puzzled. He began to say that Irish history had always been of considerable interest to him also, that it had a good story to it, its tragedy uncomplicated. But the other two didn't appear to understand what he was talking about and so he changed the subject. It was a particularly splendid autumn, he pointed out.

'Harold doesn't go in for anything like that,' Deirdre replied.

During the days that followed Harold began to talk more, surprising Canon Moran with almost everything he said. Deirdre had been right to say he was fascinated by Ireland, and it wasn't just a tourist's fascination. Harold had read widely: he spoke of ancient battles, and of the plantations of James I and Elizabeth, of Robert Emmet and the Mitchelstown martyrs, of Pearse and de Valera. 'The struggle of the Irish people' was the expression he most regularly employed. It seemed to Canon Moran that the relationship between Harold and Deirdre had a lot to do with Harold's fascination, as though his interest in Deirdre's native land had somehow caused him to become interested in Deirdre herself.

There was something else as well. Fascinated by Ireland, Harold hated his own country. A sneer whispered through his voice when he spoke of England: a degenerate place, he called it, destroyed by class-consciousness and the unjust distribution of wealth. He described in detail the city of Nottingham, to which he appeared to have a particular aversion. He spoke of unnecessary motorways and the stupidity of bureaucracy, the stifling presence of a Royal Family. 'You could keep an Indian village', he claimed, 'on what those corgis eat. You could house five hundred homeless in Buckingham Palace.' There was brainwashing by television and the newspaper barons. No ordinary person had a chance because pap was fed to the ordinary person, a deliberate policy going back into Victorian times when education and religion had been geared to the enslavement of minds. The English people had brought it on themselves, having lost their spunk, settling instead for consumer durables. 'What better can you expect,' Harold demanded, 'after the hypocrisy of that empire the bosses ran?'

Deirdre didn't appear to find anything specious in this line of talk, which surprised her father. 'Oh, I wonder about that,' he said himself from time to time, but he said it mildly, not wishing to cause an argument, and in any case his interjections were not acknowledged. Quite a few of the criticisms Harold levelled at his own country could be levelled at Ireland also and, Canon Moran guessed, at many countries throughout the world. It was strange that the two neighbouring islands had been so picked out, although once Germany was mentioned and the point made that developments beneath the surface there were a hopeful sign that a big upset was on the way.

'We're taking a walk,' Harold said one afternoon. 'She's going to show me Kinsella's Barn.'

Canon Moran nodded, saying to himself that he disliked Harold. It was the first time he had admitted it, but the feeling was familiar. The less generous side of his nature had always emerged when his daughters brought to the rectory the men they'd become friendly with or even proposed to marry. Emma, the eldest girl, had brought several before settling in the end for Thomas. Linda had brought only John, already engaged to him. Una had married Carley not long after the death, and Carley had not yet visited the rectory: Canon Moran had met him in Dublin, where the wedding had taken place, for in the circumstances Una had not been married from home. Carley was an older man, an importer of tea and wine, stout and flushed, certainly not someone Canon Moran would have chosen for his second-youngest daughter. But, then, he had thought the same about Emma's Thomas and about Linda's John.

Thomas was a farmer, sharing a sizeable acreage with his father in County Meath. He always brought to mind the sarcasm of an old schoolmaster who in Canon Moran's distant schooldays used to refer to a gang of boys at the back of the classroom as 'farmers' sons', meaning that not much could be expected of them. It was an inaccurate assumption but even now, whenever Canon Moran found himself in the company of Thomas, he couldn't help recalling it. Thomas was mostly silent, with a good-natured smile that came slowly and lingered too long. According to his father, and there was no reason to doubt the claim, he was a good judge of beef cattle.

Linda's John was the opposite. Wiry and suave, he was making his way in the Bank of Ireland, at present stationed in Waterford. He had a tiny orange-coloured moustache and was good at golf. Linda's ambition for him was that he should become the Bank of Ireland's manager in Limerick or Galway, where the insurances that went with the position were particularly lucrative. Unlike Thomas, John talked all the time, telling jokes and stories about the Bank of Ireland's customers.

'Nothing is perfect,' Frances used to say, chiding her husband for an uncharitableness he did his best to combat. He disliked being so particular about the men his daughters chose, and he was aware that other people saw them differently: Thomas would do anything for you, John was fun, the middle-aged Carley laid his success at Una's feet. But whoever the husbands of his daughters had been, Canon Moran knew he'd have felt the same. He was jealous of the husbands because ever since his daughters had been born he have loved them unstintingly. When he had prayed after Frances's death he'd felt jealous of God, who had taken her from him.

'There's nothing much to see,' he pointed out when Harold announced that Deirdre was going to show him Kinsella's Barn. 'Just the ruin of a wall is all that's left.'

'Harold's interested, Father.'

They set off on their walk, leaving the old clergyman ashamed that he could not like Harold more. It was just his grimness: there was something sinister about Harold, something furtive about the way he looked at you, peering at you cruelly out of his afflicted face, not meeting your eye. *Why* was he so fascinated about a country that wasn't his own? Why did he refer so often to 'Ireland's struggle' as if that struggle particularly concerned him? He hated walking, he had said so, yet he'd set out to walk six miles through woods and fields to examine a ruined wall.

Canon Moran had wondered as suspiciously about Thomas and John and Carley, privately questioning every statement they made, finding hidden motives everywhere. He'd hated the thought of his daughters being embraced or even touched, and had forced himself not to think about that. He'd prayed, ashamed of himself then, too. 'It's just a frailty in you,' Frances had said, her favourite way of cutting things down to size.

He sat for a while in the afternoon sunshine, letting all of it hang in his mind. It would be nice if they quarrelled on their walk. It would be nice if they didn't speak when they returned, if Harold simply went away. But that wouldn't happen, because they had come to the rectory with a purpose. He didn't know why he thought that, but he knew it was true: they had come for a reason, something that was all tied up with Harold's fascination and with the kind of person Harold was, with his cold eyes and his afflicted face.

In March 1798 an incident had taken place in Kinsella's Barn, which at that time had just been a barn. Twelve men and women, accused of harbouring insurgents, had been tied together with ropes at the command of a Sergeant James. They had been led through the village of Boharbawn, the Sergeant's soldiers on horseback on either side of the procession, the Sergeant himself bringing up the rear. Designed as an act of education, an example to the inhabitants of Boharbawn and the country people around, the twelve had been herded into a barn owned by a farmer called Kinsella and there burned to death. Kinsella, who had played no part either in the harbouring of insurgents or in the execution of the twelve, was afterwards murdered by his own farm labourers.

'Sergeant James was a Nottingham man,' Harold said that evening at supper. 'A soldier of fortune who didn't care what he did. Did you know he acquired great wealth, Mr Moran?'

'No, I wasn't at all aware of that,' Canon Moran replied.

'Harold found out about him,' Deirdre said.

'He used to boast he was responsible for the death of a thousand Irish people. It was in Boharbawn he reached the thousand. They rewarded him well for that.'

'Not much is known about Sergeant James locally. Just the legend of Kinsella's Barn.'

'No way it's a legend.'

Deirdre nodded; Canon Moran did not say anything. They were eating cooked ham and salad. On the table there was a cake which Deirdre had bought in Murphy Flood's in Enniscorthy, and a pot of tea. There were several bunches of grapes from the greenhouse, and a plate of wafer biscuits. Harold was fond of salad cream, Canon Moran had noticed; he had a way of hitting the base of the jar with his hand, causing large dollops to spurt all over his ham. He didn't place his knife and fork together on the plate when he'd finished, but just left them anyhow. His fingernails were edged with black.

'You'd feel sick,' he was saying now, working the salad cream again. 'You'd stand there looking at that wall and you'd feel a revulsion in your stomach.'

'What I meant', Canon Moran said, 'is that it has passed into local legend. No one doubts it took place; there's no question about that. But two centuries have almost passed.'

'And nothing has changed,' Harold interjected. 'The Irish people still share their bondage with the twelve in Kinsella's Barn.'

'Round here of course—'

'It's not round here that matters, Mr Moran. The struggle's world wide; the sickness is everywhere actually.'

Again Deirdre nodded. She was like a zombie, her father thought. She was being used because she was an Irish girl; she was Harold's Irish connection, and in some almost frightening way she believed herself in love with him. Frances had once said they'd made a mistake with her. She had wondered if Deirdre had perhaps found all the love they'd offered her too much to bear. They were quite old when Deirdre was a child, the last expression of their own love. She was special because of that.

'At least Kinsella got his chips,' Harold pursued, his voice relentless. 'At least that's something.'

Canon Moran protested. The owner of the barn had been an innocent man, he pointed out. The barn had simply been a convenient one, large enough for the purpose, with heavy stones near it that could be piled up against the door before the conflagration. Kinsella, that day, had been miles away, ditching a field.

'It's too long ago to say where he was,' Harold retorted swiftly. 'And if he was keeping a low profile in a ditch it would have been by arrangement with the imperial forces.'

When Harold said that there occurred in Canon Moran's mind a flash of what appeared to be the simple truth. Harold was an Englishman who had espoused a cause because it was one through which the status quo in his own country might be damaged. Similar such Englishmen, read about in newspapers, stirred in the clergyman's mind: men from Ealing and Liverpool and Wolverhampton who had changed their names to Irish names, who had even learned the Irish language, in order to ingratiate themselves with the new Irish revolutionaries. Such men dealt out death and chaos, announcing that their conscience insisted on it.

'Well, we'd better wash the dishes,' Deirdre said, and Harold rose obediently to help her.

The walk to Kinsella's Barn had taken place on a Saturday afternoon. The following morning Canon Moran conducted his services in St Michael's, addressing his small Protestant congregation, twelve at Holy Communion, eighteen at morning service. He had prepared a sermon about repentance, taking as his text St Luke, 15:32: '. . . *for this thy brother was dead, and is alive again; and was lost, and is found.*' But at the last moment he changed his mind and spoke instead of the incident in Kinsella's Barn nearly two centuries ago. He tried to make the point that one horror should not fuel another, that passing time contained its own forgiveness. Deirdre and Harold were naturally not in the church, but they'd been present at breakfast, Harold frying eggs on the kitchen stove, Deirdre pouring tea. He had looked at them and tried to think of them as two young people on holiday. He had tried to tell himself they'd come to the rectory for a rest and for his blessing, that he should be grateful instead of fanciful. It was for his blessing that Emma had brought Thomas to the rectory, that Linda had brought John. Una would bring Carley in November. 'Now, don't be silly,' Frances would have said.

'The man Kinsella was innocent of everything,' he heard his voice insisting in his church. 'He should never have been murdered also.'

Harold would have delighted in the vengeance exacted on an innocent man. Harold wanted to inflict pain, to cause suffering and destruction. The end justified the means for Harold, even if the end was an artificial one, a pettiness grandly dressed up. In his sermon Canon Moran spoke of such matters without mentioning Harold's name. He spoke of how evil drained people of their humour and compassion, how people pretended even to themselves. It was worse than Frances's death, he thought as his voice continued in the church: it was worse that Deirdre should be part of wickedness.

He could tell that his parishioners found his sermon odd, and he didn't blame them. He was confused, and naturally distressed. In the rectory Deirdre and Harold would be waiting for him. They would all sit down to Sunday lunch while plans for atrocities filled Harold's mind, while Deirdre loved him.

'Are you well again, Mrs Davis?' he inquired at the church door of a woman who suffered from asthma.

'Not too bad, Canon. Not too bad, thank you.'

He spoke to all the others, inquiring about health, remarking on the beautiful autumn. They were farmers mostly and displayed a farmer's gratitude for the satisfactory season. He wondered suddenly who'd replace him among them when he retired or died. Father Hayes had had to give up a year ago. The young man, Father White, was always in a hurry.

'Goodbye so, Canon,' Mr Willoughby said, shaking hands as he always did, every Sunday. It was a long time since there'd been the trouble about Eugene Ryan's grazing rights; three years ago Mr Willoughby had been left a widower himself. 'You're managing all right, Canon?' he asked, as he also always did.

'Yes, I'm all right, thank you, Mr Willoughby.'

Someone else inquired if Deirdre was still at the rectory, and he said she was. Heads nodded, the unspoken thought being that that was nice for him, his youngest daughter at home again after all these years. There was forgiveness in several faces, forgiveness of Deirdre, who had been thoughtless to go off to an egg-packing factory. There was the feeling, also unexpressed, that the young were a bit like that.

'Goodbye,' he said in a general way. Car doors banged, engines started. In the vestry he removed his surplice and his cassock and hung them in a cupboard.

'We'll probably go tomorrow,' Deirdre said during lunch.

'Go?'

'We'll probably take the Dublin bus.'

'I'd like to see Dublin,' Harold said.

'And then you're returning to London?'

'We're easy about that,' Harold interjected before Deirdre could reply. 'I'm a tradesman, Mr Moran, an electrician.'

'I know you're an electrician, Harold.'

'What I mean is I'm on my own; I'm not answerable to the bosses. There's always a bob or two waiting in London.'

For some reason Canon Moran felt that Harold was lying. There was a quickness about the way he'd said they were easy about their plans, and it didn't seem quite to make sense, the logic of not being answerable to bosses and a bob or two always waiting for him. Harold was being evasive about their movements, hiding the fact that they would probably remain in Dublin for longer than he implied, meeting other people like himself.

'It was good of you to have us,' Deirdre said that evening, all three of them sitting around the fire in the drawing-room because the evenings had just begun to get chilly. Harold was reading a book about Che Guevara and hadn't spoken for several hours. 'We've enjoyed it, Father.'

'It's been nice having you, Deirdre.'

'I'll write to you from London.'

It was safe to say that: he knew she wouldn't because she hadn't before, until she'd wanted something. She wouldn't write to thank him for the rectory's hospitality, and that would be quite in keeping. Harold was the same kind of man as Sergeant James had been: it didn't matter that they were on different sides. Sergeant James had maybe borne an affliction also, a humped back or a withered arm. He had ravaged a country that existed then for its spoils, and his most celebrated crime was neatly at hand so that another Englishman could make matters worse by attempting to make amends. In Harold's view the trouble had always been that these acts of war and murder died beneath the weight of print in history books, and were forgotten. But history could be rewritten, and for that Kinsella's Barn was an inspiration: Harold had journeyed to it as people make journeys to holy places.

'Yes?' Deirdre said, for while these reflections had passed through his mind he had spoken her name, wanting to ask her to tell him the truth about her friend.

He shook his head. 'I wish you could have seen your mother again,' he said instead. 'I wish she were here now.'

The faces of his three sons-in-law irrelevantly appeared in his mind: Carley's flushed cheeks, Thomas's slow good-natured smile, John's little moustache. It astonished him that he'd ever felt suspicious of their natures, for they would never let his daughters down. But Deirdre had turned her back on the rectory, and what could be expected when she came back with a man? She had never been like Emma or Linda or Una, none of whom smoked Three Castles cigarettes and wore clothes that didn't seem quite clean. It was impossible to imagine any of them becoming involved with a revolutionary, a man who wanted to commit atrocities.

'He was just a farmer, you know,' he heard himself saying. 'Kinsella.'

Surprise showed in Deirdre's face. 'It was Mother we were talking about,' she reminded him, and he could see her trying to connect her mother with a farmer who had died two hundred years ago, and not being able to. Elderliness, he could see her thinking. 'Only time he wandered,' she would probably say to her friend.

'It was good of you to come, Deirdre.'

He looked at her, far into her eyes, admitting to himself that she had always been his favourite. When the other girls were busily growing up she had still wanted to sit on his knee. She'd had a way of interrupting him no matter what he was doing, arriving beside him with a book she wanted him to read to her.

'Goodbye, Father,' she said the next morning while they waited in Enniscorthy for the Dublin bus. 'Thank you for everything.'

'Yeah, thanks a ton, Mr Moran,' Harold said.

'Goodbye, Harold. Goodbye, my dear.'

He watched them finding their seats when the bus arrived and then he drove the old Vauxhall back to Boharbawn, meeting Slattery in his postman's van and returning his salute. There was shopping he should have done, meat and potatoes, and tins of things to keep him going. But his mind was full of Harold's afflicted face and his black-rimmed fingernails, and Deirdre's hand in his. And then flames burst from the straw that had been packed around living people in Kinsella's Barn. They burned through the wood of the barn itself, revealing the writhing bodies. On his horse the man called Sergeant James laughed.

Canon Moran drove the car into the rectory's ramshackle garage, and walked around the house to the wooden seat on the front lawn. Frances should come now with two cups of coffee, appearing at the front door with the tray and then crossing the gravel and the lawn. He saw her as she had been when first they came to the rectory, when only Emma had been born; but the grey-haired Frances was somehow there as well, shadowing her youth. 'Funny little Deirdre,' she said, placing the tray on the seat between them.

It seemed to him that everything that had just happened in the rectory had to do with Frances, with meeting her for the first time when she was eighteen, with loving her and marrying her. He knew it was a trick of the autumn sunshine that again she crossed the gravel and the lawn, no more than pretence that she handed him a cup and saucer. 'Harold's just a talker,' she said. 'Not at all like Sergeant James.'

He sat for a while longer on the wooden seat, clinging to these words, knowing they were true. Of course it was cowardice that ran through Harold, inspiring the whisper of his sneer when he spoke of the England he hated so. In the presence of a befuddled girl and an old Irish clergyman England was an easy target, and Ireland's troubles a kind of target also.

Frances laughed, and for the first time her death seemed far away, as her life did, too. In the rectory the visitors had blurred her fingerprints to nothing, and had made of her a ghost that could come back. The sunshine warmed him as he sat there, the garden was less melancholy than it had been.

Beggars Would Ride

Beryl Bainbridge

*On 22 December 1605, two men on horseback, cloaks billowing,
hoofs striking sparks from the frozen ground, rode ferociously
from the Guildhall to a hill near the village of Hampstead. Dis-
mounting some yards from the summit and a little to the east,
they kicked a shallow depression in the earth. Several villagers,
knowing in advance the precise and evil properties of the talisman
they carried, gawped from a safe distance. Dropping to their
knees, the horsemen buried a small round object wrapped in a
piece of cloth. Upon rising, the taller of the two men was heard
to observe that he wished he was in front of a warm hearth; at
which moment the earth erupted and belched fire. For an instant
the men stood transfixed and then, cloaks peeled by dancing
flame, they whirled upwards, two lumps of burning rag spinning
in a blazing arc against the sky.*

On the Friday before Christmas, Ben Lewis and Frobisher met as
usual in the car-park behind the post office. Ben Lewis arrived a
quarter of an hour late and, grimacing through the windscreen of
his estate car, proceeded to take off his shoes. It annoyed Frobisher, still left waiting in the cold. When the wind stirred the
dead leaves on the concrete ground, there was a sound like rats
scampering.

'Bloody parky,' shouted Frobisher, but the man in the car
was now out of sight, slumped between seat and clutch as he
struggled to remove his trousers.

Frobisher, chilled to the bone, jogged to the boundaries of
the car-park and back again, passing two women seated inside
a green Mini, one reading a newspaper, the other noticeably
crying.

Ben Lewis emerged wearing shorts and a pair of white sneakers with blue toe-caps.

'There's two women back there,' Frobisher told him. 'By the wire netting. One's blubbing into a handkerchief.'

'Really,' said Ben Lewis.

'The other's reading,' said Frobisher. He looked down at·Ben Lewis's sneakers and smiled insincerely.

'They're new,' he said. Privately he thought them ridiculous; his own plimsolls, though stained and short on laces, were otherwise all that they should be.

Ben Lewis unlocked the boot of his car and took out a long canvas bag. 'Let's go into the bushes,' he shouted, and ducking through a gap in the fence shouldered his way into a dense undergrowth of alder and old privet.

The ground was liberally strewn with broken glass and beer-cans. 'Funny,' remarked Ben Lewis, 'how few whatsits one sees these days.'

'Don't follow you,' said Frobisher.

'Contraceptives,' said Ben Lewis, whose mind was often on such things.

Labouring over the rusted frame of a child's push-chair, Frobisher stubbed his toe on a small, round object half buried beneath decaying leaves. 'I wish', he panted, 'we could get the hang of the game. Just for an hour or so.'

Twice a week, during the lunch hour, they played tennis together. Frobisher worked just across the road in the National Westminster Bank, and Ben Lewis drove from Hampstead where he was a partner in a firm of estate agents.

'Whose turn is it to pay?' asked Frobisher, when, out of breath, they reached the entrance to the tennis courts.

He always asked that. He knew perfectly well that he had paid on Wednesday. He had a horror of being thought mean.

'Yours,' said Ben Lewis, who had no such fears.

The attendant marked them down for court 14, which was listing slowly and surrounded on three sides by trees. Though the court itself was full of pot-holes and the net invariably wound too high, it did have the advantage of privacy. Neither Frobisher nor Ben Lewis cared to be watched. When they had first started to play together, having chummed up in a pub in Belsize Park and mutually complained of being unfit, they had imagined it would be a matter of weeks before their game improved. Both had last played, slackly, at school. A year had passed and improvement had not come. Ben Lewis's service was quite good but he gained little advantage from it because it was too good for Frobisher to return. Frobisher had a nice forehand of a sort, the sort that lobbed the ball high into the air. Ben Lewis couldn't see the ball unless it came low over the net. They comforted themselves with the thought of the benefit they obviously derived from bending down and trotting about in the open air.

Of the two, Ben Lewis was the more outwardly narcissistic. He used aftershave and he hinted that he'd once had a sauna. He worried about his hair, which was now sparse, and the way his cheeks were falling in. He felt it was all right for Frobisher to sport a weathered crown — his particular height and porky-boy belly put him into a defined category — but he himself was on the short side and slender. He didn't want to degenerate into an elderly whippet with emaciated flanks, running like hell after the rabbit in the Waterloo Cup, and balding into the bargain.

'People are awfully callous these days, aren't they?' said Frobisher.

'What?' said Ben Lewis.

'The way they read while other people cry.'

'I shouldn't care for it,' said Ben Lewis. 'Not outdoors. Not in this weather.' He pushed open the rusted gate to court 14 and began to unzip his bag.

'How's Margaret?' asked Frobisher.

'Fine, fine,' said Ben Lewis. He didn't inquire after Frobisher's wife. Not any more. Frobisher's wife was called Beth, and Ben Lewis, who some years ago had directed *Little Women* for his local Amateur Dramatic Society, had once referred to her, jokingly of course, as 'Keep Death Off the Road'. Frobisher, not having seen the play, hadn't seen the joke. Far from it. He'd made some pretty silly remarks about it sounding disrespectful to his wife. Ben Lewis thought it was hypocritical of him, seeing that Frobisher had admitted to having a woman on the side. The previous summer, when excessive heat had forced Frobisher to remove his shirt, he had positively boasted about the two scratch marks Ben Lewis had noticed on his back. At the time, Ben Lewis had thought of rubbing his own back against a rose bush in his front garden, only he forgot.

'Shall we have a knock-up?' asked Frobisher. He removed his overcoat and scarf and was discovered to be wearing a dark-blue tracksuit with white stripes on each shoulder.

'That's new,' said Ben Lewis, smiling insincerely. He had the strangest notion, when he strolled into position on the court, that his new shoes had springs in the heel.

Without warning, Frobisher hit a very good ball down the line. Ben Lewis returned it, though he was dazzled as usual by the horizontal of the grimy net and the glittering rectangles of the tower block built lower down the hill. For perhaps half a remarkable minute they successfully kept the ball in play until Ben Lewis, misjudging his own strength, sent it flying into the wire netting with such force that it lodged there like some unlikely fruit. 'You won't believe it,' he told Frobisher. 'But I thought the net was higher or you were lower.'

'Optical illusion,' said Frobisher kindly, scrambling up the grass bank to pluck the ball from the wire. 'It's that jetstream.' And he indicated with his racket two white and wobbling lines stretched across the sky. He felt unusally light on his feet and remarked confidently that it was all a question of rhythm. He could feel, he asserted, a definite sense of rhythm creeping into his stroke. They were both exhilarated at this sudden improvement in form. Secretly, Ben Lewis thought it had something to do with his sneakers. Frobisher openly expressed the belief that his tracksuit had contributed to his new-found skill.

'A fellow in the office', said Ben Lewis, 'started to get into trendy trousers last summer. His wife egged him on. He pulled off a fairly complicated land deal in South Woodford.'

'Direct result, you mean?' said Frobisher.

'Nothing was ever proved,' replied Ben Lewis, and he bounced on his toes and served with quite extraordinary speed and verve.

After a quarter of an hour, an awed Ben Lewis said that in his opinion they were Wimbledon standard and possibly better than that bad-tempered fellow on the box who was always arguing with the man up the ladder. 'And you're right about the rhythm,' he said. He kept to himself the fanciful idea that they were dancing a slow fox-trot, championship standard, not a foot wrong, every move correctly timed, sweeping backwards and forwards across the court to the beat of an invisible orchestra.

Frobisher would have given anything for his wife Beth to have been watching him. She was always telling the children that he had no sense of co-ordination. It struck him as absurd that only last week he and Ben Lewis, trailing towards the bushes to return to the car-park, had openly sneered at the dedicated players on court number 12. The tall man with the sweat-band round his head, who was generally there on Wednesday and Friday, had caused them particular amusement – 'That ass with the hair ribbon', as Ben Lewis had called him. Frobisher wondered if it would be going too far to have a band round his own forehead.

It came to Ben Lewis, fleetingly, sadly, as he arched his back in preparation for a particularly deadly service, how different things might have been if he had always played like this. Only once in his life had he experienced applause, at the curtain call of *Little Women* in East Finchley. In imagination he multiplied the volume of that first, last and giddy applause, and flinging his racket to the linesman leaped, gazelle-like, over the net.

After a further twenty inspired minutes, Frobisher suggested that perhaps they should rest. Though perspiring, neither of them was the least tired.

'I do feel', said Ben Lewis, with a touch of hysteria, 'that we might be hospital cases tomorrow.' Weak with laughter they flopped down on the sodden bench at the side of the court and lolled against each other.

'Doing anything for Christmas?' asked Frobisher at last. It was better to behave as if everything was normal.

'Usual thing,' said Ben Lewis. 'Margaret's mother, Margaret's mother's sister . . . that sort of thing. What about you?'

'Nothing special,' said Frobisher. 'Just me and Death.' From beyond the trees came the fragmented screams of children running in the playground of the Catholic school.

'Do you think', said Frobisher, unable to contain himself, 'that it's the same thing as riding a bike?'

'A knack, you mean,' said Ben Lewis. 'Once learnt, never lost?'
'Yes,' said Frobisher.

'Maybe,' said Ben Lewis. But he didn't think it was. They both fell silent, reliving the last three-quarters of an hour, until Frobisher remarked generously that Ben Lewis might have won the last set if the ground hadn't been so full of pot-holes. 'Not your fault,' he added. 'It was jolly bad luck.'

Ben Lewis found that he was gripping the edge of the bench so tightly that a splinter of wood pierced his finger. He knew that if he relaxed his hold he would spring upward and in one bound rip from the rusted fence a length of wire to tie round Frobisher's neck. He said as calmly as he was able, 'I don't believe in luck, bad or otherwise.'

From the playground came the blast of a whistle. The chattering voices receded as the children flocked indoors. Frobisher stood up, and, adjusting the top half of his tracksuit, strode purposefully back to his previous position on the court. 'My service,' he called curtly.

His first ball bounced on the far side of the net at a point wickedly close to the ground. Ben Lewis, gripping his racket in both hands as if running in an egg-and-spoon race, stumbled forward and scooped it skywards. It flew over his head, over the wire, and vanished into the trees. 'My God,' said Frobisher. He stood with one hand on his hip and gazed irritably at Ben Lewis. 'You'd better retrieve it,' he ordered, as though Ben Lewis were a dog. He watched his opponent lumber through the gate and heard him squelch down the muddy path in the direction of the attendant's hut. Frobisher took a running jump at the net and hurdled it with ease.

Ben Lewis, passing court number 12, saw that the man with the sweat-band round his head had a new partner. A woman. She was crouching down, racket held in both hands, head swinging from side to side like a bull about to charge.

Having skirted the attendant's hut and entered the bushes, Ben Lewis tried to visualise the flight path of the erratic ball. He was probably not far enough back. He tried to clamber up the bank to see if court number 14 was visible, but the bushes grew too thickly. He scuffed with his sneakers at the broken glass and refuse, thinking his search was hopeless, and almost at once un-covered the missing ball. He bent down and picked it up. He was now sweating and the muscles in his legs were trembling. He found he held not only the ball but something round and small clinging to a scrap of rotting cloth. Shivering with revulsion he flung both ball and rag away from him and wiped his hands on his shorts.

He wished he was in a nice hot bath.

Frobisher, fretting on court 14, was startled by the noise of steam escaping from some large funnel. He supposed it came from the ventilation system of the tower-block further down the hill. When he looked in the direction of the car-park he observed a large white cloud drifting above the trees. He went in pursuit of his tennis partner. Struggling through the bushes calling Ben Lewis's name, he was astonished to see that the ground had been swept clear of rubbish. Ben Lewis's car was still parked near the fence. The woman at the steering-wheel of the green Mini said she hadn't seen anybody, she'd been too busy reading.

'Didn't you hear that noise?' asked Frobisher severely. 'Like a train stopping. A puffer train.'

The woman stared at him. 'Perhaps he's just gone home,' she suggested.

'He's not wearing trousers,' said Frobisher. He retraced his steps to court 14 and found it deserted.

Frobisher told his colleagues in the bank that his friend Ben Lewis had in some mysterious way disappeared. They weren't interested. Most of them thought Frobisher a bit of a slouch.

Before it grew dark, Frobisher slipped over the road to see if Ben Lewis's car was still near the gap in the fence. It was.

Frobisher went into the bushes again and this time found the tennis ball and a smooth round object lying side by side on the ground.

He wished he knew where Ben Lewis had gone.

The Interment

Francis King

'ARE YOU SURE you don't want to come?'

'Quite sure. Once was enough.'

'It's a damned nuisance, another rehearsal at an hour like this.'

Carol lay outside the bed, in nothing but pants and brassière, the shiny pale-blue bedspread tacky against her skin. She was doing nothing and she wanted to do nothing — except smoke a cigarette; but that was the one thing that she must not do in Ian's presence. He had brushed his teeth and then he had gargled with Listerine and now, dressed but for the jacket draped over the back of an upright chair, he was alternately humming and clearing his throat in that irritating way of his, while he checked that he had his music, his extra-strong mints and his throat-spray in the attaché case that she had given him the previous Christmas. She had had his name engraved on its lid; but that had been a mistake. 'Don't you think that's just a wee bit ostentatious?' he had asked, since he was modest about his modest fame. But how many people would connect the name with a singer whose reputation was still merely a national one?

'Why are you watching me like that?'

'Watching you? Am I? I suppose because there's nothing else to do in this ghastly city.'

'You could have gone out. Shopping. Or sight-seeing.'

'There's nothing cheap enough to buy or interesting enough to visit.'

He shrugged. Then: 'Promise me one thing, darling.'

'Yes, I promise. I won't.'

They both of them laughed.

'If you must do it—'

'Yes, I'll go down into the lounge or out into the street. I know.'

'Sorry to be so faddy but you know how—'

'Yes, yes! I know!'

He was as anxious about his voice as a Don Juan about his sexual equipment: a roughness was the equivalent of a dose of clap, laryngitis of impotence. Due to stand in for an ailing and ageing but still world-famous tenor at the Colón, he was like some small-town philanderer suddenly and unexpectedly summoned to the bed of an Eva Perón. It was, as his agent had said, an opportunity in a thousand; and it would be a disaster if the small-town philanderer could not 'rise' to that opportunity. His care for his voice was like that of a parent for a sickly and therefore abnormally cherished child, and it filled Carol with a mixture of irritation and pity. For that child, every sacrifice must be made, not only by him but also by her. Cigarettes were bad, but sex was even worse. Yes, he knew about those rumours of how Melba would 'irrigate' her voice before a major performance and of how the ailing and ageing tenor whom he was now replacing once told a gossip-columnist that he only gave of his best if he had spent the afternoon 'loosening up' with someone in bed. (He had not specified the sex of that someone, but the gossip was that it must be male.) 'But I'm just not like them, darling. Somehow sex drains me, *bleeds* my voice. The tone whitens.'

He stooped to kiss her, first on the forehead, then on the side of the neck, and then, for seconds on end, on the mouth. It was his way of making up for not having agreed to allow his voice to be 'bled' during the afternoon siesta that, out of boredom, they had prolonged until, with the descent of the wintry dusk, they had heard the central heating come on with a curious gasping, chugging noise, as though far below them in the basement of the small elegant hotel some antiquated steam-engine was gathering itself to set off on invisible rails.

'Shall I wait for you for dinner?'

'Not if you're hungry. I may be hours.'

'Well, I am hungry.'

'Then don't wait. Simple.'

'I *hate* eating alone.'

'Why? You might have some adventure.'

'I've made up my mind that I'm the kind of person to whom adventures never happen.' She took his hand. 'I hope it goes well.' She meant it, knowing how important this 'opportunity in a thousand' was to him and knowing, too, from her own observation at rehearsal and not from anything he would admit, that he was uneasy with the domineering black American prima donna, each of whose dresses was like some voluminous tent, with the Spanish conductor, who spoke to him so peremptorily, and, above all, with the emaciated waspish French director, who at moments of exasperation — and there were many — would run both hands back through his thick tangled hair and scream, 'Merde!'

'I hope so, too.' The tone was rueful — because he knew, as she knew and as his agent knew, that he was not really at home in that gilded railway station of an opera-house, almost twice the size of Covent Garden, and that he was not really at home in early Verdi. But there it was — that 'opportunity in a thousand' — and he could not turn it down. Yet each time that his voice, that cherished sickly child, seemed to stagger and all but faint as he pushed it out towards a receding desert of old gold and plush, he would experience a terrible despair. The small-town Don Juan was indeed impotent.

After Ian had gone, Carol continued to lie there for a time on the bed. She thought of the children and decided that, no, she would not ring the parents yet again to ask if all was well. Ian had said that it was absurd to do so night after night, at such an appalling expense, when, if anything were wrong, they would hear soon enough, God knows. She thought of the garden, wondering if, in a summer so remote from this Argentine winter and probably much colder, the neighbours had remembered to hose it from time to time. She thought of the familiar shops and the familiar cooker and the familiar sink. Odd! She thought of them with regret and a mournful longing; and yet she had always resented their daily tyranny.

Eventually she got off the bed, with the voluptuous laziness of a gorged cat, slipped into a dressing-gown and then, smiling at herself, took a packet of the forbidden cigarettes and a lighter out of her bag, hesitated a moment, and then lit up. The bathroom or the windowsill? He always detected the reek of smoke, however faint, on towel and face-flannel. The windowsill was better, even if the temperature was falling. Cigarette smouldering away between two fingers ('I do wish you'd use a holder; those stains are so ugly'), she struggled with the catch of the window and eventually slid it open. Far down below there was the courtyard of some government building, and in the dimming evening she could make out foreshortened men hurrying diagonally across it, most of them with briefcases. They arrived late, they went home early, she noticed — unlike the hotel staff, who must sleep on the premises, so constant was their presence.

She inhaled deeply, enjoying the contrast between the vitalising smoke and the numbing air on her bare throat, forehead and hands. From the room next door she could hear angry English voices, male and female. She had seen the couple, a tall young man and an equally tall young woman, who had a way of walking down the corridor hand in hand, their sharp-featured faces turned to each other, slightly smirking. They were so lovingly decorous in public that it was hard to believe that, only a short while before, they had been shouting those crudities at each other, in private.

When the cigarette had been sucked to its last bitter scorching gasp, she threw it, unextinguished, down into the courtyard, watching it shower sparks as it fell. Pretty. She would have liked it to have alighted on the head of one of those hurrying men with their briefcases, but no such luck. Another? Better not. No, definitely not. She began to dress. It was early to dine in Buenos Aires, but she was feeling hungry after the sandwiches and coffee that had made up their early lunch. ('Things are so expensive; we'll just have to make do with one main meal a day.' It was as though Ian knew that the unprecedented sum that he was to receive for his performances would never be repeated.)

The avuncular, and not the cheekily flirtatious, porter was at the desk and, on an impulse as she handed in her key, she asked him if he could recommend a restaurant. He got out a map — though he had already given her one only two or three days before — and carefully put a cross for the hotel on it and then, his head so close to hers that she could smell his sweet and pungent hair-oil, he ran the tip of his pen up one street and down another and then put in another cross. He wrote on the map 'San Bernardino', saying: 'I think you will like. All foreigners like. Not too expensive.' As she took the map with a smile and a thank-you, he went on: 'But it is very early.'

'Yes, I know. But I'm hungry, you see.'

He laughed uproariously at that, as though she had made some joke. She had noticed that, just as the British tended to regard sex as intrinsically comic, the Argentines had the same attitude to food. 'Hungry! Hungry!' She might have said that she was feeling randy, from his reaction. The wizened old man who carried suitcases up to bedrooms, summoned taxis and was perpetually mopping over the tiles whenever it was raining enough for the clients' shoes to dirty them joined in his mirth.

Flat — yes, that was the word that best described this city, even if it did bristle with skyscrapers. She had not ventured beyond its centre; but she had a sense of the narrow canyons of its streets radiating symmetrically around her, without any hills or any hollows, and then petering out in featureless suburbs, which in turn merged into plains as monotonous as oceans. Despite the grid system, she often got lost, because every street seemed to look precisely like every other street. Oh, yes, she would tell herself, it must be left turn here for the hotel, because there is that chemist's shop with those mysterious pink coils of rubber attached to a black box in its window; and now it must be right turn, because there is that statue of a general with his nose eroded as though by tertiary syphilis.

This flatness seemed to apply to the people, too. But that, of course, could only be an illusion: it was not that a people so excitable were not exciting but merely that she had mysteriously lost the faculty of getting excited by them. Ian was perpetually exclaiming 'They really are stunners!' when they passed some group of young girls emerging from a school, a shop or an office.

To follow the route marked for her by the porter, she had, at one point, to negotiate some slithery planks that covered an excavation. Some people had told her that the excavation was for an underground car-park; others, for a subway. It seemed odd that even natives of the city seemed not to know for sure. Alone like this, she felt perfectly safe, as she always felt perfectly safe when wandering about this city, whatever the hour. Yet there were people, not foreigners like herself and Ian, who never felt safe. At any moment they could disappear as completely and as disastrously as if her foot were now to slip, the hand-rail were to crumble, and she were to plunge, unseen, into the dark abyss beneath her.

This must be the restaurant. She looked through the plate-glass window and saw the huge bed of a charcoal fire, with a boy in an outsize apron, no more than a child, blowing at it with a pair of bellows almost as large as himself. There were other aproned figures, adult and in most cases heavily moustached, lugging about vast haunches of meat or hacking and sawing at them. Their sweating faces were lurid in the flames that leaped up from the charcoal grid as the boy pumped at it.

'Yes, madame.' The elderly head-waiter, the menu in its stiff leather folder tucked under one arm, might have been a civil servant taking a confidential file to his minister. How had he guessed that she was either English or American?

'For one, please.'

'For one. . . . Yes, madame.' He spoke with a faint hesitation and a frown, as though she had asked for something difficult; but at that hour the restaurant, which stretched far back under its white vaulted ceiling, was all but empty. There were some red-faced American men, who might well have been there since lunch, slumped morosely around their glasses and bottles of Bourbon; a family celebration of some kind, composed of grandmother, her grey hair twisted into a number of stiff whorls, portly mother and father, three prettily nubile girls in court-shoes that looked too tight for them and almost identical white cashmere dresses, and a bored supercilious youth with a loud braying laugh; and an elderly man drooping over a *café filtre* and a newspaper with a fatigue so extreme that it made Carol feel tired just to look at him.

The head-waiter drew back a chair for her at a table against a wall, saying 'Please' with a small, slightly ironic bow. Carol was still struggling out of her coat. When she had done so, he took it from her, folded it neatly and, instead of carrying it away, placed it over the back of the chair opposite to the one that he had drawn out for her. After she was seated, he handed her the menu and left.

Minutes then passed, during which no one took any notice of her. A number of waiters, all in evening-dress, clustered negligently around the cash-desk, chattering to the youth – no doubt the son of the proprietor – perched on a high stool behind it. An oriental, in a white jacket stained with blood, hurried past, bearing a carcase on his shoulder. The boy in the overlong apron continued to work his bellows.

At last she heard a voice behind her: 'You wish to order, madame?'

As a child, she had once said of a bus-conductor, 'Isn't he beautiful, Mummy?' to be told: 'Women are beautiful, dear, men are handsome.' But 'beautiful' was the only word adequately to describe the man who now moved forward; and that it should be the only word was all the more astonishing because he must be at least in his fifties. From the tips of his gleaming patent-leather shoes to his crisp grey curls, he had the sleekness of a champion at a dog-show. The pale-grey eyes, set wide apart, were startling above the black moustache and under the sweeping black eyebrows. He held himself erect, his cleft chin slightly uptilted and his chest thrust out. If one had met him at a Buenos Aires party, one would have assumed him to be an army colonel, perhaps even a general, in mufti – no doubt already planning the coup that would bring him to supreme power.

'Yes. . . . Thank you. . . .' She looked again at the menu. 'Have you any avocados?'

He smiled indulgently, revealing perfect teeth, and shook his head. She remembered now that avocados could be bought here for a few pence a kilo and that they would therefore be as out of place in a restaurant of this kind as faggots and mashed turnips at Claridges.

'Well, then I'll just have a T-bone steak. And a salad.'

'Tomato? A green salad?' His English was far better than that of either of the two porters at the hotel.

'A mixture of both.'

'Certainly, madame. And to drink?'

She hesitated. 'Oh, some red wine.'

'You wish to see the wine-list?'

Again she hesitated.

'Will madame leave it to me?'

She nodded, relieved. 'But only a small quantity. Not too much.'

'Of course, madame. Not too much.'

He began to laugh, and his laugh was exactly like that of the hotel-porter and his wizened satellite when she had confessed to being hungry. Involuntarily, she herself joined in.

When he had given the order to one of the sweating cooks, he picked up a tablecloth from a stack on a corner of the counter beyond the cash-desk, shook it out, and approached her table once again. Since the tablecloth before her was clean, she wondered what he was going to do with it. Without looking at her — it was as if, deliberately, he were avoiding her gaze — he carefully placed the tablecloth over her overcoat on the chair opposite to her, twitching it now on one side and now on another to make sure that it lay in precisely symmetrical folds, and then stood back for a moment to confirm that no mistake had been made. Still not meeting her gaze, he walked off.

She was puzzled by this interment of her ordinary grey woollen coat under the dazzling napery. But when she gazed about the cavernous restaurant — it had now become much fuller — she saw that at other tables other tablecloths had been draped, admittedly not with similar care, over discarded coats. In some cases, where the party was a large one, these coats, piled on top of each other and then surmounted by the cloth, looked like some slumped Arab woman under a voluminous veil.

She had been foolish to order a T-bone steak, since meat in such quantity and so little disguised always induced in her a vague nausea, even while she told herself how tender and delicious it was. Soon, as she cut sliver after sliver from it, it was standing in a pool of pinkish blood. 'Everything all right, madame?' the waiter asked, as he hurried past her, balancing at shoulder-level a vast silver salver on which a profusion of meats — liver, steaks, chops, kidneys — had been piled high. Perhaps he had guessed from her expression that all was not precisely right. 'Yes, thank you,' she answered; and soldiered on.

Soon the wine, the heat — though so distant, that vast bed of charcoal seemed to be breathing directly at her — and the noise, echoing in the white vault of the ceiling, had begun to make her feel vaguely giddy and confused. She pushed aside her plate, the steak barely half-consumed, jabbed at some more lettuce and tomato with a fork, and then pushed aside that plate, too. She took her cigarettes and her lighter out of her bag and again she lit up.

'Was everything to madame's satisfaction?'

'Yes, thank you. It was excellent. But far too much. I'm not used to such vast quantities of meat.'

Again there was that laugh. 'In Argentina we eat too much meat.' He went on to ask if she would like some sweet – a *bombe surprise*, a Mont Blanc, a cassata? – but at each suggestion she shook her head, her eyes fixed, not on those remarkable pale-grey eyes, but on those no less remarkable teeth. Some coffee, then? Yes, some coffee.

As she sipped the coffee, she watched him moving about the restaurant. Unlike some of the other waiters, who shouted their orders, snatched up dishes, and all but ran between the tables, he never gave any impression of hurry; and yet, miraculously, he forestalled all requests. A woman would be about to ask for some oil and there, just as she was raising a plump hand and opening her mouth, he would appear beside her, the cut-glass bottle in his hand. A man would want a toothpick and, even before he had started to look around for one, the waiter would arrive, setting down the holder with a flourish. When Carol herself had decided that the time had come to ask for the bill, he was already asking: 'Would madame like something else?'

There was a service charge of twenty-five per cent, but none-theless she left a tip far in excess of what Ian would have given. The waiter showed no particular gratitude or surprise, merely bowing as he murmured: 'Thank you, madame.'

As she got to her feet, he whipped the tablecloth off the chair opposite, with some of the exuberant triumph of a sculptor un-veiling what he is sure will prove his masterpiece, folded it deftly and placed it over another chair. Then he took up her coat and helped her into it.

'I hope madame enjoyed her meal?'

'Very much. Very much indeed.'

'But there was too much meat!'

'Yes, too much meat, much too much!'

They both laughed.

As she made her way back along the board-walk above the excavations, she clutched tightly at the hand-rail. Though it was totally irrational, she had a panic certainty that at any moment the planks would collapse and she would hurtle down, among splintered fragments of wood, into the darkness and dankness far below. But eventually, with a gasp of relief, she had come to the end and emerged out on to the pavement beside a busy thoroughfare.

As she walked on at a faster and faster pace, hands deep in pockets, she began to think of the sleek military-looking waiter. Yes, beautiful, beautiful. That was the only adjective that described him. Now, what would a man like that be doing in a job like that? It seemed so improbable. She was passing a small public garden, with iron hoops set in the ground to fence this area of quiet darkness off from the bustle and brightness of the street. She had seen a bench, and in order to reach it she stepped over the hoops, instead of walking round to the gate. There was no one else in the garden — no doubt because to any Argentine such a night would seem far too cold for loitering. She would smoke one more cigarette out here, in the dampness and gloom, before she went back to the hotel. 'Old enough to be your father. . . .' She could hear her mother say it of a middle-aged vet, who had been a neighbour of theirs and with whom she had been briefly infatuated, hurrying round to his premises, a school-girl of fifteen, to help him with sweeping out kennels or feeding ailing cats and dogs. In his innocence, he had never realised that it was not with animals but with him that she was in love.

Well, she'd better get back to the hotel.

When she opened the bedroom door, she found that, surprisingly, the light was on and Ian had returned before her. He sat slumped in the one armchair with a plate of sandwiches and a glass of their duty-free whisky before him.

'You're already back! If I'd know you'd be so quick, I'd have waited for you.' She took off her coat and put it over the back of the chair beside the bed, remembering how those broad hands, their nails buffed to a pinkish shine, had covered it so oddly and so deftly with that tablecloth.

'Oh, it was the usual cock-up. They didn't want me at all. Why they couldn't have telephoned. . . .'

They were all inconsiderate with him, because they knew that he was not the sort of person who had to be considered. He was not like the majestic black soprano, who was perfectly capable of announcing that she was 'indisposed' and must cancel her opening-night performance, or like the no less majestic Russian bass, who bellowed with rage and thumped anything handy, if anyone tried to thwart him or criticise him.

Carol went to Ian and put her arms around him, lowering her cheek to his.

'Have you been smoking?'

'Of course. But not in here.'

'Your hair smells of it. Filthy habit!' But he was joking.

He began to loosen her hold, putting up his hands and gripping her arms above the elbows. Then he reached for another sandwich, peered at it, and finally took a bite. 'Dry. Dry bread, dry ham. I bet you had a lovely dinner.'

'Yes. Yes, it *was* rather lovely.'

She removed her coat from the chair and went towards the cupboard to hang it up. As she placed it over a coat-hanger, there came back to her the image of those coats each interred under a white tablecloth all about the restaurant.

It was several nights later when she saw the waiter again. By then Ian was about halfway through the fourteen performances that he had contracted to give. In general, the critics had been polite but unenthusiastic: he had 'courageously' taken over the role at short notice; he showed an admirable musicianship; the voice was 'light but well-focused'. All this was what both Ian and Carol had expected and yet both were disappointed that their expectations had not been confounded.

Carol had been having a drink and coffee after an early dinner — not at the 'San Bernardino' but at a cheap snack-bar recommended by the wife of someone at the Embassy. It was ten o'clock and the opera, which did not begin until nine and was interrupted by intervals so long that it would almost be possible to eat a three-course meal during one of them, would not end until long after midnight. Even now those women glittering with far too much jewellery and wearing furs despite the warmth would be promenading with their black-tied escorts through foyers that flatteringly gave them back their own reflections from mirrors framed in elaborate gilt.

Suddenly, as she raised her glass and looked about her, she realised that the waiter from the San Bernardino was staring at her intently. He was seated with a group of men of the same age as himself but not of the same impressiveness — oh, far from it — all of them brooding silently in their chairs as though bored with each other. They might have been a group of businessmen, who had concluded whatever transaction they had had with each other and now merely out of politeness did not immediately separate and go their different ways. He was in a dark-blue pinstripe suit, with a stiff collar and the kind of tie that, in England, would indicate that he was proud of having gone to some minor public school. His feet were on the chair opposite to him, his ankles crossed, and his chin was sunk low on his chest.

Their eyes met again, and this time he gave a half-smile of seeming recognition; but she at once looked away. Soon, the intentness of his gaze had become almost insolent; she was aware of that but she resisted the impulse to meet his eyes again. His companions seemed totally unconscious both of her and of the scrutiny to which she was being subjected, as they made desultory remarks to each other, eyed the women who passed, often arms linked, beside their table, or sipped from their drinks. Yes, he was beautiful, beautiful; and she thought of Ian's firm, slim, white body and the gentle way in which he had repulsed her earlier that evening, putting her aside from him, when she had gone into the bathroom as he was towelling himself down and placed her arms round his shoulders.

Eyes still averted, she gulped at her drink and gulped again. It tasted salt and brackish, almost like blood. A young man lingered briefly beside her table, looking down at her in a bird-like way as though he were about to peck her; but, receiving no encouragement, he eventually moved on, hands deep in pockets as he

whistled 'Don't cry for me, Argentina'. The musical was forbidden
and yet everyone seemed to have heard the music.

Still the waiter stared, chin resting on his chest and the strange
pale-grey eyes fixed on her from under the black sweeping eyebrows. Had that half-smile really been one of recognition, as at
first she had assumed? Or was he merely staring at her because
she was a woman by herself and he was a man bored with the
exclusively male companions with whom he found himself? She
began to feel self-conscious and clumsy. When she poured some
more coffee out of the silver pot on the tray beside her brandy –
the handle was so hot that she had to wrap a paper napkin round
it – she slopped some into the saucer; and when she raised the
cup she had to hasten to wipe away, with the same napkin, the
drips that splattered her blouse. Suddenly, she began to shiver,
though overhead electric bars were radiating their warmth over
those customers who had opted to sit outside in this Argentine
winter evening as warm as many an English summer one.

When she next had an opportunity to do so, she asked for her
bill. There were innumerable noughts at the end of the figure; but
by now she had got used to them and they did not cause her the
same alarm as when first she had arrived. Even so, the sum was an
absurdly high one. A glass of the local brandy and a pot of coffee
and she was paying out over two pounds.

She got up, her chair scraping back on the pavement and the
nape of her neck suddenly feeling the heat of the electric bar
above her, and began to walk away slowly, without looking at
him. She had forgotten to ask for some cigarettes, as she had
intended, from the bar, but even at this hour there were countless
little kiosks and tunnel-like openings in walls where she could get
some. A wan youth leaned against a lamp-post, hands in pockets
and one foot, shod in scuffed suede, crossed over the other. She
remembered that she and Ian had passed him at exactly the same
place long after midnight when returning from the opera-house.
That he did not even glance at her with his lacklustre eyes, in a
country in which every male seemed to glance at a woman of her
age, seemed to confirm Ian's verdict ('But how on earth can you
know?') that he must be a male tart. Beyond him, she saw one of
the tunnel-like openings and entered. She pointed at a packet of

Benson & Hedges and the frail old woman with arthritic hands in mittens reached up and got it down for her. But as she fumbled for her purse in her bag, a hand came out from behind her and held out a note between forefinger and middle-finger. Curiously, though she had been totally unaware that he had followed her into the shop and even that he had been walking behind her, she felt no surprise. She knew whose hand it was and she knew why he was paying for the cigarettes. She took the packet and, without looking at him, walked past him and out of the door.

He caught her up and, beside her now as she continued to walk down the street, took her arm lightly.

'You are always alone.'

'Not always. But. . . . ' No, she would not tell him about Ian.

'It is sad to be a foreigner alone in a strange country.'

'Oh, I don't feel sad. I rather like it.'

'You are always smoking. That is because you are sad.'

'How do you know that?'

She had meant 'How can you say with such certainty that I am sad?' but, misunderstanding her, he replied: 'In the restaurant — five cigarettes. This evening, how many? Three? Four?'

She laughed. 'I've no idea. I didn't count.'

'Why did you never come back to the restaurant?'

'Because I went to other restaurants. Cheaper ones.'

'Was that necessary? You look rich.'

'I'm certainly *not* rich!'

'You look rich. Expensive clothes. Expensive perfume.'

'Well, I'm not.'

It was a strange conversation and yet nothing in it surprised or disturbed her. There was a rhythm to it, unfamiliar yet potent, like the rhythm of some dance that one has never attempted before and yet immediately masters; and there was the same rhythm to this walk, side by side, very slow, their gaze never meeting, through this canyon of the city. She had no wish to ask him about himself — Are you married? Where did you learn such excellent English? Why do you work in a restaurant? — and he seemed to be similarly devoid of any curiosity about her. Her only curiosity now was a sexual one. How would he look stripped of that pinstripe suit and that shirt with the stiff collar, and of the vest and pants beneath them? And how would he make love to her — gently or violently, noisily or in silence, approaching her by stealth or with the snap and lash of an uncoiled spring?

They arrived at the hotel and it seemed perfectly natural that they should mount the steps together and that he should stand behind her as she asked for her key. There was a bar on the first floor and she had already decided that the porter would suppose merely that she was taking this guest up there for a drink. Ian and she had entertained some of his colleagues from the opera-house in its dim-lit, slightly clammy luxury more than once.

But to her horror, he greeted the cheekily flirtatious porter as though he were a friend. 'Hey, Alfredo!'

They spoke for a while in Spanish, the porter's gold fillings glittering as he threw back his narrow close-cropped head and laughed repeatedly. She had no idea what they were saying to each other. She hoped it was nothing about herself.

The bedroom was — as always at this hour — far too hot, and, curiously, for she could smell the cigarette that she had smoked before she had left it, just as though she had acquired Ian's sensitivity. The waiter said nothing. He merely approached her and began, deliberately and expertly, to undress her as though she were some mannequin in a shop-window. The pale-grey eyes were blank. Eventually she stood naked before him, feeling no vestige of shame under that steady gaze that gave away nothing and seemed to ask nothing. He put his hands on her breasts, the coldness of them making her give a brief involuntary gasp, and then gripped them with sudden force, which made her gasp again. Then he gently began to massage the nipples. She put her hand down to feel him but he said, 'No,' shaking his head. He led her to the bed and laid her down on it. Face turned up to the ceiling, she waited, without looking at him. She heard first one shoe and then the other fall to the floor. She heard a rustle, then another rustle. That click must have been a cuff-link. A rustle again.

At last he clambered on top of her; the pale-grey eyes looked into hers. There was a crucifix round his neck and she could feel it, like a sharp sliver of ice, against her throat. For a second, she had a strange fantasy of its cutting, painlessly but deep, into the carotid artery, so that all at once her life would be spurting out of her, while he continued to look down into her eyes in total indifference.

She put her hand down again; and this time he made no protest. 'Beautiful,' she murmured. 'Beautiful.' As she said the word, the central heating started that panting and throbbing as though, somewhere far below, a steam-engine was about to start out on a journey. She could feel, with an amazing hyperaesthesia, each hair on his chest, his forearm and his thigh; each drop of sweat on his shoulder; each breath that he drew. 'Beautiful.'

When they had ended, he got off the bed and went into the bathroom. She heard the water running into the bidet and called out, 'For God's sake use the towel on the left and not on the right!' He did not answer. She heard him clearing his throat and expectorating. Then — he must have found Ian's bottle of Listerine — there came the sound of gargling. Finally, he was urinating. It was odd, she thought, to use the bidet first and then to urinate, not the other way about. All at once she felt soiled — not by the semen trickling out of her, and not by his saliva and sweat, but by this whole elaborate ritual of cleansing. It was as though he regarded her as a whore, who might transmit some disease to him, which he in turn might transmit to his wife.

He came out of the bathroom and, without looking at her, began to dress. She watched him, marvelling yet again at that beauty; but he never once glanced at her, as he hurriedly pulled on vest, shirt, pants, socks and then went over to the mirror to tie his tie before pulling on his trousers as well and reaching for his jacket. Dressed, he turned to her and at last gazed down at her for a moment before opening the door. The pale-grey eyes looked even paler than usual and still they were devoid of any kind of expression. She had seen that same kind of blankness in the eyes of a girl at school after she had had one of her attacks of *petit mal.*

'Are you going so soon? Let me give you a drink.' She raised herself on an elbow, drawing the sheet up about her in a sudden access of modesty that she had not for a moment felt until now.

But silently and swiftly he had gone, answering nothing, promising nothing, acknowledging nothing.

'Oh, you've used my towel! How often have I told you . . . ?'

But Ian was too tired, and too much discouraged by a performance that he knew to have been deteriorating night after night, to notice much. 'And my Listerine . . . ,' he grumbled at one moment; and at another: 'You do manage to get an awful lot of water on to the floor of this bathroom!'

When at last he was nestling down beside her – he was too done-in to want to eat, he said – he asked her: 'Why so early to bed?' Since they had arrived in Argentina, they had got into the habit of retiring long after midnight.

'I was bored.'

'Yes, I'm afraid it *is* boring for you. Never mind. We'll soon be home. Only another nine days.'

'Nine days!'

After five of those nine days, consumed by a restlessness that manifested itself in a number of trivial ways – she scratched and tore with each forefinger at the skin around each thumb-nail, she snapped at Ian, at the lethargic negligent maids and at an uncommonly stupid clerk in the post-office, she took long walks up and across and down the grid of the city, she was perpetually washing her hair, her own and Ian's hairbrushes, their underclothes – Carol resolutely made her way to the restaurant. It was about the same time as when last she had visited it; the huge bed of charcoal still glowed, as the sweating boy in the overlong apron exerted himself at the bellows; the head-waiter showed the same worried irresolution, as he looked around the almost deserted restaurant, before guiding her over to precisely the same table at which she had sat before. Obviously, it was not a 'good' table, so near to the cooking area and to the cash-desk; but, then, what single woman was ever regarded as a 'good' customer? Again she took off her coat and again the head-waiter carefully folded it and put it over the back of the gilt chair opposite to her, before he handed her the menu and disappeared.

She waited, her eyes fixed on the Spanish waiter, in total composure and total certainty that it would be he, the beautiful one, who would eventually come to take her order.

'Is madame ready to order?'

Yes, she had known it all along.

She now looked up and, as she smiled, the pinched, slightly disagreeable expression of her face was irradiated with a happiness that made her look almost as beautiful as the man standing above her. 'Hello!'

He nodded, with a polite irony, as any waiter might do to an eccentric female foreigner who greeted him so familiarly. 'Good evening, madame. Would madame like to order now or shall I come back later?'

She could not believe it: it was as though he were now seeing her for the first time. But then she decided that probably he was frightened of gossip if he were seen talking intimately with her — after all, she knew nothing about him and he might be married and even related by that marriage to the proprietor or the head-waiter or one of the other waiters; and so she replied quietly but with a slight tremor in her voice: 'No, I'm ready to order now.' She ordered precisely what she had ordered on the previous occasion, with each of them repeating, almost word for word, their exchanges about what kind of salad she would have and what kind of wine.

'Thank you, madame.' He bowed and withdrew.

She was waiting now for something, the next stage of this curious ritual; but at first she could not remember precisely what it was. But then, as she glanced round the restaurant, her chin cupped in the palms of both her hands while her elbows rested on the table, she saw those strange mounds of starched whiteness at every table: the overcoats covered with their tablecloths. But he brought no tablecloth to cover hers.

Well, it must be an oversight, she decided; it was too trivial to worry about and certainly not something to which to draw attention. A young couple, also obviously not deserving of a 'good' table, were ushered over in her direction by the head-waiter. The girl, who was tall, pale and not unattractive, slipped out of a shabby woollen coat, one button of which was hanging loose from a thread; the boy, who had a simian look, with unusually long, dangling arms, removed an overcoat spotted with oil at the hem. For them the waiter took a tablecloth from the heap, shook it out, brought it over and arranged it symmetrically. Then, as though aware all along that Carol had been watching him, he looked over to her, even while giving the tablecloth a final tweak, and for the first time smiled. But it was not a smile of love, friendliness or complicity, but of a contempt so blatant that it was as though he had come over to her and slapped her across the face.

Soon after that, she asked him in a low voice, as he was hurrying past the table, to bring her the bill. She had hardly touched the steak, which was congealing in a pool of blood and fat; she had swallowed only a mouthful or two of the salad. Only the wine she had finished, gulping it down, despite that same slightly salty, slightly brackish taste, as of blood.

'The bill, madame? Certainly, madame.'

He put the plate down beside her and she carefully counted out from her purse the precise sum asked. She was being mean, she knew; but she wanted to be mean.

He picked up the plate. 'Thank you, madame.' Totally indifferent.

He did not help her on with her coat; and, though she knew that the head-waiter was watching as she struggled to get an arm into a sleeve, neither did he.

'Thank you, madame,' the head-waiter said. The other had vanished.

It was their last night in Buenos Aires, and Ian said that they must have a celebration, even though there was nothing to celebrate but their imminent return to England and a cheque that, because of various inexplicable deductions for tax and stamp-duty, was for far less than they had hoped.

'What about that steak-restaurant you told me about? I feel like a large juicy steak.'

She hesitated for a moment and then thought: Why not? There was nothing to lose, since everything had been lost already.

Although the restaurant was thronged with people when they arrived — it was almost ten o'clock — the head-waiter at once hurried forward when he saw them. 'This way, please.' He sidled between tables at which, chairs thrust back, flushed diners shouted at each other in between gobbling chunks of bleeding flesh. Yes, this table was a 'good' one, set far away from the cooking area and the cash-desk and far from the door, in what was almost an alcove. The head-waiter helped her off with her coat, as he had not done on either of the previous occasions, and then took Ian's coat from him, too. He neatly folded both coats over the back of the chair between the two on which they were about to sit and then, when they were seated, handed each of them a menu.

'Are you ready to order, sir?'

She did not have to look up to know who it was.

'Yes, I think so. Yes.'

'May I recommend the mixed grill?'

'That sounds an excellent idea. How about that, darling?'

Carol remembered the silver salver, piled high with meats, that the waiter had carried at shoulder-level through the restaurant to a party at the farthest end. She nodded and answered: 'Why not?'

Eventually, without having given her a single glance, the waiter went off to deliver the order. While Ian babbled on about a telephone call that he had received about two possible engagements at Glyndebourne — his career seemed to consist largely of possibilities that never got realised — Carol watched the athletic figure in the beautifully cut dinner-jacket as it moved about its tasks.

Now the waiter had gone over to the pile of tablecloths. He raised it at one corner, as though he were in search of a table-cloth even more dazzling and even larger than any on a table in the restaurant. He at last jerked one out, and then gave it a shake, so that it opened out like a parachute before him. He hurried over with it.

He still did not look at Carol as he placed it, in that curiously reverent ritual, as though he were draping some altar, over their coats. As on that first occasion, he tweaked at a corner, stood back to examine the result, and then tweaked at another. The folds fell stiff and symmetrical to the floor. The overhead light glittered harshly on the chalk-like blankness. It glittered so harshly indeed that, as though she were staring out over the sea on a day of brilliant sunshine, she felt herself screwing up her eyes and then, slowly, a headache forming between them.

Satisfied at last, the waiter gave a friendly smile to Ian and then moved off.

'What a weird idea!'

'Yes, isn't it? But you must have seen it before. They often do it.'

'Not in the kind of cheap eating-places where *I've* been keeping body and soul together!'

'But you must remember, in that place which that conductor man took us to. . . .'

She broke off, oppressed almost beyond endurance by the sight of the strange white shapes, dotted like so many gravestones all over the cavernous restaurant. When her plate was at last set down before her, it brought a strange relief to cut deep into a kidney and to see the beads of blood ooze out, as from an ox still alive.

An Evening at the Track

Douglas Dunn

HUMPHREY MACGIBBON used to run the 400 metres hurdles
and had been good at it by anyone's standards. At twenty-three,
he broke his left leg in several places when he came off Harry
Anson's prize possession, an old Matchless 1000 cc motorcycle.

When he was standing still, Humphrey looked every bit an
athlete. He was tall, broad-shouldered and solid in the way 400-
metres hurdlers usually are. It was only when he walked, with that
jerking limp of his, that it became clear Humphrey was a man
who had had an accident. 'I'm the only man I know', he said,
with a humour that disguised his disappointment, 'who looks
more like a one-lap man when he's sitting down than when he's
walking about.'

'Look on the bright side, for God's sake,' said Harry Anson,
who was usually in a bad mood, and who had never allowed himself to admit that either he or his collector's item of a motorbike
was to blame for Humphrey's infirmity. 'At least you don't need
to feel guilty every time you go out for a drink.'

'Is there anyone here, Harry, who seriously believes I could
have taken my time down any more? I needed to lose another
two seconds to be anywhere near world class.' He looked at the
others in the club's pavilion and dressing-rooms. No one else
seemed to be listening. 'It doesn't matter.'

'Sure, sure,' said Harry Anson. He had his special reason for
wishing that Humphrey would stay away from the club. Everyone
else was familiar with Humphrey's resignation, his good-natured
acceptance of the worst that could have happened to him. But
they, too, were less than delighted to see him, although they were
welcoming when he arrived, as he did, about one evening a week.
He had been the one outstanding athlete the club had produced.

They liked him. They admired him. It was not his presence so much as the presence of his limp that disturbed them.

Humphrey watched Harry Anson put on his tracksuit. 'Why do you bother?' he asked, encouraging a laugh from the others.

'Keep the old belly in trim,' said Harry Anson, tapping his stomach. He was an indifferent athlete in whom, they all agreed, natural ability had been allowed to go to waste because of indolence, nights out, girls, beer and cigarettes. He left the pavilion. In a few minutes the changing-rooms were empty.

Someone who had trained on his own earlier in the evening was in the showers. Humphrey could hear the water running. He pulled himself to his feet, and, hobbling with the walking-stick he still had to use, went out on the veranda. He leaned against the railings for a few minutes. It was a fine evening in late May, before the competitive season had properly begun. A couple of fixtures against other clubs was all that had been held, but the first important meet of the year was coming up that Saturday, the Western District Championships. Humphrey had always enjoyed it, in spite of having more celebrated championships and matches to look forward to later in the summer. Like most athletes, he had taken a sly if modest pride in being immeasurably superior to the best local opposition. A hard-earned third place in a classy time against international fast-men from the United States, Poland, or France, was satisfying to look back on; but he preferred to remember an arrogant fifty-five seconds in the heats of the Western District Championships – a time which the second- or third-placed men, in the final, would have done well if they had matched. Towards the end of that Saturday afternoon in late May, he used to anchor his club's 4 x 400 metres relay squad. Usually, he was faced with the prospect of overhauling a deficit of forty or fifty metres. He revelled in it. On only one occasion out of five had he failed to pull it off, and even then it had been a matter of a couple of feet, having provided the best race of the day.

A smell of cut grass from the centre and outside surroundings of the track was conspicuous in the still air. A cricket team was practising at its nets. It was so still that in spite of the distance he could hear the smack of bat against ball. Five runners trotted through an open gate in the high hedge which hid the track from the road. They were the marathon and long-distance runners, setting off for their fifteen miles over the hills and lanes in the countryside beyond the edge of the suburb. Ferguson, the coach in charge of sprinters, was instructing junior members of the club on how to adjust their starting-blocks. Long-jumpers were high-kicking and bounding against space or stretching on the grass. High-jumpers were measuring high-kicks against a bar raised six feet above the ground. A dozen varieties of calisthenics were portrayed. Women athletes were coming out from their club-house on the other side of the track — always, for some reason, a few minutes later than the men. Humphrey waved, and they waved back. Round the track were three packs of runners, jogging, shuffling, warming up. A coach pulled someone out for a chat. A group laughed, sharing a joke.

Humphrey went carefully down the wooden steps to the level of the rolled cinders. Breaking into a caricature of his one-legged run, he hobbled across the track in front of a band of tracksuited runners. Peter Cairns, the club's senior coach, was consulting his clipboard. On sheets of tabulated paper, he had listed the names of his athletes, a sheet for each runner. Neatly typed were his notes on what he intended his charges to get through, day by day, week by week, various distances at various speeds, how much, how fast. All this physical arcana would be measured against one of his many stopwatches. He might have four or five watches running at the same time.

'Humphrey, would you hold that?' said Cairns, handing him the clipboard and its wads of training-schedules, leaving him free to shake an apparently deficient stopwatch against his ear. 'Perfect conditions,' said Cairns curtly.

'Yes. The wind's dropped for a change.' The weather was the way it should have been and seldom was — no wind, no rain, and a clear sky. 'I've been thinking', said Humphrey, 'that I might do a little coaching. Have you any suggestions, Peter?'

'Later,' said Cairns. He was a busy man. 'But I don't see why not,' he added, before he trotted over to where a group of athletes was waiting for him.

Humphrey followed him and stood for a few minutes listening

to Cairns' pronouncements on the evening's work-out. A few runners protested, as they always did. One said he was too tense to train on the track. He set off for a run over the nearby golf-course. The runner was a noted prima donna, a loner who found that the social endurance of training with other runners did not suit him. Cairns was angry and it took a few minutes for him to get rid of his petulance. He was fat, in his tracksuit. Humphrey supected that Cairns' belly was as dead as his own left leg.

Dr O'Neill, the club's secretary, was sitting on a camp stool on the veranda, pulling sheets of paper from his briefcase. They were entry forms for the open meets in which most of the club's runners would compete because they were not up to the standard of championship events. Humphrey was about to go and have a word with Dr O'Neill when Cairns asked him if he would hold a watch on a young middle-distance runner. 'Fine,' he said, glad of the chance to be useful.

The young runner set off from the starting-line. Seconds ticked by on the watch. A good distance away, the runner who had been too 'tense' to train on the track could be seen as a green-track-suited figure climbing the first green incline of the links. Humphrey turned his attention to the young 1500 metres runner. Fluently, with a confidence that told Humphrey that the runner either had more natural ability than Cairns had noticed, or that he had trained hard before joining the club, he came up to the finishing-mark. 'Sixty-two!' Humphrey shouted as he passed him. 'Dead on!' Cairns' schedule said that the runner should be doing laps in sixty-eight seconds, with a lap of four minutes in between each faster 400 metres.

'You're supposed to be doing sixty-eights,' said Humphrey.

'I've done this before,' said the runner. 'You can tell him what you like,' he said, meaning the coach, 'but I'm doing twelve in sixty-two.' He set off jogging a lap.

'Is that wise?' said Humphrey, but the young runner kept going, without an answer.

'Good evening,' said Dr O'Neill on the veranda. He had his medical practice in the same suburban district where the club had its pavilion. 'These chestnuts', he said, pointing with his pen, 'have come out since Saturday. Best-looking trees in the entire district.'

A young sprinter, heavy about the shoulders, went striding past the veranda. 'What's Ferguson thinking about?' said Humphrey. 'That lad ought to move up to the four hundred.'

'Twenty-two point five last night,' said Dr O'Neill, 'on a grass track. He won the Inter-Schools two-twenty. And I thought last night', he said, with a sly smile, 'that there goes another Humphrey MacGibbon. I don't suppose you remember when I told you to move up to the four-forty.' Dr O'Neill's mind had failed to go metric. He still talked of furlongs, quarters, half-miles. To Dr O'Neill, a middle-distance runner was still a miler or three-miler.

'Can he hurdle?'

'I doubt it,' said Dr O'Neill. 'But neither could you until I taught you.'

Humphrey snapped the stopwatch back into motion as the middle-distance runner set off on another lap. 'I'm no expert on the long stuff,' said Humphrey, 'but he looks pretty useful.'

'He's going too fast,' said Dr O'Neill. 'Cairns'll just burn out young chaps like that. All these foreigners that Cairns gets his fancy ideas from.'

'It's not Cairns' fault this time.'

'Then you tell him, "Make haste slowly," ' said Dr O'Neill, reiterating his favourite maxim.

'Just under thirty-one at two-hundred. The lad can judge his pace,' said Humphrey.

'Humphrey, we're having an argument,' said a sixteen-year-old, from the cinders in front of the veranda.

'Was your best time', asked the boy beside him, 'fifty point eight, or fifty-one?'

'Sixty-two!' shouted Humphrey, as the subject on his watch crossed the line again. 'Fifty point five,' said Humphrey casually, waving to his middle-distance runner, and switching the stopwatch back to its stopped zeros.

'What does it feel like? I mean, at the end, after a fifty point five?' asked one of the boys.

'It depends', said Humphrey, 'on whether you've won or lost.' He enjoyed saying such things to the young members of his Harriers club, having himself joined when he was fourteen.

'I mean, the exhaustion, what does it feel like?'

'You'll never know', said Humphrey, 'until you've been there.'

Ferguson, the sprints coach, called the two boys towards him, and directed them, like truants, to two vacant starting-blocks.

'If there was one thing I hated,' said Humphrey, 'it was rehearsing sprint starts. Now, that I don't miss, not in the least.'

'In my day,' said Dr O'Neill, 'you scooped a couple of holes in the track, shoved your feet in them, and that was that.'

The evening was now at its most animated. Cairns and others were calling out times. Jogging men athletes were making remarks to jogging women athletes. Long-jump and high-jump pits were busy. A lone hulk was shot-putting out of harm's way, on his concrete circle in the centre of the track. As always, the javelin-thrower was being advised to see an optician.

'Sixty-two!' Humphrey called out again to the young middle-distance runner.

'You'd better tell him to slow it down,' said Dr O'Neill. 'Cairns'll throw a fit if he notices what that lad's doing.'

'Ach,' said Humphrey, 'it doesn't matter. The lad's obviously done this before. We'll see if he can learn the hard way.'

Harry Anson, at the tail end of a pack, went round on one of his fast laps. Humphrey timed him, out of interest. The lap took sixty-seven seconds. Harry, bringing up the rear, did not look tired so much as bored. Cairns, his taskmaster, said nothing about it.

'Cairns', said Humphrey, 'must know nothing, if he can't see that the lad's running sixty-twos instead of sixty-eights. I mean, the difference is visible.'

'That's right,' said Dr O'Neill, who had never liked Cairns. 'An unhappy man is Cairns. There are women now who can run a faster marathon than he ever managed.'

'Talking of women,' said Humphrey, 'what's she doing here?'

'She', said Dr O'Neill, 'is a very promising shot-putter. That's how they build them these days.'

'*I* can run faster than that.'

'Not when you're carrying heavy weights, you can't,' said Dr O'Neill.

Humphrey looked and saw that, indeed, the shot-putter was carrying weights which, as she ran, she raised to the height of her chin, first one hand, then the other.

'Good God!'

'They tell me she's nifty on the judo floor as well.'

'What makes women do things like that?'

'What', asked Dr O'Neill, 'makes men want to run the four hundred hurdles in fifty point five?'

Before the light began to fade, at about eight-thirty, Humphrey's middle-distance runner finished his session. Only in the last three of his fast laps had he failed to be within a second of his ideal sixty-two seconds. 'That', said Humphrey, 'was terrific. Cheeky, but terrific. I'll look forward to seeing what you do on Saturday.'

'I'm looking for a coach.'

'Well, I'm no expert in middle-distance running, but I'll have a word with Peter if you like.'

'Couldn't you bone it up?'

'I could, I suppose,' said Humphrey, tentatively. 'But the four hundred and the four-hundred hurdles were my races.'

'I know. The thing is, you've been there.'

The coaches and Dr O'Neill cleared runners off the track. There was to be a race. The club's six 400-metres runners were to compete for the four places in the relay squad. They were already taking their tracksuits off at the start. Cairns, perspiring after his night's work, was examining his starter's gun.

'Will you think about it?'

'Sure. I'll tell you on Saturday,' said Humphrey, as the middle-distance runner trotted away, thinking about his ambitions.

Humphrey hobbled over to the veranda from where he knew Dr O'Neill would watch the race. Crossing the track, he wished the runners luck. He enjoyed his presence there, the way it acknowledged he had been faster than they could ever be, no matter how hard they trained or tried. He noticed that one of the runners was the tall broad-shouldered sprinter he had seen earlier in the evening, who had looked like an illusory memory of himself at seventeen. It made him stop. 'I dare say you could still beat me, Humphrey,' said one runner, bringing Humphrey back from whatever he thought he had seen and been absorbed by. 'I don't know why I bother.'

Light had faded into a cool greeny dusk in which birdsong was implicated, as well as a haze of late daffodils on the point of

withering which grew against a bank. Cricketers were returning to their club-house, their whites greyed by the distance. There
were a dozen people on the veranda, some in towels, others as
they had come from the track. Peter Cairns held up his starter's
pistol. He looked at it in his hand as if he liked the idea of himself as an armed man. 'To your marks!' The competitors stepped
into their blocks, apart from the man on the inside who, as an
800-metres runner, used a standing start. Two or three more
athletes came out from the pavilion to the veranda. Some wives
or girlfriends were standing at the nearest bend of the track, one
with an agitated dog held tightly on a short leash. Cairns, losing
patience, delayed the start until the dog had been shut up. On the
other side of the track, on the veranda of their club-house, the
women members of the club were gathered to watch the race. Dr
O'Neill stopped himself on the steps and waited to give the
starter and the runners the silence they deserved. 'Set!' ordered
Cairns, in a high-pitched growl, drawn out and serious until it
sounded like a threat. The gun went off.

Humphrey laughed under his breath with excitement. From
the gun, the young sprinter whom Humphrey had said to Dr
O'Neill should move up to the 400 metres began to take yards
out of the rest of the field.

As they raced round the first bend, the women who were
standing there screamed at them with that feminine enthusiasm
which, to any large crowd, adds a soprano pitch to the deeper-
voiced roar of spectators. It was a sound Humphrey used to listen
for in the days when he had been the centre of attention. The dog
barked at the runners as their spikes kicked up cinders with each
racing footfall.

'Well,' said Dr O'Neill, 'it was you who said he should move up
a distance.' He had the pretended nonchalance of an old-timer
who had seen too many runners come and go for him to have
been able to take a race as seriously as they took it themselves.
As he looked at Humphrey's tense enjoyment, he wished for the
time when Humphrey, too, would join him as an interested cynic,
fund-raising, organising the annual dances, distributing entry-
forms and being invited to officiate at minor championship
meetings. O'Neill's hero was Eric Liddell, who had won the

Olympic 400 metres Gold Medal in 1924, because the final of his chosen event was to have been run on a Sunday, and to have competed would have been to break the Sabbath. And so what, if Humphrey MacGibbon had run faster than Liddell, and on the club's own outdated cinder track?

Along the back straight, the young runner looked like a film of Humphrey. The others, by comparison, were clumsy, with their heads back, their arms flying across their chests. They were all effort and pluck and no style. They had nothing of the young runner's grace. His running had propriety, assurance; he possessed the event as, physically, his own. A distance, and speed, Humphrey knew, and as Dr O'Neill knew, were part of a physical identity. They were not chosen.

Over the last sixty metres, the young runner began to slow down. His elegance was tortured into painful mediocrity. Humphrey yelled at him, 'Fight! Fight it!' His face was as agonised as the runner's. Those who were also watching from the veranda were urging the runner on, too; but they were distracted by Humphrey's livid eagerness. As the winner broke the tape, Humphrey stopped his watch. Three others, at the finishing-line, were doing the same. Humphrey peered at the watch in the half-light. 'Forty-nine six!' He read off. 'Forty-nine six! Under fifty!'

Dr O'Neill was scrutinising his own watch. 'Five I made it. Forty-nine five.'

'You should've told me,' said Humphrey. 'I could've had a word with him beforehand.'

'I can still', said Dr O'Neill, 'spot the real thing when I see it.'

'Trained properly, he could be doing forty-eight by the end of the season,' said Humphrey, an emphatic pundit, speaking at first to no one, and then repeating himself to Dr O'Neill, who, he found, was looking at him with pitiful benevolence, as if he understood how pleased Humphrey was to have been replaced. 'That boy's a *natural* for the one-lap.'

'Another Humphrey MacGibbon,' declared Dr O'Neill to the crowded veranda. 'And I made it forty-nine *five*.'

'Forty-nine six!' shouted Ferguson, the sprints coach, announcing the consensus of the three time-keepers.

Long-distance road-runners came in from the B-roads and byeways, smelling of sweat and dusk. Others crowded into the club-house. Harry Anson came out, already showered and dressed, having finished early and ignored the race. 'Forty-nine six,' said Humphrey.

'Good for him,' said Harry Anson. 'Well, I suppose you'll be there on Saturday to see me lapped in the usual fashion?'

'I wouldn't miss it.'

'Thought not,' said Harry Anson.

The new 400 metres runner was escorted to the veranda by Cairns, Ferguson and the other 400 metres men. There was a lot Humphrey wanted to say to him but the coaches were too full of recent stimulus to allow themselves to be interrupted.

From the car-park, behind the high hedge at the back of the club-house, Humphrey heard the roar of Harry Anson's motor-cycle as he revved it up.

Steam came out of the club-house door. Shouting, laughter, and the sound of showers operating in spite of their antiquated plumbing were loud against Humphrey's ears. He did not go into the pavilion. He never did after an evening at the track. He had a dead left leg and it seemed cruel to remind everyone in there that they were susceptible to an accident. At the beginning of the evening, that did not seem to matter; but after their exertions it did not feel right that he should remind them of how everything can be taken away in one sharp high-spirited surprise. 'Good-night!' he said to someone leaving.

' 'Night, Humphrey!'

The season now appeared as something definitely to be looked forward to. There was a new middle-distance runner, and there was a new one-lap man. Forty-nine point six! At his first race over the distance! Carefully he went down the wooden steps. From inside the door, where he was distributing the entry-forms he had sorted out during the evening, Dr O'Neill could hear the tap of Humphrey's walking-stick on the steps. Then he could hear the limped rhythm of his walk over the spiked cinders.

Humphrey stopped and looked at the time registered on Peter Cairns' stopwatch. To take it back to him would have meant going into the club-house. He left the watch at the forty-nine six seconds recorded on it and put it in his pocket and walked home.

'Goodnight!' he said to the wives and girlfriends waiting in the car-park. They all knew him, if only from his stick, his limp, or his blazer, with its flagged badge of the national team. He lived only a short distance from the track, a few streets, which he could cover in nine minutes and forty-six seconds, in the dark, when no one was looking.

Modernisation

Brian Aldiss

ALTHOUGH George Laplace had been working in the Foreign Languages Institute for four months, this was the first time he had found himself invited to the Fans' flat. The Fans had taken pity on him because Sheila was in hospital.

Fan Xiaofen, the Chairman of the English Department, was a tall graceful man with a delicate bone-structure, who looked and was of aesthetic disposition. The large spectacles balanced at the end of his nose flashed with alert interest on the world. He still disconcerted Laplace by making notes of George's idiomatic usages during conversations, in an attempt to improve constantly his already excellent English.

Fan's wife, Qi Wu, was, like most of the women Laplace had met in China, subdued. She dresssed like her husband, in standard baggy pants and blue jacket, and her English was almost as fluent as his. She, too, wore spectacles, as if in a declaration of solidarity with her husband. Qi Wu had a beautiful smile and, as the Laplaces' friend Horgan pointed out, she liked to touch people, even Westerners. She was in charge of the administration of the Institute, and therefore in theory in a superior position to her husband; although her submissiveness would never allow this independence to show, she did frequently drive the department vehicle, and was an expert driver. This talent seemed to indicate in her a spark of individuality missing in many of her compatriots — or so the seven Foreign Experts attached to the Institute had decided, during their obsessive discussions of their Chinese colleagues.

Qi Wu poured Laplace some more tea. She, Fan, and Laplace had been sitting in the flat for two hours. No food or alcohol was served, only the bitter Chinese tea; Laplace had been in China long enough to expect nothing else — long enough, even, to want nothing else. He sat happily, smoking and talking, enjoying being in the Fans' modest room. They talked about China; there was no other topic. They were in Xi'an, once the capital of all China during the T'ang Dynasty; China surrounded them in every direction, physically and metaphysically. . . .

'Although the Cultural Revolution impeded our country on the road to modernisation,' Fan was saying, 'not all its effects were on the negative side. For instance, people were made to circulate, and so to reach more understanding of each other. I think I am less of a — h'm — a prig, you would say, for having been sent to work on a farm.'

'It's a question we keep coming back to time and time again,' Laplace said. 'Like most Chinese questions, we see it as being relevant to the rest of the world. If you do a turn on the farm, you understand more regarding the earth and other people's problems. At the same time, you turn a skilled postgraduate generation into farm-hands, and lose ground.'

'Chairman Mao said there should be no élites. Now we wish to have an élite to make the country competitive in the Four Modernisations, without becoming élitist. If that is possible.' Fan fell silent and rubbed his nose with a gesture Laplace had seen before; it seemed to indicate caution and puzzlement. George Laplace had a sense which often overcame him that at this point Chinese friends would say no more to Foreign Experts; as if conflict between autocracy and individualism was something that foreigners could not comprehend.

Laplace sipped his tea and turned to Fan Qi Wu. 'What happened to you during the Cultural Revolution, Qi Wu? You weren't married to Xiaofen then?'

'Of course I was too young to be married.' She smiled her bright smile. She was his own age, he knew, thirty-four, and would have been a mere child when the Revolution began. In any case, Chinese law did not permit Chinese town women to marry before the age of twenty-four.

'My experience was not so good as Xiaofen's. I was made to work for the cadres in their fields. It was hard for me. I had no friends because people were afraid to speak. The spell of exile was too long. Then the cadres put me in charge of their pigs. I loved the pigs because they were not afraid to be friendly with me.'

'Would you like a pig now, for sentiment's sake?' Laplace asked.

'Oh, it's not allowed to keep animals at the Institute,' Qi Wu answered. A good pragmatic answer; the Chinese regularly refused hypothetical questions. So much Laplace had observed, going on as usual to ask himself, was it because of a genuinely different type of thinking which placed absolutely no value on hypothetical questions (inviting a sentimental answer) like his; or were they incapable of perceiving that the question was classifiable as hypothetical; or were both sides up against a language barrier no one had as yet entirely identified; or were they too cautious to be lured into personal declarations; or were they so clever that they took every possible opportunity to remind him, quite unconsciously, that the sort of freedoms Americans enjoyed led to anarchy and got into his speech and could not be entertained even during an evening's chat between friends (so that he was being moulded, even now, to think as they did — something, incidentally, he often felt he needed, in order to solve all the pleasant mysteries which surrounded him daily — never more so than when his wife was away in hospital . . .).

'If we are not careful, we forget the bad things of the Cultural Revolution and recall only the pigs,' Fan said.

Laplace laughed. 'That's human nature. Research done in the States shows that past hardships are recalled with increasing affection the further away they get. There's a firm correlation.'

It was polite time for him to go. He had a lecture to prepare for the next day, and in Xi'an everyone rose early; it was an old peasant habit which the raw cities had yet to relinquish.

The Fans' flat was a regulation 450 square metres, divided into three small rooms and a kitchen containing a stove fuelled by coalbricks. The living-room in which they sat was whitewashed to waist height and painted blue above that. The overhead light was a hard fluorescent bar, but Fan had switched it off and lit a small low-wattage table-lamp, casting the room into comfortable shadow. The furniture was cheap and shiny, and seemed to have accumulated without thought. There were few objects about — a blue motorised fan, an alarm clock, a large vacuum flask sporting a bright picture of Shanghai waterfront, and some vases. On the wall were a hackneyed scroll picture of mountains and mist with an accompanying poem, and garish portraits of Mao and Hwa. There were also some photographs of relations and a calendar.

The only token of individuality was two rows of books, most of them in Chinese and including several works by Lenin and Mao, together with a smattering of English books, a *Webster's Dictionary*, a *Portable Hemingway*, and some short stories by Somerset Maugham. Here, thought George Laplace to himself as he rose to go, lived Xiaofen and Qi Wu, content to work hard every day, never quarrelling, never desiring other than what they had, never getting drunk, never going out on the spree or falling inconveniently in love with someone else's wife or husband, never needing a TV set, never longing for an automobile or a mad trip to San Francisco, never failing in patience or sanity. Wonderful. Maybe they turned into big black oily slug-things every midnight, just to escape human restraints.

They both shook his hand at the door. 'Don't worry about Sheila,' Fan said. 'The doctors will take excellent care of her at Number Four Hospital. It has the best reputation in Shaanxi Province.'

'Of course George worries,' Qi Wu told her husband. 'China's a foreign country to him.' She laughed. So did Xiaofen, and Laplace joined in.

But as their door closed behind him, and he felt his way down the unlit stair, he began to analyse Qi Wu's remark. Had there been a slight taunt in the lady's comment? Had he shown himself untrusting when the doctors had announced that Sheila, young though she was for the operation, stood in need of a hysterectomy, and would have it done under acupuncture anaesthesia? Yes, he damned well had. . . . But they were correct: she would be OK, and, yes, the acupuncture had left none of the unpleasant after-effects that general anaesthesia sometimes did.

Still he wondered about Qi Wu's remark. Had she implied that he treated them as foreign, alien? That was horrifying for, mystifying although he and the other Foreign Experts found all things Chinese, he felt a loving closeness for the whole culture. Or did she indicate some self-criticism by implying that she and Fan had treated him a little too cautiously? That was too imaginative an interpretation. Nor did he wish to think that they were glad that he with his foreign-ness had now left their little flat; perhaps they were already lying together on their hard bed, silently (how else?) making love in celebration of his leaving them.

That thought he repressed, or rather refused to explore further as he would have done at home; for he was less wanton than he had been, and that was China's doing. All the same, he allowed himself to wonder how long it would be before Sheila and he again made love.

Although the time was not yet eight-thirty, it felt like midnight, and the grounds of the Institute were deserted. The whole place was in a terrible muddle, and Laplace walked cautiously, keeping to the paths rather than taking a short cut over the open spaces. The block in which Sheila and he lived with the other Foreign Experts was some distance away, and elaborate buildings and demolition projects filled most of the distance. Large excavations, ditches, low foundations, scaffold poles, drainpipes, piles of material cluttered open space originally intended for basketball and football pitches. For once the Chinese ability to organise had evaporated; the entire site of the Institute grounds was a ghastly chaos and would, as far as anyone could see, remain so. It was proving increasingly impossible to teach in the circumstances, as if the external confusion reinforced or even echoed some lingering confusion within, which could not be dispelled. As the population attempted to march forward to modernisation it stumbled over its own eager feet.

Laplace had complained about the muddle to Fan, as chairman, when he first arrived, saying, 'Some of my students are unhappy about the mess – can't the new structures be built one at a time, with the entire work force concentrated in one place? Then everything will get done faster.'

'It is right for liberal students to make constructive suggestions,' Fan replied. 'But perhaps they have not studied enough what the site workers have to say. The workers may have decided on the most effective way to build, and the students may not understand their thinking. If both sides got together, they might find no contradiction. The new degenerates make anarchy by thinking selfishly, without proper consultation.'

The remarks remained in Laplace's mind. They had been mildly spoken, as Fan always spoke; but the connections between liberal thinking and degeneracy, and between criticism and anarchy, had alarmed Laplace and his wife. They had often discussed Fan's remarks, jokingly wondering if Fan, despite his modern approach, was not a reactionary, a secret sympathiser of the now-banished Gang of Four; and, as usual where Chinese questions were concerned, they had come to no conclusions.

One or two lights burned behind curtains in the block where the Foreign Experts had their flats. Bobby Wang, the Australian Chinese, was in; Laplace thought of knocking on his door and having a nightcap with him, but the idea of alcohol was less attractive than it had been — another cultural effect of working in China.

So he passed silently by Bobby's door. Since Sheila's departure for hospital, he had felt intensely alone. The Foreign Experts, maintaining their *esprit de corps*, had pressed him to join in their activities. Laplace had refused, turning instead to face a great silent presence, of which he had been aware and had eluded since his first day in China, the presence of — he supposed — the immense psyche of nine hundred million Chinese. That presence he found spooky but comforting, and he responded to it as a widower might respond to the apparition of a dead wife, and with the same result, that he became isolated from his fellows.

Laplace went slowly upstairs — there were no lifts in the whole of Xi'an, as far as he knew, not even in Number Four Hospital — unlocked his front door and entered his apartment. It was filled with the same cheap shiny furniture as Fan's flat; only here were reminders of Sheila and posters of the Rockies and Mile High Denver on the wall, in place of Chairman Mao. He settled down at the table, pulled over a textbook and began to study Chinese. As he worked through the intricate characters, he felt himself like a swimmer hobbling down a beach formed of sharp seashells, putting a toe in the chill ocean and looking out through sea mists to a distant island. One day, one day, he would get to that island and speak to them in their own tongue. . . .

After an hour's work, accompanying his reading with pencil

and paper — Chinese pencils were luxurious objects, inviting literacy — Laplace sat idly at the table, listening to the silence. How amazingly silent it was. There was no stillness like it in the States, even in the prairies; he pictured again the joke scare-headline he had once announced to Sheila in one of their early nights here: A DOOR SLAMS IN CHINA. . . . Now that Sheila herself was not here, everyone could be dead.

There was a tap at his door. Resentment filled him. He stood up, uncertain whether to respond. Perhaps they would go away. But people knocked at doors here; the building possessed no telephones. This was the Third World, as they never tired of telling you. Any phrase with a number in exerted a spell over the Han races: the Gang of Four, a hundred flowers blooming, the Third World, the Four Modernisations.

Bobby Wang, the Australian Chinese, stood outside in the passage, grinning all over his ugly and engaging face. He was a small burly man, and a great contributor to the morale of the Foreign Experts at the Institute. He was the odd man out of the seven, being unmarried; but he possessed an escape route that the other experts lacked. He could pass as native Chinese and do things the three foreign couples could never manage. At night, the Australian became a Chinese, when he slipped out of his Western clothes into local dress and mixed with the crowds in the streets of Xi'an. Next day, he would pass on accounts of his adventures, often in censored versions. The other experts, like Bobby himself, had contracted the Chinese disease: they thirsted for what they code-named China Information, for any fact, however slight, nourishing the belief that a myriad crumbs of information put together would solve the whole riddle of China for them, and everything would be understood. On that day and that day only would they feel free to go home.

'I was just off to bed,' Laplace said. 'Come in and have some tea.'

'Saw your light, George,' Bobbie said. 'I had to give you a knock. Slip your shoes on and come and get an eyeful of what I've found. It's worth it, honest to God. It'll kill you.'

'What is it?'

'The Millennium. Chinese dancing. In the Institute grounds.'

'You're kidding.'

'Get your skates on, chum. Come and look.'

He put out his light and locked his flat-door. The two men went together down the stairs. Bobby Wang led the way across the littered campus, uttering warnings of craters or other obstacles at frequent intervals. The darkness was almost unbroken. An occasional lighted window in the gaunt building blocks about them was too dim to shed radiance.

The grounds of the Institute were ringed by a high wall. Between the wall and the buildings generally stood pleasant trees, lending shade during the hot summers and colour in the otherwise colourless autumn. Under the sheltering branches, lights had been hung, straggling nakedly along a dipping length of cable. Beneath the bulbs, even as Bobby claimed, couples were dancing. The dancers were fringed by people who stood watching them. All, dancers and spectators, were almost faceless, so feeble were the lights above. Their forms seemed to melt together, their darkness to add to the darkness of the night. The lamps lit only their flowing movements.

A tango was playing. To one side was an old electric record-player, tended by two young students. Its music was soft — it would scarcely be heard over the other side of the wall, by passers-by in the street; equally silent were the dancers who embraced and turned, submerged beneath the rhythm.

'What a creepy sight!' Laplace exclaimed. 'Like ghosts.'

'No, it's lovely. They're enjoying themselves for once. They aren't just getting drunk or acting the fool, as they would be if this was Melbourne or Denver. Look how well they move.'

Laplace, as he became used to the gloom, saw that nobody was drinking, just as Bobby said. Some students carried tins of fruit juice. Because of the preponderance of male students, young men were dancing with other young men. But women were present; though all wore trousers like the men, an occasional flying pigtail was evident.

'Should they be doing this kind of thing?'

'Why not?'

'It all looks so kind of surreptitious.'

'Hang around and I'll see if I can rustle us up a pair of chicks to dance with.'

'No. Not my style.'

Bobby laughed and made no move, standing tapping with one foot to the music. As he said, the students certainly danced well, tangoing in what Laplace thought was a rather old-fashioned way. But where had so many of them learned to *tango*, for God's sake? How had the *tango* survived the Cultural Revolution? He was filled with delight: here was a first-class piece of China Information. Sheila would be fascinated when he told her of this incident at the hospital on the morrow.

The record stopped. The dancers did not leave the improvised floor, waiting quietly for the next dance. Nobody clapped. A few people looked about, smiling. Their contentment, thought Laplace . . . their innocent contentment. . . . That's one thing we've forgotten in the West. At which his native nature re-asserted itself, saying, 'What a murky low-wattage caper it is, after all!'

A couple near him lit up cigarettes. As their faces were briefly illuminated, he saw that it was the Fans, Xiaofen and Qi Wu. Jealousy filled him. They could have told him there was going to be a dance before he left them. Or maybe they had not known then — the whole affair had an air of improvisation. Only a few of the hundreds of students at the Institute were present. He remained disturbed.

As he directed Bobby's attention to the chairman of their department, he saw that Qi Wu had changed her appearance since he left her flat. At that time, she had worn the usual two pigtails, drawn back tightly. Now she had released her hair, and it hung down to her shoulders, giving her a softer and more mysterious look. She took Fan's arm and they moved forward to dance, cigarettes between their lips.

'She looks good, no mistake of that,' Bobby said.

Laplace sighed, watching Qi Wu as she moved sensuously in her husband's arms, oblivious of the onlookers.

The two men stood watching for some while, before deciding to return to their flats. Even as they turned away, the music came to an end and the lights were switched off. It was ten o'clock.

'Really spooky,' Laplace said, with relish. 'But fancy Fan dancing the tango. He's strange, Bobby. He seems to know a great deal about Thomas Hobbes and wanted me to discuss *Leviathan* with him. I must read it. Fan says Hobbes was correct, and the Chinese have proved him correct — the natural state of man is not noble, as Rousseau claims, but anarchistic, 'nasty, brutish, and short'. The Chinese have just emerged from anarchy, so he feels he knows what he is talking about.'

'Maybe, but you know as well as I do that the Chinese talk in code-words — it's just something they do. Anarchy is code for individualism. Ron Horgan was telling me that the Chinese are the most neoteric species or sub-species of mankind, most like children, but they are also the most advanced in evolutionary terms. For instance, their facial musculature is more developed and subtle than ours, so we have trouble in interpreting their expressions. Maybe their thoughts are also more developed. Hence our problems with them.'

'I like the way you say "they", Bobby.'

'Cultural confusion. Two generations in Oz and you're unfit for any thought at all.'

They got back to their block without falling over any foundations. In the hall lingered a slight but pleasant smell of vanished cooking. The constituent elements of the scene were prosaic enough — blue-washed shabby walls, bare concrete floor, well-used doors painted brown, an awkward corner cupboard housing fire-fighting equipment — but they formed as a whole a *mise-en-scène* which Laplace was still unable to take for granted as mere background to his life, almost as if he were a character in a historical novel marvelling over new street-lighting.

Bobby paused outside his door.

'How long before Sheila returns to the fold?'

'Six days.' He laughed without knowing why he did so.

'Know what, George, you should try hard to seduce Qi Wu. I have a feeling she has taken a fancy to you and wouldn't say no to a spot of amatory advance.'

'What on earth makes you say that?'

'Remember, I'm one of them, in a way. I can read the facial musculature and think the thoughts on occasion. She thinks you're the wallaby's whiskers. You'd get a whole stack of China Information, too, as well as the pleasure of the embrace.'

Laplace looked into the shadows about him. 'You're an evil man, Bobby Wang. The general abstinence in the student body around us gets home to me. I'm quite puritanical these days. I really begin to believe that the West is far too obsessed with sex. Some of that libido ought to be turned to more productive things.'

'They *have* got to you. Stay away, it might be catching!' He pantomimed fending off evil, eyes wide. 'It's having Sheila away, I suppose. . . . The Government suppresses sex. That helps with the problem of the birth rate, and it means that pent-up psychic energy can be harnessed to — it's your word — productivity. Also, revolutions are often puritanical at first, and abstinence has become a cultural norm. It's always easier to conform to cultural norms than to break them, so they're all going through a self-suppressive period at present. But that's no reason why you should let it cramp your style.'

'It doesn't do that,' Laplace protested. 'I sort of admire their puritanism. *And* the fact that sex isn't used to sell cars and floor-polishes.'

Bobby peered into his face. 'I'm worried about you, George, mate. Sex here in Xi'an is being perverted from its true course on a much larger and more organised scale than anyone ever dreamed of in the West. Strike a blow for democracy — get Qi Wu to open her sweet little legs for you.'

'You disgusting Chinese pander!'

'You barbarian Western long-nose!'

They clapped each other's shoulders and departed to their solitary beds.

The canned notes of reveille sounded over the outside broadcasting system of the Institute at six o'clock. Laplace rose at once. As he washed and shaved, he looked outside at dawn creeping over the Institute walls. It was barely light, with an autumnal haze low over the well-walked ground, yet already scholars were about, books held to their eyes or dangled by their sides with fingers marking a page, seeking refuge from their crowded rooms to study. He shaved more slowly, admiring their dedication, anxious on their behalf.

He went down to breakfast, where all was bustle. There were two items awaiting him in his post-slot in the hall, which he took in to table. Jim Lim appeared instantly, smiling, and served loquat and yoghurt; scrambled egg would follow. The students, at their tables, were enjoying the morning bowl of cabbage soup. The low-calorie diet would assist in moderating sexual impulses.

His mail consisted of a returned roll of film and a hand-delivered letter. Over his yoghurt, Laplace opened the envelope of the letter; inside was a neat hand-written note from Fan Xiaofen. It informed Laplace that the head of department considered he had been working too hard on behalf of his students, for which all were grateful. This, together with the strain of his wife's illness, made it necessary for Laplace to take a day off. The department vehicle would accordingly be placed at his disposal today, and the undersigned himself would be happy to take Laplace and any other Foreign Experts who could be spared to see a pleasant near-by antiquity. The vehicle would depart from the Institute at nine o'clock. The note was signed by Fan.

'I've got a day off — we've all got a day off,' Laplace said to Ron and Geraldine Horgan, smiling, as the other Foreign Experts arrived at the table.

With a feeling of excitement, Laplace returned to his room after the meal. The Chinese loved dishing out treats unexpectedly. A day's outing always yielded new China Information. And the Foreign Experts did work hard, putting in three times as many hours' teaching per week as their Chinese counterparts; so there was no need to feel guilty about this privilege.

He opened his colour transparencies, returned from a photographic firm in San Francisco, and slipped them into a hand-viewer. These were mainly shots of Sheila when she was becoming ill, Sheila against a background of Xi'an; the Big Wild Goose Pagoda, the Small Wild Goose Pagoda, the Museum of the Eighth Route Army, the Bell Tower in the centre of the city, the crowded alleys of the old quarter.

Through the bright eye of the hand-viewer, figures moved in a cloud. Occasionally, he could just make out Sheila's face, Sheila smiling bravely, as if confronted by a total eclipse of the sun. He was a poor photographer, and had underexposed the whole film. There was little to be seen of Sheila and Xi'an but darkness.

Laplace's annoyance stayed with him as he prepared for the impromptu excursion, for he had been looking forward to showing the transparencies, the first film he had shot since coming to China, to his wife, when he next visited her in Number Four Hospital. Downstairs, he met the Horgans and Bobby Wang. The latter said, smiling enigmatically, 'You may get your chance today, George, if Mrs Fan comes along on our trip!'

'I shall do nothing dishonourable.'

Bobby regarded him curiously. 'That's an old-fashioned remark, if ever I heard one. You feeling yourself this morning?'

The Horgans were a cheerful Canadian couple in their late twenties. Ron had a beard and a scholarly air; Geraldine was a slight girl with a sallow complexion — 'quiet but very bright' was the verdict of the other Foreign Experts. She mothered the experts to some extent, and cooked them on their birthdays gorgeous fruit cakes from old English recipes. Geraldine was the only religious Foreign Expert, and often worried because ideology had replaced religion in China. Both Horgans were devoted to their Chinese students, who in turn revered their teachers. Chris and Len Gerstein were even more devoted: they had refused to give up a day for which work was planned, and were already in their first classes. So the Horgans, Bobby Wang, and Laplace were the only takers for Fan's treat.

At five past nine, the vehicle, a little Japanese Hiace bus, nicknamed 'bread-loaf' by the Chinese, had not arrived. It appeared at quarter past, with Fan Qi Wu driving.

'This is very nice, Qi Wu,' said Horgan, as she climbed out. 'Where are we going, and where's your husband?'

Qi Wu was her usual neat self, her pigtails tied tightly behind her head. She looked a trifle flustered, and her eyes were wide behind her spectacles.

'Xiaofen has to go unexpectedly to Peking,' she said. 'So I will personally drive and act as your guide on the excursion. I am embarrassed to be late.'

Reassuring her, the four Foreign Experts climbed into the

bread-loaf. Bobby nudged Laplace and told him that now he was on to a God-given chance to be as dishonourable as he liked.

Defying Bobby, Laplace sat in the middle of the little bus with the Horgans. Bobby grinned his you-had-it-coming grin and went up to the front to sit behind Mrs Fan.

As the vehicle moved off, Laplace and the Horgans fell immediately into their usual sort of discussion. The Horgans had not heard about the previous evening's dance, and listened with interest to Laplace's account of it.

'The tango would be modern to them,' Geraldine said. 'And foreign. Sophisticated. It's hicksville only to us. Quite different connotations for them. Like rock and roll when we were kids, Ron. It was in part a political gesture. That's why we did it.'

Ron shook his head judicially. 'That's how it seems now, in retrospect. At the time, we were just keen on working up a good sweat. The Chinese are different, as they are in everything. They even sweat differently — honest, I'm serious.' He tapped Laplace's wrist to emphasise his words. 'Their sweat has no smell because the Han race lack that particular scent gland. That's one reason why I claim they're a special neoteric sub-species of mankind, biologically speaking.'

'My husband a racialist!' Geraldine exclaimed, clasping her hands and turning her eyes to the roof of the vehicle.

'That's not a racialist remark, love. Just biological. In any case, it explains why Chinese crowds — even crowds of the great unwashed — smell pleasant to our noses. . . . I wouldn't see the tango as a sign of revolt or anything like that. We're just witnessing one of the swings of the cultural pendulum. The Chinese people aren't really going anywhere, as everyone likes to believe; they are simply staying put and maintaining equilibrium by swaying slightly from side to side. At present it amuses them to court the West, Western capital and Western advice. Modernisation is simply a fad, like mysticism in the West.'

'Oh, it goes deeper than that,' Laplace said. 'I believe they have finally realised how closely linked all the peoples of the globe are, like it or not, and they are making strenuous attempts to join in on equal terms. The unbalanced years of Mao-worship are over.'

'But only for a while. I know your theory, George, that China only makes sense if you see that their brand of Communism is not Communism as preached by Marx–Lenin at all. My theory is more radical – the biological theory. The Hans are of different stock from us. Physiologically and psychologically. All their history, that long stable history, which rightly over-awes us because we cannot imitate it, demonstrates conclusively that they are a sub-species apart, which must have a father figure to dominate them on Earth. They're practical people: Our Father which art in Heaven is no earthly use – literally – to the Chinese.'

'God's always of use, if you invite him in,' Geraldine said, but George was not deflected.

'Mao Tse-Tung was just one more glorious emperor, who threw down his edicts from the Gate of Heavenly Peace in Peking like the best of them. Now Mao's dead, and they're waiting for another mighty figure to stride in and take his place. Then they'll be happy, being ordered around.'

'If that's so, then how do you account for the success and independent-mindedness shown by the Chinese in Singapore and Hong Kong?'

'Different behavioural norms.'

Laplace laughed. 'Ron, you skunk, that's a rotten get-out from an argument I suspect you yourself don't believe in. I say there's cultural evidence of change. You say, No, the evidence is biological. When I challenge that, you pretend it's cultural after all.'

'I know, I know; I couldn't think of anything better to say. The amazing success of Singapore and Hong Kong needs investigation. I'd guess you'd find that both successes rely heavily on supportive action – probably through one clan or tong in each case, the way that impressive production brigade Fan took us to comprised eighty per cent Wongs. All I'm saying is that there is a biological answer to the things that puzzle us, that the Hans are much better able to integrate with each other than the pugnacious Neanderthal strains which survive among our Western populations. Maybe if their sweat don't stink they leave fewer territorial markers. That's why their kind of Communism suits them, as well as their kind of crowded living you find in Hong Kong. What would be our pain is their pleasure. You cannot understand those facts until you suss out the underlying biological reasons.'

'Nowadays people only want political reasons for things,' Geraldine said.

'Then they'll never understand the world they live in, will they?' her husband responded.

'There are religious explanations as well as biological ones, don't forget.'

The vehicle skirted the great grey East Gate of Xi'an. The gate marked the limits of the old T'ang town, when it had been the largest city in the world, and the start of the silk route that had linked Cathay with Trebizond, Sarajevo, Venice, and the Europe of the Middle Ages. Now the silk was gone, and the original walls broken open to undam twentieth-century Xi'an, straggling untidily in all directions.

'We will go to the tomb of the Emperor Qin and see the Buried Army,' Qi Wu announced. 'Do you know about the Emperor Qin Shi Huang? He was the man who united all China two centuries before Christ, and gave his name to China.'

'Another father-figure,' Horgan said quietly.

The tomb was some distance from the city. When they had parked and were climbing out, Qi Wu said to Horgan, 'I think George is correct about saying that China wishes to take a place with other nations, though despite Westernisation we shall remain always in the Third World. You are wrong when you say that modernisation is merely a fad. We have to throw away the last shackles of our feudal thinking. That's an imperative.'

Ronald Horgan looked abashed, and combed his beard with his fingers, smiling uneasily. 'I didn't figure you could hear what I was holding forth about, up front, or I guess I wouldn't have said what I did.'

She patted his arm. 'Don't worry. We are all friends. I was interested in your biological theories especially.'

Geraldine said, 'Interested, yes, Qi Wu − so are we. But do you believe what Ron says? Is he correct, in your estimation?'

'Well, you see I am no expert in biology. I never had time to study it.'

'We've all got an amateur interest in biology,' Bobby Wang said, winking in Laplace's direction.

'Let's go and see the Buried Army,' Qi Wu said.

'Does the administration here know we are coming?' Geraldine asked.

The others smiled approvingly at the question; they recognised fishing for China Information where they heard it. Whenever they appeared at any public place, they were greeted invariably with smiles and offers of help. Money was waved aside at entrances. They were ushered to the front of queues. Tickets were never needed. Private rooms were found for them in public restaurants if ever they ventured out. Barriers invisible to them were swept aside. They continually sought to gauge the depth and extent of the privilege in which they, as Foreign Experts, swam.

Not only did the administration know they were coming; it sent a smiling young man, barely past school age, to escort them round the site and explain everything. Tickets were not required.

The great Bronze Age emperor Qin had commanded to accompany him to the Land of Shades a large army of officers, men and horses, which the potters of his kingdom had created out of terracotta, like so many golems. This army had been buried after the Emperor's death, marching in formation towards his tomb, carrying superb bronze weapons with which to deal with any barbarians they might encounter. The site had been forgotten. The army remained in the earth for over two thousand years, until discovered by accident by peasants digging a well.

Now the Buried Army was in the process of being unburied. A gigantic hall with cantilever roof had been thrown over the burial site. Archaeologists were at work, slowly disinterring and restoring the gigantic pottery figures. The four Foreign Experts stood silent, looking down into the pit from which men appeared to march. When the entire pit had been excavated, some six thousand figures would have emerged. At present, many were locked with only head and shoulders appearing from the loess earth, or were still interred in their long grave, awaiting resurrection.

'Too bad they won't let us take photos.'

'The way I take them, it doesn't matter. . . .'

They stood for a long while in silence, gazing at the figures shouldering their way out of the soil, at the eyes staring blankly after their lost warlord. At last, they emerged from the great pit, and were treated to bitter tea in a little anteroom, being served by a small smiling lady in a green Mao suit.

'I need something alcoholic after that,' Bobby observed. 'My mind is boggling.'

'We generally drink only tea in China,' Qi Wu said, perhaps but not necessarily believing the remark was addressed to her critically. 'Alcohol brings many problems to nations, as we learn in periods of hegemony. We Chinese cannot afford to drink alcohol much, so we have not picked up the habit. Consequently, we are a pretty healthy nation.'

'It's a marvellous site,' Horgan said. 'Marvellous.'

'Evidence of how strongly the ancient Chinese believed in life after death,' his wife commented.

'And how strongly they believed that you could be as practical about death as about life.'

After a silence, Qi Wu asked Laplace if he had enjoyed the Buried Army.

'The Chinese people emerging into daylight after their long darkness,' he said.

Qi Wu laughed. 'You know it symbolises nothing of the sort. It's not a symbol but a real thing.'

When they had drunk their tea, they emerged into the open air. The museum site was still under construction, with several buildings scarcely beyond the foundation stage. Paths were being laid, flowerbeds sketchily planned on the muddy ground. No one was working very hard. Behind the confusion stood Mount Li and a line of barren mountains.

'What's Lao Fan doing in Peking?' Bobby asked of Qi Wu.

'Oh, he has some business there.'

'Some place this, huh?' Horgan said to Laplace. 'It socks me. It'll be the world's No. 1 Tourist Attraction when developed, I guess.'

'That army emerging from the dirt — it's the incarnation of every nightmare anyone ever had.'

'Dragon's teeth springing up?'

'I did an India tour a couple of years back. India's extraordinary. You feel all the while you're caught in a vivid dream. But it's someone else's dream. I find myself believing these Chinese dreams are ours. It's weird. Spooky.'

'Each one of those figures has come back from the Afterlife to find itself worth a million,' Geraldine said.

'Maybe there was some demon potter working away under the earth,' Bobby suggested, laughing at his own fancy.

As they were climbing back into the bread-loaf, Qi Wu told them that they were now going to visit the Gang Liao production brigade, only a few kilometres away, where they would have a late lunch. The four Foreign Experts smiled happily at each other. A treat indeed! They knew they were in for a new stock of China Information, and could make notes. None of them had ever taken much interest in politics and, before coming to China from their various universities, would have been dismayed to think of a day's holiday being spent on production lectures while walking round a peasant farm. They had long ago broken through that barrier. With every brigade, every tally of figures, they could feel that they came a little nearer to understanding China. The very banality of life on the brigade took on a mystical quality they could not explain.

The afternoon sun shone golden on the peaceful hectares of Gang Liao; it was warm, although the month was October. They were on the same latitude as Los Angeles. With their frugal lunch they were given a small glass of wine made from local grapes.

And the visit was all they hoped for. The deputy leader of the brigade talked to them, allowing them to ask as many questions as they could devise, while Qi Wu interpreted and they took notes. After the extended briefing, they were shown all round the brigade, with a special diversion through fields of sorghum to witness how the local stream, subject to flooding in the rainy season, had been dammed by the brigade itself, to its own plan — aided, of course, by the thoughts of Chairman Mao. The deputy leader was a modest cheerful man; his ruddy face broke into a happy smile as he recalled that triumph. Back in his modest office, they inspected a photograph of him shaking hands with Chairman Mao himself, and there was that warming smile again.

The bread-loaf started on its way home as the sun was setting.

'Fantastic persimmons at lunch,' Bobby said. Everyone agreed.

Then silence fell among them. It had been a wonderful Chinese day. Full, full.

Laplace sat idly staring through the window, watching everything, storing it. No animals and few birds were to be seen, only people, peasants coming and going with great loads on their backs or their bamboo poles.

Dusk was settling. It came from everywhere, and the land yielded without protest. The road was lined with trees, whitewashed to shoulder height, so that it became darker than the open land. On the road, the traffic consisted mainly of bicycles, fairly thick at this hour, and lorries returning to brigade or team from markets in town. No bicycle carried a light, and the lorries did not use their lights. They fared through subaqueous gloom. The scene became ghostly, a negative of real life. Laplace stared in fascination, thinking that he understood now for the first time what was meant by a low-energy culture − no electricity was being used, and the chief vehicle was muscle-powered. This was how China used twenty times less energy per capita than people back home in the States.

Wherever he looked, the plain, sinking into purple evening, showed no lights. They passed a small roadside village, secure behind its mud walls; even there, he could glimpse only one light, a beige utterance that lit nothing. And then the bread-loaf stopped.

Without comment or explanation, Qi Wu climbed out and went to look at the engine. The four Foreign Experts exchanged remarks of jocular doom.

'We're going to be stuck here all night.'

'Sharing the sack with pigs and peasants.'

'Your chance to try *real* country cooking. . . .'

In a moment, Qi Wu looked round the door at them. In the gloom, the oval of her face was scarcely visible.

'The vehicle has not been properly maintained. We borrowed it at short notice from the French Department. I am afraid that the clutch cable has broken.'

They climbed down to the road with her. Bicycles and wooden carts streamed by, still unlit.

'We should push the bread-loaf into the side of the road,' Qi

Wu said. They did so, while she sat in the driver's seat and steered. They managed to manoeuvre it under the roadside trees.

'We can get a hitch into town on a truck,' Geraldine said.

'But we can't leave the van here,' her husband replied. They turned to Qi Wu. They needed a little China Information.

'As the driver, I must stay with the vehicle,' she said. 'You must go back to the Institute by a lorry.' She used the English 'lorry' in preference to the American 'truck'. 'Then you can get our mechanic to come out with another Hiace and tow this one home. Do you mind doing that? I am so sorry for the trouble.'

'That's OK,' Bobby said. 'But one of us — either George or I, I guess — will hang around with you. You can't stay here alone.'

She laughed. 'I shall be perfectly safe here. You all go together.'

'You wouldn't say that if this was Sydney. Come on, Qi Wu — besides, it's almost bloody dark.'

'It's not Australia here, Bobby,' Qi Wu replied in a tranquil tone. Perhaps she was merely stating a fact, perhaps implying much more.

After some arguing back and forth, it was decided that Bobby, with his knowledge of Chinese, would catch a lift back to Xi'an with the Horgans, and Laplace would stay with Qi Wu and the van. Geraldine kissed Qi Wu as her husband stopped the first lorry heading westwards on the dark road. Bobby dug Laplace in the ribs, his weatherbeaten oriental face creased in a sly smile.

'Now's your chance. Be dishonourable for me, OK?'

They climbed into the back of the lorry, helped by grinning workers, and the vehicle disappeared into the night.

Laplace and Fan Qi Wu stood together by the roadside. The top of her head came up to his biceps. When he suggested that they wait inside the bread-loaf, she agreed without hesitation; they climbed in and sat together on the long rear seat. Laplace brought out a packet of Yun Yan cigarettes and offered her one. By the glow of his lighter, he surreptitiously examined her face, the extraordinary Chinese design for a face, rendered rather abstract by light and shadow, with its smooth lines of brow and cheek, the cunningly lidded eyes, the curve of nose and mouth, the affecting sweep of her hair.

'You don't mind being alone with me?' he asked.

'Why should I? We are firm friends. I'm glad of the opportunity to ask you something more about the theories of Thomas Hobbes. His philosophy is something that interests us, according to how you explained it the other day.'

'I just mentioned him to Fan. I know very little about him.'

'I think you said he was a materialist. . . .'

Laplace smoked his cigarette. 'We can talk about more personal things than philosophy, Qi Wu. We have an hour together before the towing vehicle arrives. It is precious to me to have a whole hour with you — I've always admired you. I think you're wonderful.' A detached part of him listened to his words in amused anguish.

'Of course, the hour is precious to me, too. Fan and I hold all the Foreign Experts in great affection, because they work so hard for the good of their pupils, and for China. We Chinese have so much to learn, and must catch up. That's why I bother you about Hobbes.'

'I know very little about Thomas Hobbes.'

Silence fell between them. Then they spoke simultaneously:

'I watched you dancing last night.'

'How did Hobbes interpret the social contract?'

Almost angrily, he repeated his statement, adding, 'So you don't spend all your time studying and working.'

'Of course not. We relax sometimes, to come to work with clear minds.'

'Is that a precept of Chairman Mao's?'

'Yes.'

'And where did you learn the tango? Not from Chairman Mao?'

Qi Wu laughed. 'George, you are joking with me. My husband taught me to tango. Did you teach Sheila to tango?'

'We don't dance. . . . You looked so inviting when you danced. With your hair down. . . .'

After a silence, where only their glowing cigarette-ends fended off all the darkness in China, he said, 'What would you do if I kissed you, Qi Wu?'

Pronouncing the unlikely sentence was enough to tell him he would never attempt what he suggested.

'I would be embarrassed to meet Sheila afterwards.'

'But at the time — would you enjoy it?'

'I would be anxious all the time.'

He put his arm round her waist. 'Come on, relax, give me a kiss, let's try it at least.'

She pushed him away. 'Please stop, George. This is not·like your behaviour. I do not understand you, or why you are doing this. Sheila will soon be out of hospital.'

'Not tonight she won't, baby. Forget Sheila. Don't you ever do anything spontaneously? A bit of individual action?'

She wriggled energetically and pulled his hand away. 'Your silly questions! To be an individual is to be anarchistic, isn't that right? What you would do would make us miserable. Who would trust us afterwards? We should be discredited for acting dishonestly. It would spoil our good influence with the students.'

'OK, Qi Wu, I'm sorry. Forget it. I got carried away by your proximity. It was just going to be a kiss, not a political act.'

She patted him almost as if he were a dog, a dog she wished to placate. A vehicle passed with dim headlights burning, revealing her momentarily, doll-like in her tunic and trousers, gazing towards him. Feelings of guilt, failure and resentment, a thoroughly unpleasant mixture, stirred in him.

'Don't you have sexual feelings, Qi Wu?'

'How can you pretend to be friendly when you insult me with such questions?'

He flushed.

'I'll get out and leave you alone if you find me so unpleasant. You think I'm a barbarian, don't you? Really, you figure all foreigners are barbarians, don't you? Be honest.'

'Don't be offended, George. I simply think that to kiss would be to start on a wrong path. We have different cultural patterns. That is why I am interested in the theories of Thomas Hobbes. He taught that men and women should submit themselves to the will of the State — not for the good of the State, but for their own good. Is that correct? Have you read *Leviathan*?'

The lust for China Information overcame his sulks. 'And is that how you visualise the theory of China at present?'

She paused. 'Honestly, I believe that we have submitted ourselves for the good of the State, not for our own good. It's hard for us to decide. I think we submit too much.'

He sat absolutely rigid in the dark, his frustration and shame gone, transfixed by what she said. Terrified of scaring her back into reticence — was she giving him a dole of truth to compensate for rejecting his advances? — he said, almost in a murmur, 'And does Fan feel as you do about that matter?'

Another pause. She gripped the seat in front of her. 'Fan didn't go to Peking today. We were seen last night, dancing with our students, and some unfriendly person reported us. So Fan had to go this morning for some criticism. That's why we decided to get you away from the Institute for the day, so it would be pleasanter for you.'

'You mean, we'd have been criticised as associates of Fan?'

'I don't know what would happen. Not that. We did not want any unpleasantness to touch you.'

'And what will happen to Fan?'

'Nothing. It is different from formerly, under the Gang of Four. People were tortured then, you know. But we have occasionally talked too much about freedom with our students. We may have confused them. Fan will need a little self-criticism.'

Laplace stood up. 'Qi Wu, I'm glad you told me this. You know we respect you greatly — and Fan — and the Chinese in general. But of course we feel you have very little freedom, to travel, or to criticise, or even to marry when you feel like it. Will you and Fan make an issue of this arrest — stand up for your rights? Many people must feel as you do.'

'We can't make an issue. Our conscience won't allow. We have to obey the law even if we don't agree. You do, too, in your country, you know. That's the sacrifice we made. . . . As a result, we have some prosperity and good security, and are respected by our friends abroad. We can defy hegemony. We have escaped from anarchy and must pay some price for it.'

'A tyrannous state! Is that the price you are prepared to pay?'

Patiently, she said, 'No, not tyrannous, George. You are too fearful. Artificial, with artificial restraints. That's what Hobbes said. "This great Leviathan, which is called the state, is a work of art." We must persuade ourselves to be artificial. Society has always been artificial.'

He threw his cigarette-end out of the open door into the road.

'We — I mean, the Foreign Experts — will all speak up for Fan, if you want.'

'No, no, George, please don't think it. That would bring us all trouble. I made a mistake to tell you. Fan will return tomorrow. He has gone there before.'

'And you're worried.'

'Well, no, not really. A little. We are short of teachers. We have to catch up in everything. And they know that Fan is a good teacher.'

As he sat down by her again, a heavy vehicle thundered by, rocking the bread-loaf. He put his hand on her knee.

'Sorry about the pass I made. You're so attractive.'

'You must do some self-criticism for your lack of self-control. If I had done what you wished, you would represent anarchy, and so you would get in the way of my modernisation.'

That was the sentence of hers he repeated to himself most frequently afterwards.

'Modernisation! You mean repressing yourself.'

'No, I mean controlling ourselves. Why do you criticise us so much when you so much lack control?' She spoke levelly, almost sorrowfully. 'Your culture has so many good things we envy, yet your lack of control makes you miserable. We are happier than you, I believe. You have difficulty understanding that, don't you?'

They do take us for barbarians, he told himself, and I can see that from Qi Wu's point of view I tried to shape up like one. Why can't they distinguish between individuality and anarchy? And why can't I distinguish. . . . between whatever it is I can't distinguish between because I don't see it and they do? The barrier between us — it's not ideological, though ideology further confuses the issue; nor is it true to say it's merely cultural. Ron Horgan would say it was biological.

Perhaps I should go in for some heavy self-criticism. Maybe life in the West is more deeply sexualised than we perceive, and maybe that has caused us to forget or neglect other values, just as the opposite applies to the Chinese, I'd estimate. I sure can see how greatly behavioural norms shape our thinking. They place the same value on modernisation as we do on self-expression, which scores zero on their chart.

'Why don't you answer, George?'

It occurred to him that she and Fan might collect Foreign Information the way he and the other Foreign Experts went for China Information. But, no, that was crazy. In China, China was the only subject.

'I was thinking. . . . That's the big problem everywhere today. The citizens throw out God and you throw out the kings and emperors, the representatives of God on earth, and then you're left with the question of who rules the citizens. Does the State exist for the individual or the individual for the State? That's been the hot-potato question ever since the Italian Renaissance, I guess. . . .'

Silence fell. Lights were flashing ahead. Headlights. They're here, he thought dully. I wouldn't really have had time to do anything properly. We were nearer Xi'an than I estimated. I thought we had more time. Qi Wu, if we had a week stuck in this damned vehicle on a desert island, would I get through to you then? The lights swept by and were gone.

With some relief, he said, 'Now you're not answering, Qi Wu.'

'George, you know that with the Cultural Revolution and the bad activities of the Gang of Four, we have missed many things of importance that happened in the rest of the world.'

'Sure, I know that. That's why we're here — to help you catch up. Believe me, it's a profound pleasure — you inspire us. I'm sure you will catch up and — who knows? — in a couple of decades you'll probably own the whole world.'

'We have no ambitions beyond our own frontiers — you know that. We wish only to undergo the vital process of becoming more up-to-date. So will you please tell me — what is this Italian Renaissance? What does it mean?'

He was trying to explain, and they were smoking another Yun Yan, when the breakdown truck arrived.

Why Should Not Old Men Be Mad?

Julia O'Faolain

IT WAS a ridiculous occasion. The beginning of the row did nobody credit, and Edward could not for the life of him remember its end. Over the years, his memories of the thing were to curdle, growing spotty and sulphurous until they put him in mind of the reflections one sees in mirrors which have hung in damp haughty old houses and perpetuate their gloom.

The evening got off to a bad start. Jammet's, for decades Dublin's smartest restaurant, had, towards the end, accumulated a stable of rickety old waiters with hamburger faces who that night — here memory sharpened to a knife-edge — snubbed the party's host.

Jim Farrel, a student fresh from the country and unused to restaurants, had chosen to spend half a term's allowance on dinner for four men he didn't know. The guests were Edward, who had just been elected to the Senate, Monsignor Macateer, later to become Bishop of Cloyne and Ferns, a German theologian, and an English Catholic MP who was in Dublin for a conference. The four knew of each other but did not know Farrel, who had led each to suppose that one of the others had asked him to arrange the gathering. His white lies were exposed when he came to pay the bill, and his guests overcome by awkwardness, mirth and doubt as to whether he could possibly have found their conversation worth the expenditure. Had they, they covertly asked each other, sung sufficiently well for their supper? They must, Edward privately supposed, be feeling like an inexperienced young girl who has been treated too sumptuously by a suitor. What, she as they must wonder, would now be expected?

Perhaps it was to bridge this ticklish moment that the German offered a round of brandies and that Edward, feeling light-hearted, resolved to consult Mikey Macateer about his marital problems. Discreetly, man to man — he had known Mikey since school — he brought up the matter of an annulment. Two annulments. Both Jennifer and he were married. The year was 1958. Was there, he asked Mikey, any chance?

The Monsignor rounded on him like a snake.

Possibly, he had found the evening a strain? The German, an ascetic with advanced ideas, was not the sort of man with whom Mikey felt at ease, and he must have been on pins and needles lest Edward, a Civil Liberties supporter, let the country down in front of the English MP. Annulments were the last straw.

Mikey's lips had quivered like the cardiogram of a wildly pumping heart. Between them his tongue wavered forth, as he asked in a hiss of enraged and spittly Gaelic whether Edward was deliberately giving scandal to foreigners. Trying for annulments was an erosion of the system, said Mikey. It was a factor for disorder, a time-bomb placed at the heart of Mother Church who, whether Edward knew it or not, was going through risks and trials unknown since the days of Martin Luther.

Tics sucked Mikey's cheeks inwards as though it were being pierced by sewing-pins. Edward, he said, was a fornicator and he a man who called a spade a spade.

'Spayed is what you are,' Edward had answered in English. 'Hiding', he had shouted, 'behind your dog collar.' The Irish clergy, said Edward, reaching for old invective, were living in the Dark Ages, leaving no choice to the laity but between total abstinence and having six children.

'Sex', wondered the German doubtfully, 'children?'

'Six,' Edward corrected him.

After that, the level of discourse sank. Appearances ceased to be kept up. Scandal was given, but memory drew a veil. Edward's recollection of the end of the business was a blank. Luckily, he had no further occasion to meet anyone who had been present that evening and his host, Jim Farrel, faded utterly from his ken.

News did, however, continue to reach him of Mikey Macateer's rise. Over the years, the fellow was made a bishop, called to

Rome, given a place in the Curia and there alleged to be a man of influence. It stuck particularly in Edward's craw to hear that, after Vatican Two, Macateer became a big progressive, famed for his fight to ditch the cult of abnegation and find the human face of Catholicism. He was hot for reform, it seemed, and instrumental in making annulments easy to get — too late, of course, for Edward and for Jennifer, who was by then so seized up with arthritis that she had had to go and live in Palm Springs.

'Fuck,' mourned Edward when he thought of this.

It was eighteen years after the Jammet's row that someone in Edward's hearing mentioned Macateer as possibly *papabile* — at any rate, a Power in the Vatican, a dexterous string-puller and an *Eminence Verte.* This was at the Irish Embassy in Rome, so Edward allowed for exaggeration. Still, no smoke without fire. There must be some flicker of truth to it. Edward felt green-eyed — well, why wouldn't he? There *he* was, having to turn his mind to retirement and hobbies while that ecclesiastical turncoat slithered upwards in his pride and power. To be sure, churchmen paid a price for their long span of active life: no sex, no kids, loneliness — *what* loneliness? There'd be precious little loneliness for chaps who had made a go of it. Peaking late, they had the best of both worlds in the end. There was Mikey surrounded — Edward supposed he was surrounded — by priestly boot-lickers, pious catamites, a court, and snowed under by invitations.

Edward refused to attend a lunch where the ambassador — a busybody — had hoped to bring the estranged friends together. Having pretended that he had to press on to Venice, he was then obliged to leave the Eternal City earlier than planned. This too stuck in his craw. It wasn't that foolish old business at Jammet's which made him refuse to see Mikey. That was water under the bridge. After eighteen years you buried — or drowned — hatchets. No, no, but, oh, somehow, the invitation had found him in low fettle. He'd been feeling his age. Rome mocked him with memories of old adulteries — it had been a favourite venue for them and, maddeningly, the props were still there: mimosa, *carrozze,* that piss-poor wine that in the old days had not tasted pissy at all. He remembered saying to Jennifer that it was like drinking bottled sunlight.

So, 'No,' he told the embassy chap who rang. 'Sorry.'

It seemed unfair; it seemed *wrong* that Macateer should be reaping what he hadn't sown: esteem, good fellowship and the company of youth, when Edward, who had given so much of himself to so many, was alone.

Two years went by. Then came a letter from Macateer, apparently back in Ireland. It was a summons to visit, and Edward disregarded it. The twit was clearly puffed up with self-esteem. Celibates got that way. Proponents of a married clergy should make use of the point. Hammer it home. Edward thought of saying this in a card to Mikey since *he* was now such a reformer. Instead, he forgot about him.

Weeks later, casting about for gossip with which to enliven a letter to a favourite cousin, he remembered him. Susan was the last attractive female in Edward's entourage and he cherished her with a sad ironic gaiety. Like himself, she suffered from withdrawal symptoms. It wasn't that she or he were withdrawing from anything. No, things were withdrawing from *them* and at such a clip that this time Edward could think of no news to tell her. He fell back on working Mikey's summons into an anecdote and, having done so, began to believe that maybe there *was* more to it than met the eye. Jaundiced spectacles? Perhaps.

'His Grace the Bishop of Cloyne and Ferns', wrote Edward, 'writes from an ecclesiastical loonybin somewhere near Athlone, i.e. in the soggy middle of the country, saying he would like a visit. Princely command? Cry for help? What is His Grace doing in a bin in the bog? A Beckettian fix – unless he's running it. But even then what a come-down from the corridors of the Curia where, they say, he was *un très Grand Manitou*. His nicknames tell much: Macchiatelly, because of being smooth on the box, Macateer the Racketeer, inevitably, Mac the Knife. Has someone got their knife into Mikey? I shall go, see and report. Hope I whet your appetite for further bulletins?'

It was all fantasy, including the nicknames – or was it?

Elation at having managed to make something out of nothing led to a doubt that there might be something where he had at first seen nothing. Edward, a virtuoso barrister, had in his prime been able to convince juries of anything he chose. Now, cut off

from the medicinal cynicism of day-to-day reality, he found that
he could all too easily convince himself.

Satan fodder finds for idle minds — or so Mikey and he had
been told in kindergarten.

He wished — God, how he wished — that he was still racked by
intimate doubts and choices. For years his letters to Susan had
been mined with anguished questions: Should he leave his wife,
who would pine incapably if he did, and take off with Mil? Leave
Mil for Jennifer? Sell up this house and follow Jennifer to Palm
Springs? Return to his pining wife before she died? No alternatives
left now. Susan held his hand in a desert awful with the lack of
them. Oh shit, oh *shit*! Well, *there* was one function left to him
still and quite satisfactory, thanks.

'Life', he wrote and probed an ear with his pen while wondering
what to write next, 'here is as calm as a gold-fish tank with one
half-animate inmate: me. A silvered one. My hair pales and drops,
as I soon shall myself. Contemporaries drop like flies and my
address-book turns into a graveyard guide. I have to keep pencilling
out names for fear of gaffes like the one I made with poor Martin
Clancy last month at the Yacht Club. "How's Mil?" I asked. He
looked at me in shock: "Mil's been dead three years." Had I
known? Suppressed and blinked away knowledge? Perhaps.
Like black tennis-balls smashed at you across a net, like objects
dark against the sun, news like that darkens the mind and sets up
a refusal. Silly Milly Clancy — you won't remember, but thirty
years ago her beauty was breathtaking — Mil dead? Mil laid down
in Glasnevin and rendered to a compost fit to blow half Dublin
skyhigh. Or just gone? Whoo, like a puff of air. Whee, like the
intervocalic Latin *t* that became a *d*, then disappeared: *vita, vida,
vie. La vida es un sueño,* so why, as Willy Yeats rightly if rhetori-
cally demanded, should not old men be mad?'

Edward supposed he was being literary, but what the hell?
He felt weepy, too, and to yield to *that* would be worse. In one
corner of his eye, Milly Clancy lurked in luminous tennis-dress and
a rainbow casing of teardrop: like Snow White awaiting a kiss in
her glass coffin. Get away, Mil! What else was I — ah, yes, madness
and the Case of Mikey Macateer.

Old grudges had dissolved into a ferocious solidarity with

Mikey, a possible victim of Vatican foul play. Could he have been nudged from his Curial niche? He could. He could. Priestly machinations were infamous and ditto the ruthlessness of today's youth. Edward was in a position to know, having been edged out of his own firm by his own sons — well, he'd *let* himself be edged out. The three were too dim to make a living on their own, and perhaps he was trying to repay their dead mother by being soft with her sons? Blood was thicker than water, though *they* didn't strike him as having a drop in their veins. Put the three through a mangle and he'd be surprised if anything came out: blood, juice or jism. Plastic men. Their passions were for crosswords, beagling and messing with small intricate boats. Small, mark, nothing on a scale to accommodate the lurch and sway of seaborne loves. No, tinkering with stalled engines was what they liked. They rarely left the harbour.

To be fair — fairness had been Edward's loadstone — *they* found him trying. His flourish embarrassed them. He knew. He saw. Fresias in his lapel, the length of his cuffs. Even his concern with human rights struck them as spiritual social-climbing. 'Pragmatic' was their favourite word. Economics, they instructed, was what mattered now. No, *not* in the Marxist sense. Forget words like 'left' and 'right'. Ireland had never had it so good. In the convex diminishing-mirrors of their eyes, he saw himself as a sentimental old codger fighting the fights of long ago.

An Americanised generation, they admitted to boredom when not working. Yet all three had married and were, as they were quick to point out, nicer to their wives than Edward had ever been to their mother. So alien were they that if she'd had it in her to take a lover he'd have thought them bastards. She hadn't. Maybe they'd been sired by gamma rays on evenings when she'd been sitting back, legs apart, watching reruns of *Peyton Place*?

Edward was seized by an urge to see old Mikey Mac who, in another era, used to climb on his shoulders to sneak back in over the seminary wall after the two had stayed out till dawn dancing at a Ceilidh.

Wet furry fields lay like the stomachs of soft animals bared to the sky. The train, with Edward in it, tore masterfully through the flat lands of middle Ireland. He felt zesty and wondered whether Mikey needed help. Edward was still President of Civil Liberties. Had some Lilliputian bureaucrats pinned Mikey down? Ah, look out there for the old war-horse twitch, Edward. Delusions of grandeur! Watch it, do! It was a typical daydream to fancy that you were needed by the powerful. Since Aesop's mouse, God help us, all mice must dream of saving lions. And what worse dreamer than the mouse emeritus?

He took a taxi from the station, arrived unannounced and gave his card to the porter: Senator Edward O'Hourraghan, President of Civil Liberties, hon. sec. of this, that and the other. He was in the honoraries these days, thought of the condition as akin to the DTs: shivery syllables, a ghostly status. He wanted, he told the flunkey, to see the Bishop. The man was a bit ghostly himself: cobweb hair, dandruff powderings, a silhouette from eighteenth-century farce. Which bishop? he asked. How many had they got, then? Edward briskly inquired. 'Cloyne and Ferns,' he bullied, 'Bishop Michael Macateer.' He knew how to inject authority into his voice.

Twenty minutes later he was in an institutional parlour — all angles, vacancy and reflecting surfaces — facing a silver-haired Mikey dressed in velvet pants and the sort of purple poloneck you might expect to find in a Jermyn Street shop. Failing to determine Mikey's status, Edward wondered whether this was trendy wear in the Vatican.

'Are you here for long?' he probed.

Mikey's palms were like powder-puffs and his eyes had the bloom of sloes. How good of Edward to have come, he marvelled, and held Edward's hands between his own as though they were infinitely precious. 'At our age one should hasten to repair bridges, don't you think?' He gazed intently and in a rather Latin way at Edward. 'What'll you have?' he asked. 'Wet your whistle?'

Edward chose whiskey and, when Mikey opted for tea, wondered might the Bishop have come here to dry out discreetly.

A man in a white coat hovered, summoned the porter to bring a trolley with refreshments, then took himself off to a window-seat. Mikey made some inadequate introduction which Edward failed to catch and the man kept looking out of the window in a way which made it unclear whether he was to be included in the conversation. At one point he turned and disconcerted Edward by the energy of his stare. It was targeted on the tea cup which Mikey had raised to his lips. Edward, following it, expected to see a palsied quiver, but Mikey's hand was steady. His complexion did, perhaps, suggest drink? Priests, being denied one outlet, turned traditionally to the other. The surrogate, accepted in Ireland, might shock in Rome. Bloody Ities, thought Edward, high on sympathy for Macateer, whose stamina should not — any more than Edward's own — be put in doubt over a matter of tippling. The man in the white coat was about the same age as Edward's sons. What was he? Doctor? Minder? Terrible for old Macateer to be under scrutiny. Edward, on a surge of brotherly feeling, slapped his old sparring partner on the back before the cup was safely returned to its saucer. Drops slopped on to Mikey's trousers and Edward's sleeve. Slow reflexes there, Edward acknowledged. Mikey was getting slow. His own mind was a bit murky suddenly. Was the minder watching *him*? he wondered, but was embarrassed to check.

'Well,' he mustered heartiness. 'It's grand to see you.'

Mikey confessed that he had been hurt that time when Edward had avoided him in Rome. He'd put the ambassador up to issuing the invitation, so the refusal had been something of a slap in the face. 'One needs old friends,' he said sadly. New ones tended not to be disinterested.

Edward couldn't have agreed more. Feeling emotional, he dredged up the old lie about how he couldn't have stayed in Rome that time. Wanted to. Couldn't. Believing himself, he swore that the thing had been out of his hands.

'Oh, I never held it against you,' said Mikey. 'It goes back to that night in Jammet's when I was so bloody-minded. I've often wanted to apologise for that. Times change, eh? New criteria. Besides there were things on my mind. You wouldn't know this, but the lady in question. . . .'

'Jennifer.' Edward was annoyed by Mikey's terminology. It came straight from police files. It was a tongs for picking up dirt. 'Jennifer Dooley,' he said firmly.

'Her sons', said the Bishop, 'were pupils of mine at Gonzaga.'

'I never knew that.'

'They were. Nice boys. Vulnerable. Still, I suppose I was a bit straitlaced. Fighting doubts of my own. The toughest hour comes before the breakthrough, and I took it out on you. I've always regretted that.' Macateer's forthright look seemed a touch too good to be true. 'How is she now?' he asked.

Edward, hardened rather than softened, found himself testing Mikey's apology, mentally fingering it for flaws.

'A nice woman,' said Mikey. Jennifer had never been that. 'How did you say she was?'

Edward hadn't and wasn't going to. There was a sinister symmetry to poor Jennifer's condition. Arthritis sounded like an old penance for making too free with your limbs. She, who frolicked in alien beds and meadows — for a moment he smelled flattened grass — she, whose bum once flashed like milk or mushrooms, shall be confined to a wheelchair in a desert city in the circle of the Californicators. He imagined rows of raddled, leathery, legless old things. Or was Palm Springs in Nevada? Surely not? That name suggested snow. Niveous belly. Snowy thighs. Once smooth as egg-shells — were they scrambled now?

Edward's distress brimmed for Mikey too, who had his own afflictions. Anguished, he found he'd finished the whiskey which he'd been planning to nurse. He hoped drinking in Mikey's presence didn't upset him. Trying to slide the glass out of sight, he found that he'd only succeeded in attracting the attention of the doctor or minder who asked would Edward like a refill.

'No, no.' Edward repudiated excess. 'Thanks, though,' he conciliated and was shocked to receive a wink. The man in the white coat stared with a poker face at Edward then, for a second time, coolly and deliberately winked at him. Edward shifted his gaze hurriedly to Mikey who, sitting with his back to the doctor, was discoursing on how happiness was the goal of marriage, the fleshly bond a hold one and the day fast approaching when the Church would admit a dead marriage to be dead. 'Or so', he wound up, 'I fervently hope. *I've* been fighting hard for that. Too hard for my own good.'

Edward looked at the whiskey-bottle and saw spots in the amber. Black, like flies congealed, they moved when he shifted his gaze. This new weakness appalled him. Had that man winked or hadn't he? The laity, he heard Macateer state, were far more backward than the clergy. Women, especially, were frightened of divorce.

'Think of farmers' wives in a place like this.' Macateer waved out at lush pasturage beyond the Institution lawn. A cow stared in at Edward, its mouth moving from right to left and back. 'What does divorce mean to *them*? That some young strap could catch their man's fancy and take their place on the farm. Have them put off the land. Evicted. Turned into landless vagrants.' The racial and sexual terrors there, said Macateer, ran deep. The Church had to consider the needs of the bulk of the people, the more traditional as well as those impatient for change.

The maggoty things in the whiskey leaped like letters on a screen. 'Impatient,' Edward heard and decided that Macateer thought that he, Edward, had been impatient because he'd known he'd soon be past it, now *was* past it and could look forward to no new embraces. Macateer mentioned the hare and the tortoise. A judicious clergy would not, said Macteer, and *should* not try to keep up with the wilder elements, the hares. . . .

'By the time the tortoise reached the goal,' Edward remarked. 'the hare had probably either left in disgust or gone mad with impatience. You can't please *everyone*.' No sooner was the word 'mad' out of his mouth than he saw his gaffe. You didn't say that word in a madhouse any more than you said 'rope' in the house of a hanged man. Nervously, his eye met the minder's and in confusion he stretched out his glass and accepted the refill he didn't want. Change, said Macateer's imperturbable voice, *would* come. There was no *doctrinal* objection to divorce. . . . Edward stopped listening. Could the man really imagine that he wanted to hear all this? That he would find solace in being told *now* that he might as well have left his wife and run off with Jennifer? Could he? In Edward's prime it had been professional suicide in Dublin for a man to defy the Church, and Edward had had no choice but to knuckle under. His needs, it seemed, had been subordinated to those of the wives of randy farmers. To avoid a quarrel he tried to change the subject. 'Tell me about Rome,' he said. 'What's the state of play there? No,' he amended, 'I mean in the Vatican.'

Rome, sweet Rome, was something else, at least for Edward it was. A cruel fleshy town. Mentioning it had brought its crusty flavours to his tongue: meat cooked till it fell off the bone, rosemary twigs tied to the legs of lambs slaughtered when they were no bigger than a cat, spitted skylarks. Jennifer had once confessed to feeling guilt over her greed for these birds so unsportingly netted on their migration southwards. A blithe but not spiritual pleasure, she'd admitted, while wiping flecks of charred songbird from her nose and chin. Shame, she'd reminded shrewdly, gave eating that extra tingle usually peculiar to sex, and she and he, in all that enormous Roman *rosticceria*, would be alone in feeling it: a bond. He had kissed her sucked and greasy fingers.

'Keats isn't our tradition really,' he'd argued.

Open fires, turning spits and flushed faces gave the place a look of old-time visions of hell.

'Eat the carcasses,' a waiter had shouted at them, laughing in sensual empathy. 'They're the tastiest part. Hold them by the beak and chew the heads.'

Edward's mouth was dry with memory and tears pricked at his eyes. In places like that, Jennifer and he found bliss tuned to perfervid pitch by their nervous adulterers' yearnings. It had been on a Roman weekend that they had admitted to each other that they would never make the break.

'So what's the news from the Vatican?' he asked again.

Raising his eyes, he saw that behind Mikey's head the man in the white coat was vigorously shaking his own.

'The news' — Macateer tilted his broad boxer's chin — 'is that I'm giving you a chance to return good for evil.' The chin jutted. It always had. Mikey led with it, but its aggression now was subverted by tremors. 'I take it you're still head of Civil Liberties?'

The man in the white coat could have been directing a tangle of traffic. Stop, menaced his gestures: careful. Or was it deaf-and-dumb language? Maybe *he* was the inmate and Macateer in charge?

'Are you?'

'Yes.'

'In the past, you and I have differed over definitions and indeed over the desirability of freedom, but today', said the Bishop lucidly, 'I am asking you to help me to regain my own in its basic, physical form.' The word seemed to set off a reflex. 'Fizzz-z-z . . . ,' he faltered in a spurt of hilarity. 'Physical.' Mirth drained from his face as quickly as it had come. 'I want you', he ended quietly, 'to get me out of here.'

Edward feared that a laugh would be inappropriate. One had, however, got halfway up his throat.

'You may question my right to ask,' said Macateer. 'It is the right of the helpless.' He jabbed a finger at Edward.

As though reading subtitles, Edward peered to where the man behind seemed now to be exhorting patience. With whom? Was Macateer bonkers, then? And, if he was, then why was he allowed to write *and post* imperious letters? It was an outrage that a man of Edward's age and station should be dragged halfway across the country at a madman's whim. Embarrassing, too.

Yet Macateer was the picture of sanity. He smiled at Edward then, reproaching himself, shook his head. 'I've sprung it on you. Tss.'

The chap in the coat was familiar from somewhere. Where? The puzzle kept popping into the foreground of Edward's mind, distracting him. He wished the chap would leave the room, or else that Mikey would. Then he could ask one about the other.

Mikey, anxious lest Edward be harbouring grudges, was launched on a history of his own doctrinal waverings. Where he had ended up, he told Edward, was in the same boat as himself, with the other side out to get him.

Get whom?

'Me.' Macateer added that, though Edward might think him a Johnny-come-lately to the cause of liberalism, this was far from true. There was a tide in such movements and to anticipate it could only be counter-productive, self-indulgent and, in a sense, yes, mad. Was Edward being called mad now? It seemed he was. Mikey's face had grown supercilious. It reminded Edward of some portrait of a doge. Was it in the Wallace Collection? he wondered, but thought not. His attention kept dodging and scampering. It was the intensity of Mikey's onslaught. Made one back off. 'Voltairian rationalism', he heard Mikey sneer, was all liberalism could be in the context of the forties and fifties when Edward was a liberal. Later, on the other hand. . . . Bullying rhythms drummed. Mikey's fingers formed a knot as taut as a cricket-ball ready to lunge out and bash the bails off all obstacles to Mikey's will. Edward, inevitably reminded of the dogmatic old Mikey, saw that the memory showed, for, perceptibly, the tones softened and gave way to ingratiating ones so wrong for Mikey that Edward, teeth on edge, felt a panicked urge to plead: 'Stop, don't do this to us. Don't humiliate yourself.' Maybe, in fairness, he *should* do this? But wouldn't it be *more* humiliating for Macateer if he did? As a compromise, he tried to catch his eye, but its beam was wavering evasively over Edward's shoulder.

'You don't like me,' said Macateer surprisingly. 'Isn't that a good reason why you *should* help me?' Now his eye did catch Edward's in an iron-blue clench. 'Isn't that the liberal ethic?' he challenged. 'I have served an institution,' said Macateer. 'You fight the tyranny of institutions. What about taking on this one?' He gestured at the walls of the room. He had always admired Edward's gutsiness, he said, which was why he was appealing to him now. In the past Edward had stood up and been counted, defending sacked schoolteachers and other radicals and, at the risk of damaging his practice, held out against a domineering Church.

The bathos made Edward wonder if he was being mocked. 'Are you', he checked, 'making fun of me?'

'Fun?'

'We achieved so little.'

'You kept the idea of liberty alive.'

The man's face puffed with assurance. What did he believe? Now the man in the white coat was listening with interest. Edward's struggles, said Macateer, reminded him of the dissidents in the Soviet Union.

'You embarrass me,' said Edward. 'We have no Siberia in Ireland.' He laughed at the ridiculousness of this.

'No, but people can', said Macateer, 'get committed to asylums! Not that the agency which committed *me* was Irish.'

There was a silence. A sweaty gleam, hovering, halo-like, about the Bishop, could come from strain or the stimulus of drugs. The white-coated man guffawed with sudden violence.

'Ah, now, yer Grace, yer not comparing the Vatican to the

Kremlin, I hope?' He winked at Edward, who again was shocked.

Macateer ignored him. 'Would Civil Liberties', he asked Edward, 'take on the Vatican? Just to the extent of opening an enquiry? It would not, you understand, be limited to my case?'

'You've turned against the Church?'

'A certain church.'

'You mean', Edward pressed incredulously, 'that you would take legal action against . . . some agency . . . in the Vatican?' The man was deranged, he decided with relief and a feeling of let-down. His fighting spirit, roused like an old horse taken too briefly from its paddock, was all a-tremble. He looked at Mikey, an awful old man, the spirit of smug Irish Catholicism personified, and saw no reason why freedom-lovers should fight for him. Mad or sane now, he had in his day been as repressive as he had had the power to be and was unrepentant. Mikey's mind was tidy, his commitment extreme. Once, it had been expedient for the Church to be traditionalist and tough. Now Mikey saw it as wise to move the other way. 'Wise' meant politic.

'I am no defector.' Mikey's eyes were blazing, his cheeks concave. Fragility reached a taut climax in him as in a windblown candle. Edward was responsive to this passion of the flesh as he had not been to Mikey's words. These, however, came grating and panting out in a gravelly torrent. A man loyal to his institution, said Mikey, arguing with the fluency of habit, did not refrain from criticising it when necessary. Neither did he leave it. He laboured to change it from within. Went *into* labour to produce a new version of it. To leave was easy — and ineffective. Defectors became enemies. 'To stay and struggle', said Mikey, his eyes bulging painfully, 'is the test of loyalty.' Here Mikey's discourse grew obscure, black, thought Edward, like the tip of a smoking candle-flame. He had been persecuted, it appeared, had roused unworthy passion, courted isolation, trouble, personal animosities which — well, all communities harboured such. Edward must understand. Edward didn't. Conspiracies were hinted at. Mikey smoked and fumed.

Suddenly, the man in the white coat had taken a glass of water from the trolley and, walking over to the quivering Macateer, handed him a coloured pill. 'Mustn't excite yourself,' he admonished. 'He gets worked up,' he told Edward. 'Dangerous at his age, don't you know. Here,' he harried Macateer. 'Remember our agreement?'

Macateer snatched the pill and swallowed it with a gulp of water. 'Sycophant!' he shouted.

The minder went back to his window-seat.

Macateer tilted the back of his head at him. 'Bet you don't know who *he* is? Our genial host: Jim Farrel. Name mean nothing to you?' Macateer's angry eyes stabbed at Edward. 'Had us all to dinner,' he prompted. 'Twenty years ago? Remember? Poured champagne, buttered us up and footed the bill. Throwing a sprat to catch a salmon, mm? He's the original Platonic pragmatist and parasite.' Macateer paused. When he spoke again it was with diminished energy. 'If you help me,' he told Edward, 'Jim'll play ball. He likes to be on a winning team. If you don't. . . .' He pointed his thumb downwards.

Farrel winked. 'A joke,' he said. 'His Grace likes to—'

'Toady!' Like a schoolyard insult, the word pebbled over Macateer's shoulder. To Edward he spoke quietly. 'Jim's mum had a hardware shop down the country. A tidy little concern. He has the sensitivity of cast-iron *and* its toughness. *I* found that useful, mind. I took him to Rome with me — aha, you didn't know that? Yes, yes, he was my minion there for years. My cat's paw. Forgive the quaint diction. He's a quaint creature. Turned his coat. In the end he helped my enemies certify me. Why not? From his and their point of view, a man who ceases to know his own interest is mad, and I, feeling my time run out, ceased to bide it. Thus they could think that I would be best off in my native island with my old slavery enslaving me. Italian journalists are inquisitive; it was best to get me out of reach. He's tapping his forehead, isn't he?' Macateer, without looking round to where Farrel was indeed making this gesture, mimicked it perfectly. The hand tapping his high papery forehead was covered with raised brown moles. Macateer seemed older and more overgrown by the moment. A loser? 'My crime', he told Edward, 'was your own failing: intemperateness. Also', Mikey smiled without gaiety, 'love. Love of my family, which is and was the Church.'

Edward's brain buzzed. His stomach was making itself felt.

Drink and excitement were lethal at his age. He should get out of here. But a quick withdrawal could look heartless. Antagonistic forces tugged. Emotionally, he could have been being quartered by wild horses. Sectioned. Minced. Eagerness pulsed in him: that lethal itch to live. Poor bloody Mikey! *Mon semblable, mon frère!* Yes? No? Issues which Edward had long thought settled and jelled beneath the veneer of age's mellowness had begun to toss, jumbled like notions in an adolescent's brain. The sensation was nostalgic and disagreeable.

'Don't excite yerself, now,' said Jim Farrel, perhaps speaking to both old men.

Procrastinating, Edward decided not to catch the train tonight. He'd stay in a local hotel he'd seen touted by the gastronomic guides.

'You're not going?' Mikey was aghast.

'Must.' Edward tapped his watch. 'Only to Ballylea House. I'll come again tomorrow.' This was a false promise. He'd have to see. When he pressed Mikey's hand, it felt like spaghetti: a mess of veins. Mikey's eyes looked at him with equally soft appeal and unearned comradeliness: Not many of us left, Edward. Who's 'us', Mikey?

Farrel took Edward to the front door, then through a port-cullis of rain to canvass the car-park for lifts. He dashed back with news that a Dr Ryan would be dining at Ballylea House and could take Edward there.

'Was it you posted his letter to me?' Edward managed to ask as he was being settled into the car.

'It was, yes. He has high hopes of you, Senator.' Farrel's face was a blurr magnified by the wet window and his tone a concerned nanny's. Edward wondered would he be mad to involve Civil Liberties in this intricate sub-world. 'Phone if you're coming tomorrow,' Farrel shouted as the car drove off. 'Ask for me, Senator: Jim Farrel.'

Dr Ryan accepted a drink in the hotel bar. He was a fresh-faced gossipy psychiatrist and revealed that Farrel wasn't. Wasn't a psychiatrist? Not even a doctor? Edward, remembering Jammet's, and Farrel's weakness for slipping a rung or so above his station, asked, 'A male nurse, then?'

His guest conciliated. 'You could say that. More of an inmate, actually. *You* wouldn't know, to be sure, but in places like this. . . .' The lines, it seemed, were fluid, the outfit run by priests, not doctors. 'Oh, ours is definitely a subsidiary capacity.' He mused. 'Odd customers wash up on Irish shores. Gulf Arab girls come here to study nursing. Our reliable chastity is why. Equally, our pious discretion brings anonymous prelates to the Institution. Enough said,' said Ryan, lowering a lid. Farrel, he admitted, *was* an inmate, though of a special sort. 'Mind, it's not my department. All hearsay. But it seems they came together from Rome:Master and Man.'

'Surely both can't be mad?' And what, Edward wondered, about the white coat? The pill?

'Farrel's good with patients.' The doctor tee-heed. 'Listen, he was a medical student in his youth. We lay man-traps for men like that. You can't imagine how short-handed we are. So, he's humoured, let have the coat and the parlour. Staff in places like this is impossible to get. I married a local girl myself or I'd never have stayed. Then I like the horses. I'm a country type. But I'm unusual.'

'Is anyone in the Institution clinically mad?'

The doctor made the most of this cue. Was Edward a Laingian? He discoursed on madness, quoted Foucault. On wet nights, it seemed, he read. Sure, wasn't it all relative? A matter of being out of step with your immediate community? And hadn't some societies seen madness as divine? Mind you, Pope's crack about great wits being near to madness had especial relevance in the context of the Church. With abstract men subjected to great pressure – especially, now, my God, with all the controversy – you'd *expect* breakdowns, wouldn't you? Moments of uncertainty. The Institution specialised in distinguished key thinkers who came here to recuperate. *Sub rosa.* Much could hinge on their emotional health.

'Not mental?'

'Mental, emotional – some may just need a rest.'

'Or to be kept out of the way?'

The doctor – now on his third whiskey – whispered, 'Ah, now, Senator, mum's the word!'

Could he be a semi-inmate himself? Or was Edward succumbing to an insidious folly: believing himself alone in his sanity in a world of lunatics? Ryan, face fat with alcohol, continued his chat. Important with innuendo, he grew big on it, amplifying gestures, grinning, nudging ribs.

'Ah, but silence is golden, eh, Senator, what?' Edward's title seemed all of a sudden to set off a train of thought, for the face shuttered itself at speed. Ryan's mouth twisted, like a key in a lock, as he revealed that he was anxious about his dinner and had better phone his wife pronto. She was late and the table booked for half an hour since. Sorry, Senator, must be off. Great privilege to meet you. Thanks for the drink.

Later, Edward saw him dodge across the lobby under the wing of a woman. Not acknowledging Edward's wave, he scuttled into the dining-room.

Alone in the bar's dimness, Edward was assailed by memories of the decades — his middle ones — when Dubliners had scuttled from him in droves. The town, when he was not yet a senator but already active in Civil Liberties, had been populated with citizens made in the mould of glove-puppers, each equipped with dissimilar sides to his face. The side for public viewing was pious and non-committal. The private side, a glitter of keyed-up bravery, peered, in the shadow of raised collar and lowered hat, like a rabbit from his hole. 'Keep up the good work, Eddy,' these secret fans hissed furtively. 'We'd back ye all the way if it wasn't for the aul' job, don't ye know, the wife, the kids, the pension. Sure you know what it's like yourself. Cross the priests in this country and you're a goner. But we're with you in spirit. You're doing Trojan work!'

He remembered the public ostracism with a cold shudder which he had never let himself feel at the time. In the heat of the fight, pugnacity kept you going. And his swagger had appealed to women. He had enjoyed, even exploited, being odd man out. Now he would get nothing from it. An old man needed approval, needed the goodwill of acquaintances to tether him to a receding world.

What *right* had Mikey to come whining to him? Let him take his come-uppance. According to his own reckoning, the man who played against the odds was a fool.

And what about Edward's reckoning? Wasn't abandoning a principle a way of letting death steal a pass on you? Was it? It was. You became less yourself. Ah, to hell, Mikey wasn't worth fighting for, and it would be a terrible fight. It could bring Civil Liberties into disrepute and stir up untold scandal. A caper like that could lead to not one but two old men being thought demented.

Edward's bladder was bothering him, and he set off for the gents. Passing the dining-room, he saw Ryan's face duck behind a menu in pretence of non-recognition. The light in the men's room was dusty neon, cold as a twilit sea. In a tidal mirror, the face floating towards Edward was fearful, peppered with the marks of doubt, clenched, shifty, explosive and — it struck him with a slow surge of pleasure — vehemently alive. As he came closer, a pink flush began to give it a healthier glow; the lips parted in amusement and a fist lunged ahead of it, pronging two fingers aloft and erect in a waggling V-sign.

He decided to have a bottle of Château Haut Brion 1970 with dinner. It was good neither for his liver nor for his wallet, but seize the moment, seize the day. He'd drink in it to his own and Mikey's intemperate future.

Next morning he was up early. Nowadays, he scarcely slept anyway, and dreams sparked off by his day's doings were best suppressed. He was aware of them slithering back now beneath a mud of oblivion. Good! Foreward!

The breakfast-room was a splatter of neon. Tables were icefloes where guests who last night had stayed too long at the bar flipped open napkins and lowered dispirited walrus faces towards their kippers. Edward, however, was brisk. Purpose enlivened him, and his grapefruit was a zesty pleasure. He chatted with the waiter, deciding to walk to the Institution which, the man assured, was no more than a mile off as the crow flew.

It proved a bracing stroll, and he was breathing pastoral air with relish when, halfway up the Institutional avenue, Jim Farrel emerged from the ambush of a rhododendron.

'I had an idea you mightn't phone,' he reproached. 'Listen, Senator, I need a word with you.'

He needed many, it turned out, for Edward would have to be put in the picture if he was to be of any use to Macateer.

'For his sake,' Farrel appealed, 'you should hear both sides.'

Edward, the old lawyer, had to agree that, if there were indeed sides, he'd better take a look at both. He let himself be led through foliage towards a rustic tea-house. The estate had once belonged to members of the old ruling class and bits of pretty pomp subsisted. A lake, visible from where they sat, was fenced off by wire netting.

What Edward must know, said Farrel, was that the Bishop's folly was not personal. 'Madness' — Farrel's face streamed with excited sweat — 'has the whole bloody Vatican in its grip. It's an infection, Senator: a disease. You'd have to know the place to understand. It's very closed off. Patronage and slavery are rampant. You heard our friend call me a hanger-on and worse. Well, that's what I was, and the place is full of men like me: men who carry other men's briefcases for a decade or so, open car-doors for them, dust down their rosaries, live on hope. Hope is the disease, hope and impatience, and the top men are not immune. *They* hope for something else maybe: the Kingdom of Heaven on earth with freedom to love and live carnally extended to all. A new reformed God comforting His creatures with apples of all knowledge and licence.' Through Farrel's tones came a flicker of quotation marks. Clearly, this was parody of something or anyway an echo.

'Macateer?' wondered Edward.

'Aye. You heard what he said: he used to fight it and then he succumbed to it. That's not uncommon, Senator. Look how the old witch-hunters grew fascinated by the thing they were suppressing. There's scholars will tell you that they invented it, that all we know of witches comes from the witch-hunters' reports and that maybe there were no witches at all.' Farrel grinned shyly. 'You pick up queer lore. Well, to come back to the present, the dream that's haunting the place now is old, too: an old heresy. This time, though, it's biting right into the heart of the Church. Right to the *sanctum sanctorum* — and when that happens who's to condemn it?' Farrel's grin grew wolfish and his eyes glittered with an appetite for scandal. 'They say', he whispered, 'that in the last couple of years *two* popes had to be knocked off. One for sure was done in. Eliminated for the greater good. Can you credit that, Senator?' Cunning pause. Insinuating smile. How far will you go with me? asked Farrel's long streamer of a face. Flecked with dimples of darkness, it flowed whitely in Edward's troubled vision – the tea-house was dusky, and Farrel's presence had an unsettling effect on him. The chap was actually swaying like a cobra in his excitement, and this impeded Edward's apprehension of what he was saying.

'Men like me', confided Farrel, 'get to know things that the red hats themselves don't know, let alone the bishops. In a sense, we run the place. Why else would we put up with the sort of shit you saw me take from Macateer? We know our worth and that it depends on not being known. Eh, Senator, can you believe that it was men like myself who arranged for those two popes' disposal – men that I maybe know? Doing someone's bidding, to be sure – but tell me this: what's a head without a hand to do its bidding? It's not much, is it? Listen' – he gripped Edward's arm – 'how do you imagine he was got out? Our friend? Mm? Brought over here? By whom? Why? I'll tell you: it was I did it and for his own good. For his safety. Better a spell in the bin than what *can* happen, mm? To be sure, he's in no state to appreciate this.' Farrel paused, waited, but Edward had nothing to say to him. 'You'll have guessed', the fellow went on, 'that there are factions. What you mightn't guess is how ruthless the fight has to be. No holds barred. The dreamers *have* to be stopped. He – our friend – is the one who taught me that. He was an institution man himself. Trained me up to think like him. Well, it's common sense: when you're afloat in a boat you don't drive a hole in its bottom and you don't let anyone else do it, either. Right? But then he joined the dreamers: started wanting the fruits of eternity in the here and now. Like those popes I mentioned. No need to name names. Impatience, Senator, is a hazard of the profession. Listen, sit down, it's only fair to hear me out. I want to make sure you have things clear. Then you can judge. Sit down, sit down. Have you understood, Senator, that the man in there,' Farrel gestured in the direction of the Institution, hidden behind trees, 'that the Macateer in there is a changeling?'

'I've got to go.'

'I'm speaking metaphorically.'

'Let me pass.'

'In a moment, a wee moment, there's plenty of time.'

'I have a tight schedule.' Edward waved his wrist and watch.

'What's madness, you may ask?' Farrel thrust his face into Edward's, barring his exit from the tea-house. 'Maybe its worst strain is altruism?'

'Let's discuss this later. I want to see Macateer now.'

'You're suspicious of me?' An urchin's humour twiddled at the corners of Farrel's mouth. 'These things are hard to take in.' The cobra sway of Farrel's head made Edward's spin. Right, left, right swayed Farrel, like a goalie guarding his goal. He was in fact guarding the door. 'What have I to gain by hurting you?'

'Is that a threat?'

'Senator!' Farrel was every inch the reproachful nurse — nanny or nursery-school teacher. 'It is because of my deep respect for you', he spoke with formality, 'that I'm appealing to you on his behalf. He had to be made to see sense first, *then* restored to his former position.'

'So that he'll restore you to yours?' But Edward was not interested in this dialogue. Its premises were absurd. On the other hand, he hesitated to push past the man, fearing to let things get physical. He wondered would anyone hear him if he were to shout. No, probably not. 'I need', he improvised, 'to go to the bathroom.'

'Take a leak in the bushes.'

'That's not what I need.'

'OK, then, OK.' Farrel, a policeman's grip on Edward's elbow, walked him in custody back towards the avenue. 'First we must talk sense to him,' he explained, while pushing foliage out of Edward's path, 'then help him legally. He has a strong case, but must be persuaded to behave with prudence. Otherwise, things will just start up again the same way. We'll be back to square one. The Progressives are just not going to be let wreck the Church. I wish I had more time to make this clear to you, Senator. I know you find it hard to believe. The new is strange and the strange seems mad — but ours is a time of polarities. You, an old liberal and a man of the middle, owe it to us to hold the ring.' In his excitement, Farrel was backing Edward into brambles and had made him lose his balance. 'Oh, Jesus, I'm sorry,' he shouted and caught the lurching Edward in his arms. 'Steady now, Senator. You don't think *I'd* hurt you, now do you, surely? Me?'

'Why not you? Who are you anyway?'

'I'm your spiritual son. I picked you out twenty years ago.'

'What rubbish.'

'Not rubbish. You remember the dinner at Jammet's? You must. You do. The Bishop mentioned it yesterday. Well, why do you think I gave it? I'd picked you out: you and him. You represented the two sides of my tradition: the Irish heritage. I wanted to apprentice myself. I was looking for a mentor. My father died early, you know. Anyway, he was a limited man. I had ambitions. I wanted short cuts: an adoptive father. One adopted by me who could instruct me, give me a leg up. I planned to get to know you and the Monsignor, as he then was, both. That's why I gave the dinner. The two foreigners were bait. I knew you'd want to meet them — well, I hardly hoped you'd want to meet *me*. But, normally, you should have extended some hospitality after accepting mine. I counted on that. If it hadn't been for the fight you had with Macateer — you'll remember that? — it would have worked. As it was, I had to choose between the two of you right off. I could have brought you home in a taxi — drunk as you were. But your wife would have been there. She wouldn't have let me stay. So I plumped for him, stayed on, flattered him, became his factotum. Secretary. Well, you know all that. But I've often wondered what it would have been like if you'd been my patron. Here we are. You said you needed a bathroom.'

They had reached the door of the Institution.

'I want a taxi,' said Edward. 'I'm leaving.' He couldn't bear to see Macateer now, or indeed anyone else. The fumes of Farrel's unbalanced eagerness made him feel unbalanced himself. It was like getting drunk off another man's breath. He had to be alone for a while.

'He's expecting you. He'll be disappointed. At least say "hello".'

'I'm too old for all this.'

'Too old to turn away from it. The young don't need you. Do your sons need you?'

Edward was astounded at the chap's knowing insolence. Had he been ferreting out information? Gossip? Into that madhouse he was resolved not to put foot.

'I'm going.' He turned, stepped down some steps, hastened, as he heard Farrel come after him and, losing his footing, fell and rolled down the rest of the flight. Feeling the fellow try to pick him up — his leg ached where he had perhaps pulled a muscle — he was impelled by pain and fury to lunge for the bloody ass's face. His knuckles hit something hard — teeth perhaps? — and he felt blood on his fist. Was it his own? He could have wept with exasperation. Feeling himself being further manhandled, he lunged again and realised that he had managed to break his own glasses. Splinters ran into his palm and he could see nothing but blurr. Voices reached him confusingly.

'What's up? What's it now? What's the matter?'

'. . . gone berserk. Here, give me a hand.'

'Who is it?'

'A visitor. I know him. Gently now.'

'Who did you say?'

'Drunk?'

'. . . do himself an injury — or us. A friend of Farrel's, is he?'

'What set him off? Here, Pat, Joe, we need help. Those buggers are never there when you need them.'

'Quiet now, Senator . . . need to give him a shot of something. Tough old bastard, isn't he? Music in the old bones yet, what?'

'A damn sight too much. What was it you said . . .?'

'Off his head — doting.' That was Farrel's voice.

'A shot of something. Someone call Dr Ryan.'

Struggling and captive like a newborn infant, Edward felt himself carried in the door.

Rags and Bones

Nadine Gordimer

A WOMAN named Beryl Fels recently picked up an old tin chest in a junk shop. When she got it home to her flat she found it contained letters.

She telephoned friends and had something more amusing to exchange than news of business trips and children's colds. 'What do you do with other people's letters?' 'Take them back' — but that was a stupid answer. Back where? The old man who ran the shop wouldn't know to whom they belonged; these rag-and-bone men wouldn't tell a buyer, ever, where they found the things they scavenged from house sales, pawnshops, and people more in need of money than of possessions whose associations they either did not know or no longer cared about.

'Read them. Oh, of course, read them.' The antiquarian book-seller was at once in character; he was good fun, this permanently young man of forty-five, homosexual and bibliophile. He and Beryl Fels went to the theatre and avant-garde films together, a plausible if inauthentic couple.

'Burn them, I suppose. What else could one do?' — the lying rectitude of a most devious woman, who eavesdropped on her adolescent children's telephone conversations.

'What did you want a tin chest for?' — this from someone who had no leisure to spend Saturday mornings pottering about among bric-à-brac and making trips across town to some special shop where one could buy a particular cheese or discover a good inexpensive wine not easy to get.

Beryl Fels had thought the chest would be the thing to hold spare keys, fuse-wire, picture-hooks. Living without a man, she was efficient as any male about household maintenance, no trouble at all to her, although her hands were creamed and manicured, as perfectly useless-looking as any man with an ideal of femininity could have wished for. She had been looking out for something that would clear from her lovely yellow-wood desk (another Saturday-morning find) a miscellany that didn't belong there.

Some of the letters were banded together, and probably all had been, once. All were addressed to the same name, a woman's, and to a box-number in one town, or *poste restante* in other towns and even, she saw, in other countries. She had not thought of the chest as a receptacle for letters. But, of course, if one were to have so many letters to keep! She counted: 307 letters and 9 postcards. And telegrams, many telegrams, some stuffed into their original orange window-envelopes. There is something queer about preserving telegrams. She held them: at once urgent and old, they don't keep. She read one; telegrams are hardly private, the words counted out by a post-office clerk under the public eye. It was terse and unsigned, a date, a time, a railway station platform number, a cryptic addition whose message was not very difficult to guess. *Yes yes yes.* A lover's affirmation. What can 307 letters be but love letters? And it seemed that probably the person they belonged to had not put them in the chest – some were wadded as if they had lain pushed behind heavy objects. Someone had found them, perhaps, and tossed them into the tin chest that the woman to whom they had been written didn't own. Beryl Fels saw, as she tipped them all out, that they had been thrown in carelessly in reverse order, the top of the pile was at the bottom of the chest, and there was the very sheet of paper (the old foolscap size) with the instruction that would have met the eye of anyone on opening the drawer or lifting the lid of the place where the letters originally would have been kept. *These letters and documents are to be preserved unread until twenty years after the date of my death, and then are to be presented to an appropriate library or archives.* The signature was the name on the envelopes. The postmarks – the letters were not in chronological order any more, so one would have to go through the lot to see how long the affair had lasted – were from the late 1940s (which explained why the telegram she'd read gave a railway station platform number rather than a flight number). If the woman had died then, the embargo was lapsed. If she were still

alive, she certainly would have destroyed her letters rather than
let them out of her hands.

Beryl Fels began to read while she drank her coffee late on Sunday
morning. She did not get out of her dressing-gown or make her
bed or tend her balcony herb garden to the sound of Mozart or
punk rock (she was interested in everything that was a craze or
passion in other people's lives), as she usually did on Sundays.
She had had two invitations to lunch at the homes of couples,
one hetero- the other homosexual, options she had left open to
herself if a preferable third — she was a free agent — did not turn
up, but she did not go out and ate no lunch. At times, while she
read, her heart made itself heard in her ears like a sound from
someone moving about in the flat. The tendons behind her knees
were tense and her long-nailed forefinger stroked the wings of
her nose, which felt warm and greasy. The woman to whom the
letters were written was not just anybody; the man who wrote
them was her confidant and critic as well as her lover. He wrote
most passionately when he had just had the experience of hearing
her praised by people who did not know he knew her. He wanted
terribly to make love to her, he said, when he saw her up there on
the platform giving a lecture, with her glasses hiding her eyes
from everybody. He felt himself swelling when he saw her name
in print. Whole long letters analysed the behaviour of people who
would, he felt, do this rather than that, express themselves in
these words and gestures rather than those, were 'there' or 'simply
not there'. It became clear these were characters in a novel or
play: she was a writer.

And he — he seemed to have been a scientist of some sort,
engaged in research. It was difficult, without having access to her
letters to him, to discover what exactly it was he hoped to achieve,
what it was that he was climbing towards over the years the
letters covered. There was the impression that the specialised
nature of his work was something his mistress did not have the
type of intellect or education to follow, despite her brilliance,
attested to in every letter, and her success, which was as strong an
erotic stimulus as whatever beauty she might have had ('. . . against
that field of female cabbages your face was stamped out like a

fern' — he strained to be literary, too). But that she was ambitious for him, that she jealously bristled when others received promotions, awards, honours that he was in the running for, was plain from the passages in his letters calming her with his more stoic, cynical view of talents and rewards in his field. To her he unburdened himself scatologically of all the malice he felt — *he* and *she* felt — towards those who advanced themselves by means he certainly wouldn't stoop to. She also consoled; he found endearing — and did not deny, since no doubt he knew his worth — her assurances that, whatever small kudos others might pick up on the way, he would get one of the Nobel Prizes one day.

At some stage he did receive some signal honour for his work; as a lover he took what evidently must have been her stern triumphant pride as a new and particularly voluptuous kind of caress between them; and at the same time he was concealing from himself, in order to enjoy the triumph unalloyed, the knowledge that she was not fitted to judge the scale of such achievements or the significance of such honours. This last came out in certain small embarrassed phrases, and half-sentences scored over but not made illegible (as if he couldn't bear to have secrets from her, not even those he was concealing for both of them). The stranger, reading, took up the pathetic cunning of these phrases and half-remarks, whereas between the distinguished man writing them and the distinguished woman to whom they were addressed the grit of doubt would be enveloped in emotion and mutual self-esteem as the lubrication of the eye coats tiny foreign bodies and prevents them from irritating the eyeball.

The distinguished woman schemed to attend the ceremony at which her lover was to be honoured; letters covering the wrangling of a whole month between them first persuaded, finally implored her to give up the idea. 'Even if you could approach Fragar through Ebensteain, how can he not smell a rat? A bedroom rat, quite frankly, my love. Only members of the Society and their wives will be present. The press! They don't come to things like this. It's not exactly a world-shaking event. They get a handout, perhaps, with the list of awards, afterwards. And since when have you been known as a journalist? Why on earth should you suddenly express great interest in the proceedings of the Society?

You'd be recognised at once by someone who's seen your photograph on your books, for God's sake! Someone would start sniffing around for a connection, the reason for your being there. And how could we *not* look at each other? You know it's impossible. You're not just anybody, even if you sometimes want to be.' And in answer to what must have been resentful disappointment: 'There are some things we can't have. As you often say, we have so much; more than other people can even dream of, I'm superstitious to spell it out, not only "us", our great joy in each other's bodies and friendship, but success and real achievement — certainly you, my darling, I am well aware, quite objectively, you are one of the great names coming. . . . If we don't suffer the attrition of farmyard domesticity, then we can't have the sort of public display of participation in each other's achievements married couples have — and most of the time it's all they do have. Why should you want to sit like some faculty wife (like mine, whose husband doesn't want to sleep with her and can't talk to her any more) wearing an appropriate smile for the occasion, as she does a hat. . . ?'

Again, she must have wanted to dedicate a book to him. He tormentedly regretted he must forgo this. 'No matter how you juggle initials or code-names known only to us, you give away our private world. You acknowledge its existence, to others. Let's keep it as we've managed to do for nearly five years. Separately, we are both people in the public eye; it's the price or the reward, God knows, of what we both happen to be. Let the media scrabble and speculate over those. I know that book is mine; and it is my posterity.'

At five in the afternoon Beryl Fels read the last letter. It was not one of the momentous ones — reflected no crisis — nor was it the type of note, strangled terse with erotic excitement, that immediately preceded planned meetings. He was writing while eating a sandwich at his desk; he was thinking about his damned lecture for the Hong Kong conference; he'd read only five pages (this must refer to some piece of her work she had given him) but could not wait to tell her how moving in a new way and at the same time witty . . . hence the scribble. . . .

Beryl Fels stood up. Belches kept rising from her empty stomach. Outlines in the room jumped. Thirteen cigarette-stubs — she counted dully — in the ashtray. The dazedness came from the change of focus for her eyes: there were her other 'finds' around her, to establish the equilibrium of her own existence. She gazed at her beautiful yellow-wood desk, subdued in its presence as if, entering into the past of other lives, she had dislodged the order of her own and retrogressed to the shallow-breathing stillness of being caught out, brought back to the angles and polished surfaces of the headmistress's study from blurred fearful pleasures in an overgrown corner of a garden. She put her hands to her nose, the child sniffing the secret odour on the fingers.

Running a bath, making her neglected bed, and choosing one of her silk shirts to wear with trousers provided the routine (she often bathed and changed at this time of day, just home from work) that accomplished the shift from the experience of reading the letters to an interpretation appropriate to her well-arranged life. Like the other finds — the desk perfectly at home between balcony door and lyre-backed chair — this one found its place. It became one of her interests and diversions as a lively personality. A pity the day was Sunday; she could have telephoned the public library to ask if they had any of the woman's books. She could have gone down at once herself, to read up about her. Perhaps the identity of the man was known to people more widely read than she was. If not, the letters might be even more important — a discovery, even a literary sensation, as well as a find. She telephoned her bookseller friend again and again, but of course he would always be at some party on a Sunday evening; he was asked everywhere. Having overcome an unusual (for her) reluctance to talk to anybody — it just showed how one needs to get out and among people, how quickly solitude takes hold — Beryl Fels impatiently awaited Monday morning.

In the week that followed, she asked her antiquarian bookseller friend and the chief librarians at the public library and a university library (both aquaintances) about the woman writer. None of these had heard of her. Each was cautious to say so; each uneasy, unless this pat ignorance should prove to be a professional lapse, the name that of some esoteric but important writers' writer he should have known. But library catalogues revealed not a single book by anyone of the name was on the shelves or even in the store, the morgue stacks from which books no longer in general demand were taken out for borrowers on special request. The antiquarian bookseller did dig up, in some old publisher's catalogue, the title of one book by the woman, thirty years out of print. The title rang no bell for anyone.

Determinedly, so good at tracking down things she wanted, Beryl Fels got someone to introduce her to a professor in the science faculty at the university. She did not show him her find but jotted down for him all the facts gleaned from the letters that could lead to an identification of the other personality who made up the pair of distinguished lovers. There was no one, no one at all fitting the given period, field of activity (quickly established as geophysics), and country of origin whose work was sufficiently original or important for his name to be known. There was certainly no one, in the list of Nobel Prize winners for science, who could have been or could be him — should he still be alive.

The antiquarian bookseller said she should keep the letters anyway. 'Beryl darling, for our grandchildren — if any.' He was conducting one of the unruly lunches expected at his table, and timed the laugh, pausing not a second too long. 'Even letters written by ordinary people become saleable if you wait fifty years or so. Like old seaside postcards. Laundry lists. Don't I know? How else could I afford to give you all such a good meal? People will collect anything.'

Ladies' Race

Angela Huth

ON THE THIRD ANNIVERSARY of the death of their friend
the chief mourners, perhaps the only mourners left, visited the
graveyard with their customary bunch of early daffodils. They
wore black coats, signifying the formality that had insinuated itself
into their lives — a thing they were both aware of, fought against
but seemed unable to change. The man, hands crossed over his
crutch, wore bright new leather gloves. The woman's hands, also
crossed, were bare: the nails bitten away, flaky, lustreless. They
remained in uneasy silence for some moments, heads bowed, eyes
on the simple headstone that was engraved with the two names of
their friend, the date of her birth and the date of her death.

The man shifted. Relieved, the woman took his arm. She regarded this annual gesture of respect as pointless. Surely they
should forget, not remember. But Gerald was insistent, and she
had learned not to cross him on important matters. All the same
she could not resist observing how she felt: Gerald should know.

'Anyone would think this was the most important anniversary
of the year, to you,' she said.

Gerald made no reply. They turned towards the path of pale
sharp stones that ran stiffly between the graves. Leaning against
each other, like people older than their years, they began to walk
towards the gate. It was cold, in spite of the thickness of their
coats. But, heavy with marriage, it was no time to hurry. These
visits always bared their memories, troubled them for a few hours,
or days, or even weeks.

Gerald met Lola first. She was tall, head above most women at
the party. It was a cold house, and while others gathered shawls
about their shoulders Lola was impressive for her long bare arms

and the warm-looking flesh of her neck and half-exposed bosom. Gerald, who had had no lover for two years, partly for the good of his soul but mostly for the lack of suitable women, found himself inclining towards her. As he fetched her a glass of wine and another plate of haddock kedgeree — her third — he considered the possibility of breaking his vow of self-inflicted chastity. The thought was an unformed uncoloured thing: the merest web that flung itself across his tired mind. But registered. Meantime, as a patient man, he was surprised to find himself annoyed by the queue at the buffet. He had left Lola alone in a corner and could see a gathering tide of men beginning to converge upon her. But she greeted him on his return with the kind of quiet pleasure that evaporated her new admirers. Not that she had much to say to Gerald. She seemed quite content to sit silently by him, wolfing her kedgeree, apparently hungry. Gerald, dry with weariness from weeks of overwork, was grateful for her lack of demand: he was in no mood to bewitch, or even entertain. He felt at ease in her silence, and grateful for it.

Much later they walked down the frosty street to his car. Lola wore no coat, said she never felt cold. Gerald was briefly shot with the desire to feel her flesh, to prove her boastful warmth. Instead he put his hands in his pockets and kept his distance. The filmy stuff of her dress blew about as she walked, making her seem fragile, for all her height. In the seat of his old sports car she had to bunch up her long legs: Gerald found himself apologising. Sarah — what years ago *she* suddenly seemed — had always managed to stretch out her miniscule limbs with great comfort Lola laughed, easing the nervousness Gerald always felt when a new woman entered the sanctity of his car. She lived, it turned out, quite near him.

Some days later, by the gas fire in his muddled sitting-room, Gerald discovered his first impression of Lola had been quite wrong. There was nothing frail about her. No: she was an athletic girl with calves of lively muscle and wristbones that were handsome in their size. While she ate her way through his last supplies of Dundee cake and shortbread, she told him something of her outdoor life: she had played tennis one year at junior Wimbledon; she ski'd each winter, sailed every summer, rode at weekends, jogged around Hyde Park three mornings a week before break-fast — hated her secret job at the Foreign Office. Gerald was momentarily alarmed by the thought of such outdoor energy: worlds that were far from his. But then she smiled, brushing crumbs from her chin with the back of her hand, and he felt relieved again.

'I suppose you think just because of all that I'm very hearty, don't you?' she said. 'I learned judo till I was fourteen and I could fling my older brother over my shoulder easy as anything.' Her eyes sparkled over Gerald's weary body, hunched deep in his armchair. 'As a matter of fact, I expect I could still. . . .'

'I'm sure you could,' he said.

'Shall I try?' She was both mischievous and serious. Gerald was torn between not wanting to disappoint her and wishing to preserve some dignity.

'Is this quite the place?' he asked, glancing about the piles of books.

'Oh, anywhere'll do, won't it?'

Lola was already up, enormous above him, smiling her enchanting smile as she pulled him to his feet. He sensed scaling up the side of her as if in a fast lift; flat stomach, mounds of bosom beneath wool, thin neck, pretty teeth. Just for a second his eyes were level with hers. Then, the crash. He was grovelling on his own Turkish carpet, the small square of ugly reds and blues that for years he had meant to change, had never been forced to study so closely before. He heard the sound of falling books, felt pain in elbows and knees. Lola was laughing, helping him up again.

'There. . . . Honestly. I told you. You all right?'

'Fine.' Gerald had cupped his face in one hand, was pulling at the blue skin beneath his eyes. 'You're still very good,' he said.

'Well, it's nice to know I can still do it. Self-defence is very important these days. Of course, you aren't that heavy.'

Gerald returned to his chair, to hide his affront. 'And I was scarcely attacking you,' he said.

'No. But you might have been. Anyhow, you were very sporting.'

'Thanks.'

Lola bent down and kissed him quickly on the temple. One

bosom rubbed his nose. Her jersey smelled slightly of violets. He watched her, in her kneeling position on the ground again, pour more tea and finish the cake.

'You should meet my friend Rose,' she said. 'She's the real one for judo. Though you'd never guess her strength, just looking at her. She's only half my size.'

By the time Lola left it was almost dark. She claimed she had to be somewhere far away by six, and must hurry. From his first-floor window Gerald watched her run down the front path. She left large footprints in the new snow — it must have snowed during the afternoon. Funny they hadn't noticed it. Rubbing his elbow, Gerald wondered where she was going. He turned back to the fallen piles of books. Attempting to rescue some order, he tried not to think. The evening ahead seemed long and empty. The warmth of the room, always to be relied on, had gone with Lola. The thief, he thought. The impudent thief. He wouldn't let her go, next time.

There followed a week of absence. Lola was away on some secret mission. But she rang, as promised, on her return — within half an hour of her return, as a matter of fact, Gerald noticed. She asked him to supper next evening. Just a stew, she said, and Rose might drop in.

Gerald spent a day of happy anticipation, enjoying the patience that comes with knowing there are only a few hours to pass. He tried to get used to the strange sensation that in time he and Lola might become proper friends. He bought two expensive bottles of wine, one white, one red, and rather hoped Lola would be alone.

But Rose was already there, peeling potatoes, exuding an air of efficiency that Lola altogether lacked. She was small and curvaceous with pale wavy hair that kept falling about her face, changing its shape from moment to moment. She had vast yellow-green eyes that slanted cat-like, and one dimple when she smiled. The warmth of her was so powerful that for a moment Gerald saw Lola as a cold and distant mountain. Then the mountain laughed in absolute delight at his extravagant wine, and his lonely week without her turned to dust.

Over dinner in the small hard kitchen with its dreadful strip-lighting and the vegetable-patterned curtains, Gerald learned that

Rose and Lola were childhood friends. They had been brought up together in Dorset, gone to school together, shared a love of sport and (much laughter in recalling incidents) even a boyfriend in their teens. They still met at least once a week and, Gerald supposed, confided to each other the intimate secrets of their hearts in that peculiar way that girls seem unable to resist. They spoke of their sporting life, of course, praising each other's qualities of stamina and speed.

'Rose can run miles and *miles* without getting out of breath,' explained Lola. 'She always won the cross-country at school. There was no one to touch her.'

'Ah, but Lola's high jump,' declared Rose. '*That* was something. She broke all records.'

Gerald enjoyed the evening. The girls, chattering on almost as if he was not there, made him relax and smile. Having drunk most of the excellent wine himself, and having been persuaded to eat far too much of the heavy stew, a delightful sleepiness came upon him. Lola and Rose, immersed in their memories, didn't seem to notice his drooping eyelids. He could watch them unobserved. With some incredulity he reflected how only ten days ago there was no woman in his life with whom he would have wanted to spend the evening. Now here he was enjoying himself with two new ones, relishing their quite different attractions, and their friendliness. It was not the night, however — as during the afternoon he had vaguely thought it might be — to lay a gentle hand on Lola. For some reason he would not want Rose to know any such thought had crossed his mind. And were he not to leave before her she would be bound to guess his intentions.

So he left early, mumbling about an early start next morning. Rose and Lola were dismayed, but understanding. They both kissed him warmly on the cheek.

In his chilly bed, two hours later, Gerald was still thinking about them: Rose's eyes, Lola's smile; Rose's waist, Lola's full bosom. Both had rippling laughs, soft voices. Forced to choose between them, though, Lola would be his. She had a rare quality of calm, for all her mischievous fun, that gave him strength. Besides that, she was a creature of extraordinary sensitivity: in the laughing discussion they had had about judo she had given

Gerald a look but made no mention of the event that proved her skills had not rusted. Gerald would always be grateful to her for that. Lola, Lola, for he said to himself: it's a cold night without you.

Then he heard the ringing of his front-door bell. He hurried downstairs, puzzled. He was not a man on whom unannounced visitors eagerly called. Something must be wrong. Gerald felt the excitement of fear.

Rose, muffled in a fur coat, stood on his doorstep. She held out his grey wool scarf.

'You left this behind. . . . Sorry. Have I woken you? Thought I'd drop it as I was passing.'

'Good heavens. No. Yes. I mean, well — look, do come in. Afraid I'm in my pyjamas.'

'Are you sure?' Rose was already in the hall, snowflakes on the fur glinting in the dim light.

' 'Course. We'll have some whisky.'

He put on his dressing-gown, she kept on her coat. They sat on the floor by the gas-fire, listening to its quiet buzz, aware of the full moon through the window.

'Sorry it's so cold,' said Gerald. 'I keep meaning to put in central heating but can't face all the palaver.'

'That's all right.' Rose shivered and smiled. 'That was the most heavenly evening, wasn't it? I can't think why, but I know I'll remember it as a particularly nice evening. Won't you?'

'Yes,' said Gerald. 'Think I probably will.'

'Lola says you've only met twice.'

'That's right.'

'She's the best person, actually, I've ever met.'

'Ah,' said Gerald. 'I can see she seems a — good sort.'

Rose laughed.

'What do you mean "a good sort"? I've never heard anything so pompous.'

In the fraction of the second that her eyes were closed with laughter, Gerald flung himself awkwardly against her, pushing her flat on to the floor. He kissed her with all the hunger that had been pent within him, festering, for two years. She wriggled furrily beneath him, murmuring something about knowing the moment she saw him it would end like this.

'But can't we go somewhere more comfortable?' she said.

They spent the night in Gerald's bed.

Rose stayed three nights and three days. During that time she tidied Gerald's flat, changed the sheets and bath-towels, brightened the place with Christmas roses and winter leaves. Gerald would come back in the evening and find her cooking casseroles that smelled of past holidays in France, a butcher's apron belted tightly round her tiny waist. Each evening he found himself unable to wait for the pleasure of her until after dinner, and later at night he would fall deeply asleep in her arms.

On the fourth morning she announced she had better be getting back to her flat. Gerald, whose reasoning was never at its liveliest at breakfast, struggled with himself. He reflected on the speed with which a man could turn from solitude to cohabitation, and with what ease the new state of living together can feel like an old habit. He thought of asking her to stay, to live with him for a while. But she had already packed the small case she had fetched from her flat. She was washing the breakfast things with an air of finality. An invitation to stay, at that moment, would have seemed presumptuous. So Gerald let her go, all smiles and thanks for the happy time, anticipating a welcome return to his solitary state.

But when he got back to the flat that evening, still smelling of Rose's scent, the breakfast things where she had left them tidily on the table, aloneness seemed less desirable. He lit the fire, whose hiss had become confoundedly nostalgic, and a small cigar. He poured himself a drink and tried to concentrate on his briefs for the complicated case next day. But there was no heart in his concentration, no appetite for the cold food Rose had thought-fully left in the fridge. Damn the girl. He found himself humming a tune from a musical of twenty years ago. At the age he had seen it the words had held no meaning for him.

> I was serenely independent
> And content before we met. . . .

And he would be again, given a few days. It wasn't as if he had wanted her, or any woman, to insinuate herself into his well-structured life. In forty-three years of bachelor life he had learned the art of subtle evasion and self-protection. Rose had merely stirred some superficial desire in him, vulnerable after two years' chastity.

All the same, by nine o'clock he decided to ring her and tell her to come back. Just to talk. As he moved to the telephone, hesitant in the knowledge of his weakness, it rang. Rose, then, was even weaker than he. Gerald was glad.

'For Christ's sake come back quickly,' he said. No time to think of more reticent words.

'Come back? It's Lola, not Rose.'

'Lola? I'm sorry. How nice.' He had almost forgotten Lola in the last few days.

'Rose has had to go home to Yorkshire to nurse her mother, who's dying of cancer.'

'Oh. I'm sorry. I wonder she didn't tell me herself.'

'She thought about it, but decided the news would be inappropriate during the last few days.'

Gerald silently marvelled at Rose's sensitivity.

'It might have made a difference,' he agreed.

'I mean, one doesn't want to burden new friends with serious problems, does one?' There was a remarkable lightness in Lola's voice.

'No, of course not. Look here . . . what are you doing? Why don't you come round for a drink?' The invitation was an unconsidered reflex action. Having heard himself make the fatal suggestion, Gerald suddenly relished the idea of instant innocent infidelity. Lola could tell him more of Rose, of her dying mother. Lola, platonic Lola, Rose's friend . . . all parties would understand.

'I just might,' said Lola, with maddening cool. 'I'll see how I feel.'

She arrived two hours later, took her customary position on the floor as if she had never been away. The room was full again. Gerald poured glasses of wine. Almost at once Lola broke the news.

'Rose loves you,' she said. 'Exceedingly.'

Gerald raised an eyebrow. He reflected with some wonder on

the swiftness of communication between women friends. Lola was smiling, sympathetic.

'Oh, yes,' she was saying. 'Rose hasn't been so bowled over for years. Ever, perhaps. I had a feeling, didn't I, you two'd get on together?'

'I remember.' Gerald sat down, rather enjoying himself. He wouldn't have minded hearing more. He searched for some way to convey his own modest feelings about the whole matter. 'Isn't she being a little . . . precipitate?' he asked. Perhaps he should have said 'rash', 'daft', or 'infatuated'.

'Good heavens, no. How unromantic you are. I mean, you just know some things immediately, don't you?'

Gerald, who was always unsure of his initial reactions, had not the heart to disagree.

'Perhaps,' he said feebly. 'But she indicated nothing of this to me, though she was very kind.' He glanced round the room at the neat piles of books, the vases of flowers. 'She — kept you in touch with activities, did she?'

'Oh, we tell each other everything. Always have. That's why I didn't ring, knowing she was here.' It might have been Gerald's imagination, due to the lateness of the hour, but he detected the slightest falter in this explanation of her silence. Lola now lowered her eyes. 'She told me you were potentially marvellous in bed, if a bit out of practice, and wonderfully considerate in most other ways.'

'Did she indeed?' Pride mixed with fury rose within Gerald. Was there no such thing as a discreet woman? A woman who had some respect for private moments? Struggling for control he murmured, 'I'm forced to believe that events can only be confirmed in a woman's mind by reporting them. A man has faith in his own private reflections, memories. They can be real to him alone. That seems to be the essential difference between the sexes.'

'Are you cross?' Lola looked at him. Such innocence.

'Cross? Not cross at all. Flattered, perhaps, I should have been the subject of all your talk.' He bent forward, stretched a hand to the back of Lola's neck. Had she not been Rose's friend he would have ravished her on the spot. As it was, her quiet presence filled him with a nameless longing that the past days and nights with Rose had done nothing to dispel.

'Rose', said Lola, apparently unaware of his hand, 'is the most remarkable girl I know.'

'That's what she said about you.'

'Oh, we're very loyal.' Lola gently removed his hand. 'Poor Rose. Her mother's been a burden one way and another all her life.'

'Will she be long dying?'

'She might be.' Lola lowered her eyelids again.

'In that case. . . .'

'For heaven's sake don't make some crappy suggestion about consoling each other while she's away.'

'Of course not.' The sharpness of Lola's tone suggested to Gerald it was time he became master. Against all instinct he stood up. 'I think you'd better go,' he said. 'I've a hard day tomorrow.'

'I'm sorry,' said Lola. For a split second she screwed up her eyes, disguising an almost incredible look of pain. She rose to her feet. 'I won't keep you. You must be — exhausted.'

Gerald followed her to the front door, head bowed. His attempted brusqueness, meant to conceal his own temptations, had misfired. He had hurt, inadvertently, where he had meant merely to warn: to indicate he was a man of high principle where friends were concerned.

'I'll ring you,' he said gloomily.

'Oh, if you feel like it.' Lola ran down the path into yet more spinning snow. Back in his room Gerald had two more drinks to induce sleep and to clear his mind. Eventually, dawn paling the snowy windows, he fell asleep, a confused man. The images of two girls raced behind his eyes — sharply, at first, figures from memory. Gradually they dissolved into the stuff of dreams: interchanged, beckoned, laughed, teased, and faded when he touched them.

Days went by. A card came from Yorkshire. *'This business may take some weeks,'* wrote Rose. *'Please don't quite forget me.'* Gerald wondered if her echoing of Katherine Mansfield's dying words had been intentional. *'I won't,'* he wrote back. *'Memory of your presence lies uncomfortably in my flat.'* He was unsure whether that was the whole truth, the explanation for his restlessness. But he posted the card and rang Lola. Her silence was frustrating. But her evident pleasure, on hearing him, was cheering.

He drove her to Hungerford, on Sunday, for lunch at The Bear. She, like Rose, had a fur coat: older, softer. She refused to take it off till halfway through lunch.

'But I thought you never felt the cold,' said Gerald.

'I did today.' She sounded sad. She struggled reluctantly out of its arms. Beneath it she wore an apricot silk shirt. Gathers from a deep yoke swelled over her breasts. Gerald swore he could see one of them moving, thumped by her heart. He wanted to touch it. Instead he dug into his treacle tart, eyes down, not daring to look further.

'Rose misses you *dreadfully,'* Lola was saying. 'She rings me up most evenings to ask how you are. I keep telling her I don't know, I don't see you. She keeps saying *do* see him, and let me have some news. That's why I came today, so that I can report back.'

'Oh.' Gerald allowed himself the merest glance at Lola's hazel eyes, the long thick lashes cast down to indicate her seriousness.

'I suppose I shouldn't be telling you all this.'

'Probably not.'

'Do you love her?'

'Love her?' Gerald was thinking about the middle-aged couple at the next table. What had induced the woman, dressing that morning, to choose a pink velour hat, manacled by brown feathers, for a November lunch in Hungerford? 'Love her?' he repeated. 'Well, I like to think the onset of real love, when it comes, is quite clear. For the moment I'm confused by Rose, so that can't mean love.'

'But I suppose that means some *hope,'* said Lola. 'I suppose that means some reason for optimism on Rose's part.' She smiled enchantingly. 'I mean, confusion could always *broaden out* into absolute clarity, couldn't it?'

'I suppose it could,' said Gerald, not wanting to disappoint her. Then he suggested large brandies against the cold of the afternoon.

They walked on the Downs making tracks through the snow.

Each kept their hands deep in their pockets. The sky, thick with approaching snow, was broken on the horizon by zests of yellow cloud. Gerald, surprising himself, flung his greatcoat on to the ground. It made a strange patch of colour on all the white.

'God couldn't find any matching material,' giggled Lola, voicing succinctly the vaguely similar thoughts he had been having himself. He watched as Lola lowered herself on to the coat, gathering her long legs under her arms. She was protected by a hedge of snow a few inches high. Looked up at him, concerned. 'Aren't you cold?'

The wintry chill seeped through Gerald's tweed jacket, a strange pleasure.

'Not at all.' He sat down beside her.

'As a matter of fact, there's nothing more elusive than clarity,' she was saying. Again, Gerald's own thoughts, though he felt there would be feebleness in agreeing out loud. He moved his eyes from the valley beneath them, the black-boned trees, softened by the distance, to Lola's flushed face. He felt his way beneath her fur coat, beneath the warm silk of her shirt. The sky crushed down low over their heads. Gerald was surprised to find his hand, suddenly on a bare thigh, pinned there by flakes of snow. He felt them melting, the water trickling between his fingers. Lola gave a shriek as it reached her flesh. There was a small thread of sound from a distant train. The bellow from an invisible cow, startling. 'This isn't right,' said Lola. But she lay back, eyes shut, snow covering her so quickly Gerald was forced to move himself on top of her to protect her from the thickening flakes.

They returned to The Bear for tea. Lola was ravenously hungry. The lady with the feathered hat sat drowsily by the fire, cup of tea in pink hand, exhausted by the indolence of her afternoon. Her companion, a small grey-flannel man, pecked at a pipe, staring at some private distance. At the sight of Gerald and Lola he looked for a moment quite shocked, as if something about them caused painful nostalgia. He tapped his pipe so savagely on the hearth the fat lady murmured, 'Whatever is it, dear?' When he made no reply she patted her hat for comfort so that the feathers stirred broodily and the bald patches of pink velour showed beneath.

'You must think very carefully about Rose,' said Lola, spreading honey thickly on to warm toast.

'I will, but not now.'

'You must realise she's very good at loving. She could make you extremely happy, believe me.'

Gerald put his hand on Lola's knee. She removed it at once. Exactly an hour ago she had encouraged it so hard Gerald had felt clear madness. Now there was confusing sanity. He sighed. 'What's the matter?'

Lola was quite impatient, interested only in her food. 'Don't let's talk about Rose any more today. I'll think about her when you've gone.'

'Good. You'll have a bit of time. I've got to be in Paris for a week.' A perverse thrill shot through Gerald.

'Then I might even go and see her.'

'That would be best of all. You might realise.' Lola swallowed a long draught of tea, sounded practical. 'But please don't do it in the snow.'

' 'Course not. Idiot. What do you think I am?'

'An unintentional menace,' she said, 'trying to please us all.'

Gerald was not quite able to keep his word. In Yorkshire the following weekend, her dying mother in a bedroom upstairs, Rose reacted to his presence with such exuberant pleasure he wondered how he had survived the last couple of weeks without her. She managed to disguise the strains caused upon the household by illness. He admired her for that. All she asked, in deference to her mother, was that he should keep to his own room at night. To this Gerald unwillingly concurred, increasingly desirous of the warm, slightly plumper Rose, so strong in her concealment of melancholy.

On the Saturday afternoon they went for a walk on the moors near Haworth. The earth was scarred with the last remnants of snow: there was rain in the wind. They clung to each other, faces stinging in the cold. Scarcely speaking, they tramped for several miles, then took shelter from a heavy shower under the trees. Gerald lay his coat on the hard dry earth: the familiarity of the gesture reminded him of his promise, and of the recent coupling on the wintry Downs. He hestitated only for a moment. Rose was kissing his hair, scrabbling at his shirt, muttering words of love. Succumbing to her, he heard only the rain on the leaves: no thought of Lola.

Later, wiping rain from Rose's cheeks with his handkerchief, came a moment of revelation. Rose was the girl for him: nothing had ever been so clear in his life. Desire quite sated, he felt love for her, though he said nothing for fear of her overbrimming with pleasure. She had mud on her mackintosh and tears in her eyes: had never looked more vulnerable and trusting. He wondered if he should make an instant proposal of marriage, while the inspiration was upon him. Then Rose sneezed, smothered her face in a damp handkerchief, and the moment had gone.

'I expect you and Lola,' she said, and paused. 'Have you?' Gerald said nothing, made an attempt to twist his cold face into an expression of surprise. Rose took his hand. 'Not that I mind,' she went on, mouth turned down. 'Don't ever think that. Lola's my friend. All I'd ever ask is the truth, that's all. I can't bear the idea of deception.'

'Quite,' said Gerald, and the clarity he had felt only minutes before disappeared. He watched a black cloud roll across a nearby ridge of land, obscuring it, and was suddenly depressed by the sound of rain. It occurred to him that the post he had been offered in Rio might be the solution. If he went abroad for a couple of years, he would forget them, they would forget him. He'd come back to find them both married, be willing godfather to their children.

'Lola likes you very much indeed,' Rose was saying. 'You must know that, don't you? Really, she'd be much better for you than me. She'd keep you guessing for years, never wholly committing herself. That's what men like, isn't it? Seems to me the last thing in the world they want is the whole of someone: only selected parts. That's where Lola's so skilful. She'd never burden you with the whole of herself. Afraid I could never be like that. Loving someone, I can't resist offering them the entire package, keeping nothing back. I suppose that's awfully boring but I can't help it.' She laughed a little. 'So, really, there should be no confusion in your mind.'

Gerald remained silent for a few moments, struggling to do up the knot of his tie. Then he said: 'It's a little overwhelming, after two years with no one in my life, suddenly to find two new friends who seem so kind and caring.'

'Two new friends,' repeated Rose. 'But you met Lola first. You liked Lola first.'

'I made love to you first.' He tried to be honest. 'Feel closer to you.'

'Really?' Rose pressed herself against him, soft with relief. He wished she would get up, change the conversation.

'Don't see why there should be any complications,' he said, finally. 'Shouldn't we be getting back? We're both frozen.'

Rose had the good sense to agree at once. They spoke no more of Lola, spent a peaceful Sunday by the fire, both aware of a new bond of understanding.

Gerald returned to London with reluctance. He missed Rose as soon as the train drew out of the station. But, back in the silence of his flat, his thoughts turned to Lola. It was she he wanted, most urgently, beside him in the room. He rang her flat but there was no reply. So instead he rang Rose. Her surprise and pleasure cheered him, though his confusion remained. Wearily, he went early to bed and dreamed of the freedom of Rio.

Rose returned as soon as she could to London after her mother's death. She arranged an immediate meeting with Lola.

They sat in opposite corners of a battered sofa that had come from Lola's nursery, and for years had been their favourite place for serious talk. Each noted the other's pale face. They equipped themselves with large drinks, which was not their normal custom.

'I only got back from Paris last night,' said Lola, 'so I haven't heard from Gerald how it all was.'

'Harassing. She seemed to go mad, the last week. Insulted me hour after hour but wouldn't let me leave her bedside. Gerald came up for a few days. He was. . . .' She paused, wanting to say loving. 'Noble,' she said.'

'I can imagine. It must have been difficult for you, the house so gloomy and quiet.'

Rose came near to smiling. 'We slipped off', she said, 'for the occasional reviving walk. Over the moors.'

A long silence. Their eyes did not meet.

'Was it snowing up there?' Lola asked eventually.

'Snowing? Well, there was snow on the ground. No, but it rained a lot. Why?'

Lola thought for a while. She decided, for the first time, that the whole truth would not benefit her friend.

'He said he particularly liked going for bitter walks in the snow.'

'He's a funny one, all right,' said Rose. 'What are we going to do about him, Lo?'

Now Rose had come to the point, Lola stretched her long legs with relief. The gin was beginning to turn her blood warmly to quicksilver. It would be quite easy, now, as such old friends, to be practical. They could solve the problem very quickly.

'It's quite clear we both love him,' she said, 'and it's quite clear he loves both of us. All we've got to do is force his hand in making a choice. Procrastination is the destructive thing. Hell, the greatest friends on earth could hardly be expected to survive the misery he's causing us, waiting for his decision.'

'To be fair, he's only known us a couple of months, hasn't he? Perhaps' — Rose smiled, incredulous — 'I mean, it could be he doesn't want *either* of us.'

'Nonsense,' scoffed Lola. Rose copied the brusque practical tone of her friend's voice.

'Well, *my* position is quite clear,' she said. 'I want to marry him.'

'Do you? *Marry* him? Marry him? I suppose that's what I'd like, too,' said Lola.

'He's the only man on earth I could possibly contemplate marrying, and all that that entails.'

'Well, you're ahead,' said Lola. 'He feels closer to you, easier with you.'

'But you frighten him more, and that intrigues him. You're the mystery figure. I'm the warm open book.'

They both laughed.

'Put a shotgun at his head and there's little doubt who he'd choose,' said Lola. 'Oh, God, why on earth did this have to happen? And, more interesting, what is it that we love him for? Sometimes, I just can't think.'

'Nor I,' said Rose. 'After all, he's balding, unfit, drinks too much, pompous, vague, and possibly deceitful.'

'Too short,' added Lola. 'Awful breath after Sunday lunch, hideous shoes, drives dangerously, boasts boringly about his lack of friends. There's absolutely nothing I can think of, on the face of it, to recommend him.'

'Except that his sympathy is overwhelming, and he makes me laugh.'

'And also', said Lola, screwing up her face with the effort of choosing the right words, 'he has this extraordinary understated relish in perfectly ordinary things. In his presence you feel the urgency of every day, somehow: the pointlessness of wasting time. Do you know what I mean? We've never discussed any of this, of course. He'd be loath to do any such thing, I'm sure, and so would I.'

Rose nodded.

'In a subtle way,' she added, 'not by paying obvious compliments, he boosts the morale. Makes you feel *better* than you imagined you could about yourself.'

'All of which', said Lola, 'cancels out the mild deficiencies.'

They both smiled, and were silent for a while.

The telephone rang. Lola leaned back on the sofa, eyes shut, not moving. When eventually it stopped, she turned her head almost sleepily to Rose.

'You deserve him,' she said. 'I can just back quietly out. Not see him any more till you're married or whatever.'

'Nonsense,' said Rose. 'He'd be far happier with you. Endlessly intrigued. Honestly.'

'Rubbish,' said Lola. 'I'd drive him mad.'

'He'd be bored to tears by my constant enthusiasm. Smothered by my open love. He'd be—'

Getting up, Lola cut her short.

'This is utterly ridiculous, Rosie,' she said. 'Why not let's resolve it immediately?' She looked at her watch. 'He must be at home. Let's go round now, make him come to some conclusion.'

'Isn't that a bit unfair, giving him no warning?' Rose, for all her reluctance, stood up.

'It's less unfair than carrying on like this. It may all end in disaster, but at least you and I can go back to where we were. That's what I really mind about.'

'Me, too,' said Rose.

Giving themselves no time to change their minds, they left the flat very quickly.

Gerald spent a most disagreeable evening. The gas-fire produced no heat in his bitter room, there was nothing but stale cheese in the fridge. He was depressed by the unmade bed, the dust, the mess, the general lack of care that had increased since Rose's departure. He rang her, feeling a decent amount of days had passed since her mother's funeral: a little housework would take her mind off things, and he would reward her with a delicious dinner in some expensive restaurant. When there was no reply from her flat a vague uneasiness disturbed him. Where was the girl? Just when he needed her most. He rang several times, became increasingly irritated by the lack of reply. Finally, angry, he ate cold baked beans with the cheese, and rang Lola. Her presence, suddenly, seemed even more desirable than Rose's. She wouldn't offer to clear up, but her funny smile, in her place by the fire, would restore tranquillity. Besides, it was high time they renewed their carnal acquaintance in a place more comfortable than a snowy Down. Lola must be there, and come quickly. Godammit, he loved the girl. The fact was astoundingly clear. He must do something about it quickly, before he booked himself a passage to Rio.

But there was no reply from Lola, either. He was let down on all sides, deserted, forlorn. Implacable. With no heart to study his briefs for the court case next day, or to read a book or listen to music, Gerald poured himself a large whisky and burrowed into his chair by the hissing fire. In the bleak hours that followed, moon glaring through the windows, some semi-wakeful dream of a composite girl teased his mind. Wearily, he followed her movements: watched the heaving of Lola's bosom, the twinkle in Rose's eye — found a hand in his he could not identify, smaller than Lola's but larger than Rose's. There was a singular flash of pure Lola as she was the first night he had seen her, tall and aloof, scorning the winter air that made others shiver. This was followed by a view of Rose, too, alone, radiating in the sombre hall of her mother's house. Then the two figures merged again, confusing, taunting.

'To hell with you both,' he shouted out loud, stirring himself, the words flat and blurred in the silence. He reached for yet another drink but found the bottle empty. His hands were stiff and cold: he rubbed them hopelessly together, trying to summon the energy to go to the cupboard for a new bottle of whisky. Then from the profundities of his desolate state he heard the far-off ring of his front-door bell. He let it ring several times, to make sure it was not a further trick of the imagination, then struggled to his feet. He experienced a moment of being grateful to his education and upbringing: when called upon, however low, a man can and must make an effort. He straightened his tie, adjusted the look of discontent he could feel dragging at his face, and with supreme effort cast self-pity aside. Whoever was calling at his door would see a calm and satisfied man, a man whose own resources were enough. Pleased with this sudden transformation of his person, the gallant Gerald made for the stairs, new confidence ensuring a firm and eager step.

Lola and Rose stood there, inevitable snow on their hair and shoulders. Something united about them, something determined. Gerald forced a smile.

'Come in,' he said. 'Come in, come in, come in.'

They followed him up the stairs in silence, kept on their coats, took their places on the floor in front of the fire. Gerald poured three drinks, took his place in his own chair. Through the confusion in his head he sensed their silence was a little ominous. Perhaps they had some important matter about which they wished him to adjudicate: he was their friendly listener, after all. But, if this was the case, Gerald felt perversely unhelpful. He would do nothing to broach the subject of their difficulty. From a befuddled distance he would watch them struggle, sipping his drink all the while. Might even enjoy himself. But they said nothing. Eventually, his natural instinct to assist overcoming less charitable feelings, Gerald muttered:

'Well.'

Lola drew herself up then, her long neck a gleaming white stem in the dim light. Her nostrils flared as they did sometimes, Gerald had noticed, when she was worried. A line of boyhood poetry came back to him. 'The camels sniff the evening air. . . .' Shelley, wasn't it?

'We've got to get this sorted out, Gerald,' she said.

Gerald heard his own sigh of relief. All his life, people had required him to sort things out. In his childhood, with the drone of bombers over High Wycombe, there had been the matter of his socks. These, in the opinion of his old Nannie, needed sorting out most days of the week. Gerald obliged, of course, without demur, rather enjoying marshalling the balls of red, blue and grey wool into strict soldierlines in his drawer. And Nannie had always praised him. In his teens he had something of a reputation at sorting out fights between dogs – owing to a combination of his quick draw on a soda siphon, and his authoritarian voice. After his father died, having sorted out the muddled will, he turned to sorting out his mother's lovers, placating the rejects and warning the present incumbent that his position was likely to be temporary. Little wonder, then, he eventually turned his skills to professional use. Only a decent humility kept him from reflecting upon the number of his grateful clients, whose complex problems he had successfully sorted out over the years.

Whatever Lola had in mind, then, would be a routine matter.

'How can I help?' he asked, recognising the sympathetic tone he used in the office when meeting with a new client.

'You can decide.' Lola's response was quick, fierce.

'You can clear up the confusion once and for all,' followed Rose, 'and put an end to this misery.' She, too, was unnaturally fierce.

'Confusion?' asked Gerald, mystified.

'Don't try to be silly, Gerald,' said Lola. 'Don't try to pretend you don't know what we're on about.'

Gerald tipped back his head into the familiar comforting dip of a velvet cushion. He shut his eyes. The old thought came to him that there is a deviousness about the demands of women that confuses the straightest man. To deal seriously with them, superhuman patience and tact must be called upon. It was very late at night to summon such energies, but Rose and Lola were his friends. He would try. He could cast aside all the burning logic of his own mind and attempt not only to understand, but also to feel, the torments of theirs. That way, as he had come to learn in his practice, is the best short-cut to sorting out.

He opened his eyes. 'If you could tell me more,' he said, 'perhaps I could. . . .'

'We both love you, idiot,' Rose interrupted, 'and it's plain you love both of us. Which one of us do you want?'

Gerald looked from her face to Lola's. In both their beautiful eyes he saw the same naked love glowering through a thin film of hostility. He shivered, repeated the question silently to himself. Funny how he had not confronted himself with the actual question before. Now, faced with it, his responsive mind, for all the whisky, was concentrated wonderfully. Which one did he want? If indeed he wanted either. And if he did, what would he want her *for*? Life? Marriage? A divorce wrangle in court in ten years' time? God forbid: it would be better to remain friends with both. Platonic, if need be. If that was what was depressing them, the sharing of carnality. Women friends, as he well knew, had their limitations when it came to the sharing of a man.

'There doesn't seem to be much problem, does there?' he said, his voice unconvincing. 'Surely there's no need for any such severing choice. Surely we can carry on as we are, all good—'

His final feeble word was lost in their hoots of derision, their scornful laughs.

'How can you *demean* yourself with such a suggestion?' shouted Lola.

'Does it never occur to you', shrieked Rose, 'what you are doing? Lola and I have been friends for *years*, you know. For God's sake, you've made gestures to us both. You've turned to us both, relied on us both, indicated you love us both. . . . Which one do you want?'

They gave him a moment's silence in which to reflect and reply. But when he made no response they started up again, interrupting each other, repeating themselves. The questions came so fast there was no hope of Gerald contributing a thought, had he had anything to say — which for once in his life, when it came to sorting out a problem, he hadn't. He was aware of a great desire to laugh. The situation, from his point of view, was highly comic: two beautiful women screaming at him to choose one of them, fired by their presumption that he loved both of them. Well, he did in a way. But love for anyone is an irregular graph and, while he would not deny that at times his feelings for both of them had whizzed up the chart into astonishing peaks, for the moment they had caught him at a real low — tired, hungry, depressed, a little drunk. The warm adrenalin of certainty, which he presumed should accompany any major decision a man takes concerning the binding of his life to one women, was far from him. All he desired was that they should leave him in peace, now. He would think about the matter for the rest of the night, and write to them both in the morning. He could book a ticket. . . . They were glaring at him, silent at last.

Gerald heard himself give a small friendly laugh, and felt his dry lips crackle into a small matching smile.

'Well,' he said at last. 'Why don't you toss for me?' His suggestion charged the silence with explosive fury.

'We're in no mood for jokes, Gerald,' said Lola.

'No, we're not,' said Rose.

Gerald wished they could see their own faces, wizened and glowing with anger. God, they were beautiful, each one in her own way. He felt terrible desire for them both. Then, in the moment of fighting that desire, an inspiration came to him. There was no time to prepare its presentation. He would put it very simply, eyes shut to make it easier.

'You could run a race for me,' he said.

When eventually he opened his eyes, two new expressions confronted him: indignation, yes; but indignation softened at the edges, as if *possibility* danced lightly in the background.

'Run a race for you?' Lola's huge mothy eyes enlarged in a very good show of incredulity.

'A race for you?' echoed Rose. 'But we're so unfit,' she said quietly.

'We haven't run for years,' agreed Lola.

Taking these observations for some kind of concession, Gerald saw his way ahead was no easier.

'There could be *time*,' he suggested generously. 'Heavens, there's no hurry, is there? You could train. A month, say. Two, if you like. Meanwhile I'll work out a nice little cross-country course. Nothing too strenuous. About five miles. . . .'

'*Gerald*.' Lola's voice was weak, her head bent so appealingly on one shoulder Gerald was much tempted to lean over and restore it to its rightful upright position, kissing her all the while.

'Gerald, really,' said Rose, who was always less sparing with words, and a single tear slid down her cheek.

Filled with new strength, heartened by the attraction of his own idea, Gerald felt he should make some effort to console, comfort, convince.

'It may seem an absurd plan on the face of it,' he began, with all the sparkle of one who doesn't believe a word he's saying, 'but if you think of it – it's probably the only solution. I mean, the only fair solution. You see – and forgive me if this sounds lacking in courage, but I'm inexperienced when it comes to deciding about women – I wouldn't like to hold myself responsible. I wouldn't, I couldn't choose. You must see that, don't you? You must understand what a dilemma you've caused me.' He took a deep determined breath. 'You must see what . . . affection I have for you both. How pleased I'd be to be married to either of you.' Both girls gave small snorts of protest, but the fight seemed to have gone out of them. 'In the circumstances, for my own part, I'd be quite pleased to carry on as we have been: all three of us friends. But I do see your point, of course I do. I understand the difficulties. So it seems to me my solution isn't a bad one. It might even be rather fun.' He looked from one to the other of them. 'But then again, you might have all sorts of objections. In that case . . . I suppose the only thing to do would be to say goodbye to you both. I'm very tempted by a job in Rio. With you both gone, there'd be nothing much to keep me here.'

It was by now nearly five in the morning, the sky through the bare windows a grimy colour, the girl's faces drawn and shadowy. Lola, in her usual position on her knees by the fire, let a small silence pass when Gerald had finished speaking, then swivelled a defiant head towards Rose.

'What d'you think, Rosie? I'm game.'

Rose gasped.

'*Lo*. You can't . . . I mean, you realise what it'd involve, the result? Whoever won — whoever got Gerald — it would be the end of us.'

'I know,' said Lola.

Rose's acceptance was barely audible.

'Very well,' she said. 'But it's the most terrible plan I've ever heard.'

'It is,' said Lola, with such bitterness that Gerald's heart briefly contracted with fear, 'but on the other hand, Gerald is right. Too feeble to make the decision himself, we have to make it for him. We might as well give him a little amusement on the way.'

'I suppose so.' Rose was equally hard. She looked at Gerald. 'But anything rather than Rio.'

'Yes, well, that's decided, then.' Gerald feared more discussion might undo the decision. But his fears were allayed by Lola's tone of practicality as, standing, she said: 'A month, then. Rosie was always faster than me cross-country. A minute's start would be fair for me, wouldn't it, Rosie?'

'Quite fair.'

'It'll all be *scrupulously* fair,' assured Gerald. 'I'll plan the course with incredible care. We'll all walk round it together the day before.'

'*Wonderful*,' said Lola.

'Very considerate,' said Rose.

'Oh, you can rely on me,' said Gerald.

They left him then, with no kiss on the cheek, none of the old cheerful promises to meet soon. At his gate they paused for a moment, both cold in the unfriendly dawn, though Lola let her fur coat fall open when she saw Rose pulling hers tightly round her.

'It would probably be better, Rosie, wouldn't it, not to be in touch till the day?'

'Probably it would.' Their eyes met.

'Sorry. I'm sorry.'

'For God's sake, Lo, all these years! It's ridiculous.' Rosie, near to tears, shaking with cold, was shouting. 'It's the maddest plan I ever heard. Why don't we just turn our backs, both of us? . . . Leave him?'

'We can't do that.'

'But he doesn't deserve you, me, anyone.'

'No.'

Rose looked up at her tall determined friend. She thought how precarious is friendship: how hopelessly threatened by things unworthy to destroy.

'Till the race, then,' she said, and turned away.

From his window Gerald watched the girls part. He felt quite awake now, the clarity of his insane plan firing him with energy and glee. Only for a moment did the idea of abandoning the whole project, writing it off as a poor late-night joke, cross his mind. A man must go ahead in his decisions. There was much to be done. Funny, though, to think that his last few weeks of bachelorhood would be spent pouring over Ordnance Survey maps. And come to think of it, where were those damn maps?

Gerald went to his desk, began rummaging through drawers. Enthused by the whole project of planning an interesting route — a route which would tax, but not weary to excess — Gerald was able to spare no thought, that busy dawn, for his competitors. If they were returning troubled to their beds, he could not conceive of their unease. He himself had no experience of the severing of friendship: a mere visitor to many, he had always been a friendless man.

For Lola, the training meant increasing her morning runs from three to seven days a week. Besides this, she gave up all alcohol and went to gym classes in the evening. Within a week she felt the difference in herself: strong, alert, fit. There was no breathlessness in her runs around Hyde Park now. In the bitter frosty mornings, unripe sun the single spot of colour in the grey air, she relished her calm, her vigour, the final reserve of energy that allowed her to sprint with astonishing speed over the last lap, from Knightsbridge Barracks to Hyde Park Corner. She had no doubt that she would win the race. As teenagers, it was true, Rose had both exceptional stamina and speed. But nowadays she took little exercise. She was plump and unfit. In fact, to be fair, when the time came Lola would refuse any start. They would begin as equals and the best one would win the trophy of Gerald.

Now her training was in full swing, the absurdity of its reason had curiously evaporated from Lola's mind. She thought much of Rosie, but with little guilt. After all, she had met Gerald first, had introduced them. When Rose had seduced Gerald, Lola had honourably disappeared to give them a chance. It was not her fault Gerald had not made something of his opportunity. It was to promote Rose she had accepted lunch that Sunday and found herself in an unlikely position on the Downs: an event which made clear to her the extent of the feeling she had been at such pains to conceal. Rose would make Gerald happier, of course: she was better equipped with all the conventional aids to marital contentment. But Lola doubted if Rose would love him more. God knows why, but the idea of the rest of Lola's life without him was inconceivable. Perhaps she should have indicated this some time ago, and she would have won him without having to go through all the madness of this race. But Lola was cautious of proclamations. The uncertainty that silence causes lovers is often a more lasting bond than declared certainty. On the other hand, it, too, can be misinterpreted. Lola hoped Gerald had not misunderstood her — well, if he had, there would be a lifetime in which to make amends. For the moment she missed him intolerably. They spoke occasionally on the telephone, about matters pertaining to the race: no suggestion was ever made that the whole thing should be cancelled. And so the bleak wintry days went by, the increasing strength of her limbs Lola's only consolation. In her weaker moments she thought of Rose with regret. She missed her. One day, perhaps, there could be forgiveness all round, and they could be friends again. Meantime, the object was to beat her.

Jobless for the present, Rose decided to leave London. If the race was to be cross-country, she decided there could be no better place to train than her native moors. So she returned to Yorkshire, to the cold cheerless house that awaited a new owner, and set about her task with a sad determination. The old housekeeper was still in residence. She welcomed Rose with all the warmth of someone starved of human company for too long. The old-fashioned kitchen flared into life again as Mrs Nickols steamed and baked to satisfy Rose's customary hunger. But Rose had no appetite. She was aware that to lose many pounds of flesh was the first necessity if she was to have any hope of winning Gerald. Besides, an icy desolation acted on her stomach like poison, so that food sickened and the long nights were sleepless. She rose early every morning, shivered into the bitter drizzly air in a thin tracksuit, and began her long jog over the dewy moors. She increased her time and distance every day, and within a week was able to rejoice in the result; all her old speed and stamina were returning. Sprinting up a steep slope, she could arrive at the top without panting for breath. On rocky stony ground she found herself to be surprisingly surefooted. And her speed on the flat, at the end of a long run, increased both her confidence and pride.

Her hours on the moors were free from pain except when she passed close to the place where she and Gerald had sheltered from the rain. Then, longing for him returned acutely, but could be subdued by the physical act of running. It was the hours between that caused the real torment: the dreary afternoons in the deserted house, the silence, the missing of Gerald and Lola. Rose forced herself to do exercises recommended in a keep-fit manual, and went almost hourly to her dim mirror in search of some change in her appearance. Here she was soon rewarded. Hollow cheeks and a flat stomach indicated new fitness. The scales showed she had lost nearly a stone in two weeks. Her speed over the moors secretly surprised and amazed. Pessimism changed to optimism. One morning she woke with no doubts left: she was going to win after all. Lola was an ungainly runner with a huge stride. She had no chance against Rose in her prime, and Rose was making sure the physique of her prime was returning. She confided to Mrs Nickols, who encouraged her in the long kitchen evenings.

'You'll win, Miss Rose. There's no one with determination the like of yours. You've always won.'

Gerald rang her sometimes. She took her chance to express her unaltered love for him, in the belief that the most sensitive man is

incapable of guessing accurately the measure of love he is receiving. His response was not encouraging, in that he seemed more
eager to discuss matters pertaining to the race. But Rose understood: having initiated such an event, it must preoccupy his mind.
Once it was over there would be a lifetime in which to regale him
with declarations. She tried hard not to think of Lola, and the
sadness of the future without her. But, given the simple choice,
who would give up a lover for a friend? Still, Rose missed Lola.
Really, the whole thing was very regrettable. But of course she
could not be the one to suggest they went back on the decision.
One day, perhaps, there could be forgiveness all round, and they
could be friends again. Meantime, the object was to beat her.

In a pub near Hungerford, Gerald was unable quite to refrain
from revealing his plans, and he became something of a local
hero. He found himself describing the contestants of the race,
and bets began to be placed. Several people who lived locally
suggested to him routes — routes which would include the kind
of tests that meant real excitement: high slopes, knotty wood-
lands, stony ground, heavy plough. . . . But the last stretch of the
race was Gerald's own inspiration. The girls would end at Coombe
Gibbet, the old gallows. Dwarfed by its outstretched arms, they
would for a moment be etched against the winter sky. All that
would be left then would be the gentle downward slope to the
winning-post. (Gerald had already bought a red and white
chequered flag.) Yes, it would be a dramatic end. There would be
champagne, of course, and a marvellous lunch for all three of
them. After that . . . Gerald's imagination clouded. The joke over,
what would happen? He would have to rely on the sportsmanship
of the loser: hope she would go quietly on her way, no fuss, no
tears. God knows what he would do with the winner: see her a
good deal, he presumed. Get used to her. Hope that eventually
she and the loser would resume their friendship. Because, in truth,
the idea of losing completely either Rose *or* Lola was too terrible
to contemplate. Not that Gerald spent very much time contem-
plating at the moment. He was wholly occupied by the planning
of the route. Evenings in London were spent in the meticulous
study of Ordnance Survey maps. Every weekend he walked the

proposed route, rejecting various stretches and replacing them with others. Finally, he was satisfied. The five-mile run was full of interest, slight hazards calculated to intimidate but not to hurt. Gerald's acquaintances in the pub chuckled and agreed. They would be out in force to cheer the girls on. It would be a novel sport for a Saturday.

His plans finalised, Gerald rang Rose and Lola to break the news. He detected a certain coolness in both their voices, but put this down to nerves. Neither could consider it dignified, of course, to show enthusiasm for such an unusual venture. And both insisted on walking alone round the route with Gerald. This, he felt, was a little unreasonable: to make a man walk ten miles when he need only walk five — and heavens knows in his careful research he must have walked fifty miles by now — showed some meanness of spirit. However, bracing himself, Gerald complied with good grace. Dates were arranged.

Lola came first. Huddled in her fur coat, wool cap pulled low over her face, it was hard to tell the state of her fitness. Gerald welcomed her with all his old warmth. Lola did not respond. 'Let's get on with it,' was all she said. Obligingly, Gerald opened a gate.

'Won't be opening it on the day,' he grinned. 'You can get over it any way you like — jump, vault, climb—'

'Quite,' snapped Lola.

From time to time on their walk round the course Gerald attempted to make a joke, to assume lightheartedness. But, met with total silence, he eventually gave up, and was reduced merely to explaining the way. Back at the winning-post at last, the afternoon sky low with threatened rain, he gave Lola a map with the route thoughtfully marked in red pencil. So she could learn it off by heart, he explained. But now, how about some tea at The Bear?

Lola declined at once, and moved towards her car parked in a nearby lane. Gerald opened the door for her, brushed her cold hard cheek with his lips. She softened for the merest second.

'Oh, God,' she said. 'You know this is insanity, Gerald, don't you?'

'Don't worry,' said Gerald. 'Thing is, don't take it too seriously. It'll be a lot of fun.'

When Lola had driven away, three prospective betting men,

gumbooted and heavily clad in mackintoshes, appeared in much good humour from behind a hedge. They had been studying the form, they explained: nice little runner, this one. Lovely flanks, strong legs. Much laughter over subsequent drinks. They, at any rate, had entered into the spirit of the thing. It was only later, as he drove back to London, that Gerald recalled Lola's parting face, and wondered if secretly she was afraid.

Rose came two days later. Fur-coated, too, but hollow-cheeked.

'Taken your training seriously, have you?' Gerald inquired. But Rose responded with no more warmth than Lola. On their walk round the course — and Rose bounded along at an impressive pace so that Gerald found himself quite puffed trying to keep up with her — she only broke her silence once to inquire about the crossing of a stream.

'Are we meant to jump it or run through it?' Gerald had given no thought as to which he required, but felt it best to be instantly decisive.

'Jump,' he said, noting the slippery banks. That would make for a little more fun. Rose screwed up her enormous eyes: Gerald had forgotten their intense green.

'Jump?' she repeated in a small voice.

'Or you could . . . ,' he wavered.

'No, no. It's all right. Jump, you say.' She seemed a million miles away.

Back at the winning-post, Rose, too, was offered tea and declined. She wished instead to be driven straight back to the station. In the car she said, 'I'm terrified I'll never remember the way.'

'You study the map,' advised Gerald, 'and you'll know it by heart. Besides, there'll be signs. White flags, pointing. Also a few people, I dare say, to cheer you on—'

'People?'

'Well, you know how it is. Things get around. It'll add to the excitment.'

'God Almighty,' said Rose weakly. 'I thought it was going to be an entirely private matter.'

On the empty platform she looked peculiarly small.

'Don't wait,' she said. Gerald turned to go, understanding he was genuinely not wanted. 'But do say goodbye.' He turned back to kiss her, confused. 'I'll love you for ever, anyway,' she said. 'Don't forget that.'

Hurrying off to meet his new friends in the pub, Gerald felt a distinct and alarming hunch: he knew who was going to win, and tears hurt his eyes. Of course, he could be wrong. He needed to know what the others reckoned. They had studied Rose, too, from their position behind the hawthorn hedge. Having done so, what were the odds on her? Gerald drove recklessly fast through the town to the pub, keen to know.

The morning of the race Gerald arrived first, an hour before it was scheduled to begin. He had made sure not to ask either competitor how they were transporting themselves to this remote area of the Downs — it was none of his business — and he had no idea what to expect. He felt briefly guilty about Rose. She did not have a car. But no doubt a taxi could be found at Hungerford station.

It was a cold bright morning. Sharp sun, pale sky: earth hard from overnight frost, bare branches still glittering where the rime had not melted. Perfect conditions. Gerald, clumsy in his old army greatcoat, banged his sides with his arms, stamped his feet and blew on his hands. He watched the globes of breath launch forth bold as Altantic balloonists, only to disintegrate without trace seconds later. He smiled to himself, well pleased.

He collected things from the car — stopwatch, Ordnance Survey map with the route meticulously marked in red, flasks of coffee and brandy. These would keep him going till lunch. He had ordered Black Velvets, and steak-and-kidney pudding to be waiting for himself, Rose and Lola in The Bear. God knows what sort of a lunch that would be, but there was no use in speculating. With any luck, the joke over, they would all go their own ways. Gerald had refrained from thinking about the future — uneasy subject in the circumstances — but in the back of his mind was a plan to visit his mother in Ireland. Time would be needed for reflection. On return he would get in touch with the winner, being an honourable man, and see how things went from there.

A Land-Rover arrived. It discharged four men in tweed jackets and sturdy boots. They had placed considerable bets on the race. Two of them carried binoculars, the others prodded their shooting-sticks into the earth, testing its hardness. They banged Gerald on the back, offered him brandy from their flasks and made jokes in loud voices. They were out for a good morning's sport and Gerald, responsible for their pleasure, felt himself something of a hero. Cheered by the sudden companionship, he entered into the spirit of the thing, and presumed himself temporarily to be among friends.

Others arrived. The news, it seemed, had travelled. They stood about, thumping themselves to keep warm, asking permission to study Gerald's map spread on the bonnet of his car. Gerald heard only one dissident voice among them. A fierce lean girl in leather went from group to group haranguing them about being male chauvinist pigs; but she was powerless to spoil their fun. 'Ah, it's a bit of sport, girl,' explained one of the tweedies, gently punching the breastless leather jacket. Alone in her opinion, she eventually went away.

At five to eleven, no sign of the competitors, Gerald felt the first stirrings of anxiety. There were jokes about sudden withdrawal. New bets were placed about whether the runners would turn up at all.

But at eleven o'clock precisely, Lola's red Mini drove through the gate. Amazed, Gerald watched both her and Rose get out of the car. As far as he knew, they hadn't communicated since the night of the decision. The implications of their drive from London together was suddenly moving. He gave himself a moment to recover before striding over to greet them.

Both girls wore thick fur coats, bright wool socks, and expensive running-shoes, very new. Both had their hair scraped back and large, unmade-up eyes. They looked about at the gathered spectators, registered horror. Then, unsmiling, turned simultaneously to Gerald.

'We thought this was to be a private event,' said Lola.

Gerald shrugged.

'Well, I'm sorry. You know how things get about.'

'It's appalling,' said Rose.

'You'll be quite unaware of them', explained Gerald, 'once

you get going. Anyway, it's rather encouraging, isn't it, to have an audience cheering you on?'

Neither girl replied. Gerald offered them coffee, brandy, biscuits. They refused everything. They stood closely together, arms just touching, a little sullen. Noting their faces, regret, sudden and consuming, chilled Gerald more deeply than the raw air. He would have given anything to have withdrawn from the whole silly idea. . . . But then Lola gave him an unexpected smile, and he detected Rose's look as almost compassionate.

'Come on, then, let's get it over,' said Lola.

Gerald's spirits returned. He should have had no worries. They, too, saw it as no more than a lark: something that would make a good story for years to come.

'I've ordered a stupendous lunch for us all at The Bear,' he said gratefully, and was puzzled when they conveyed no gratitude in return. Brusquely, they flung their coats into Lola's car. Their clothes beneath were almost identical shorts and tee-shirts. Lola's had I'M NO HERO stamped across her large bosom. Rose's tee-shirt bore the message LIKE ME. Gerald wondered if these messages were part of some private plan between them. He noted the paleness of their limbs, and the way their skin shrivelled into goose flesh. Rose hugged herself, shivering. Lola left her arms at her side, characteristically defying the sharp air. Both looked remarkably fit. Rose was much thinner. Muscles rippled up Lola's long thighs.

Gerald took off his tie, which was to be the starting-line – an amateur detail symbolising the *fun* of the whole thing, he thought. He walked a few paces up the slope, placed it on the ground. Standing again, he took in the sweep of the misty countryside beneath them, shafts of sun stabbing into plough and trees.

'Now, you know where you have to go?' Both girls nodded.
'No problems about the course? Don't think you can go wrong. There are signs all alone the route. Put them up myself yesterday.'

He bent over to tweak the tie, make certain it was straight. The girls were prancing up and down now, bending their knees and sniffling.

'Right,' said Gerald. 'I understand you've decided Lola shouldn't have a start after all?'

'Right,' said Rose. 'She'll gain up the hills.'

'There's absolutely nothing between us,' said Lola.

'Quite sure about that?' Gerald was determined to be absolutely fair.

'Quite sure,' they both answered.

'Very well, then. Are you ready? – Good luck to you both.'

Simultaneously Rose and Lola both crouched low over the tie, fingers just touching it. Gerald let his eyes travel up and down their spines, knobbly through the thin stuff of their tee-shirts. He remembered the feel of both their backs.

Standing to attention at one side of the tie, he saw Rose's bent knee wobble, and a drip on Lola's nose. Never had either girl looked more desirable. But nothing in his voice – his old Sandhurst shout suddenly called to aid – gave any hint of such sentiments.

'On your marks,' he bellowed. 'Get set. *Go.*'

Both girls leaped up, matching flames, Gerald thought. Breasts thrust forward, heads back, nostrils wide. They ran slowly away from him, side by side through silver grass. A cheer went up from the crowd. Laughter. Melting frost still sparkled. Gerald kept his eyes on the competitors, almost out of sight now, buttocks twinkling in their identical white shorts.

When they had rounded the first bend, Gerald returned to his car. He drove to a wood half a mile away from which he knew he would be able to see their approach from a long way off. Other spectators had reached the wood before him. They cheered as his car passed, waved with menacing glee. Sensing a small flicker of shame, Gerald ignored them. Did not wave back.

His parking-place was deserted. Relieved, he sat on the bonnet and focused his binoculars on the distant path. Sunbeams knifed the fading mists about him, jabbing through branches and tree trunks, so that for a moment he suffered the illusion he was trapped in a cage of slanting gold bars.

The distant crackle of undergrowth: through his glasses Gerald could just see them, now in focus. Lola, a little ahead, mud-splattered legs in spite of the hard ground – strands of escaped hair across her brow. Rose's thighs were alarmingly pink, mottled with purple discs. Gerald felt himself smiling. They made a fine pair, and one of them would make a fine wife. Unbelievable, really, to think *they were racing to win him. He was to be the trophy, the husband.* Did he care which one became his? At this moment, he did not. They both looked equally touching, running so eagerly. Either would do.

As they approached, neither Rose nor Lola glanced his way. Good girls: that was the way to win races. Concentration. And conservation of energy. For the moment, both seemed to have plenty of that in reserve. They were admirably calm, controlled.

They were past him in a flash: such a pretty sight — breasts bobbing, eyes sparkling, the pair of long legs and the pair of short legs matched in rhythm as they snapped at the frosty ground. This was a story the children would want endlessly repeated — the story of how two beautiful girls ran a race for their father. And how the fittest, or luckiest, became their mother . . . . The foolish smile remained on Gerald's lips. He was glad to be alone.

Just past Gerald, Rose slipped on a muddy path of woodland track. She lost her footing for a moment. Recovering, she saw Lola had increased her lead. For the first time, fear bristled through her, weakening her churning legs which, in wonderful response to all the training, had seemed till now prepared to pump on for ever. She knew that within a half a mile they would be at the stream. Leap it, Gerald had said. Suddenly she quailed at the thought of leaping. She would slip, fall — something would go wrong. Better to run through it and risk being disqualified. The decision made, Rose put in a burst of speed. In a moment she was just behind Lola again: could hear her breathing and see dark shadows of sweat on the back of her tee-shirt.

At the stream quite a crowd had gathered. Rose heard cheering and more laughter. They were hollow echoing noises. Mocking. Sharp with relish for an unusual sight. Rose hated their beaming blurred faces.

Oh God, and now the stream. It looked so wide this morning. Black water furred with melting ice and cracking sun. And suddenly, in an effortless leap, Lola was over it. *Racing up the bank the other side.* Increased cheers. Sickness in Rose's chest. She splashed into the water, felt the ice burn her calves, the mud slip beneath her feet. But somehow, then, she regained *terra firma*, clutching at clumps of prickly grass as she scrambled after Lola up the bank. Another cheer.

Upright again, her feet felt squelchy, soggy, heavy. It had been a foolish thing to do. It had lost her precious seconds.

Lola was ten yards ahead.

Lola had dry feet.

Lola would be Gerald's wife.

They were only halfway through the race, and already it was the end for Rose. Sad and angry tears flew from her eyes. She let them trickle down her burning cheeks. Spurred herself on, on. Maybe there was still a chance. Just in case, she could not give up trying.

Gerald's next position was the corner of a ploughed field. Two-thirds of the race over. Both girls tiring. Pace much slowed by the heavy black mud. Clothes and bodies darkly spattered, feet badly clogged. As they passed close to Gerald — Rose by now only just behind Lola, having made a remarkable recovery since her setback at the stream — Gerald could hear the duet of their breathing, and smell sweat in the clear air. Irreverently, he was reminded of their different smells in other conditions. Poor girls, poor girls. In the warmth of his fleece-lined jacket Gerald felt his heart expand with a strength of compassion that was strange to him. Well, he would make it up to them. One his wife, the other his friend. It would be all right. It was only lighthearted fun, after all, wasn't it?

Gerald turned to hurry along a short-cut to the five-barred gates. These, he had stipulated, must be jumped or vaulted. If Lola cleared hers as easily as she had cleared the stream, the winner was in no doubt. Poor Rose. Dearly beloved Lola. Gerald felt for the flask of brandy in his pocket. He took a swig as he hurried towards his vantage-point. A toast to them both, really. A toast of love.

Lola was less happy in the open. The winter shadows of the woods had been protective. Now the expanse of opalescent sky pressed intimidatingly upon her head. Two worries concerned her: she had been constantly, easily in the lead. That, surely, was a bad omen. And a quarter of a mile ahead was the five-barred gate. Years ago no gate could have daunted her. She had always been a good vaulter. Now, she felt the energy required to heave herself over seeping from her body. It seemed a terrible obstacle.

The sun, much stronger, was in her eyes. Her feet were heavy with mud from the plough. That had been a stupid idea of Gerald's, the plough — guaranteed to slow them both up. Just behind her she could hear Rose's heavy breath. They were running downhill, an easy field of cropped grass. At the bottom the two gates were set side by side in the hedge. Lola was to take the right, Rose the left. They had decided that without telling Gerald. No doubt he was expecting to enjoy their confusion. Well, he would be disappointed.

Lola saw a large crowd at the gates, heard the braying laughter and cheering from the well-scarfed throats. Damn them. They were waiting for a fall, disaster. She hoped neither she nor Rose would reward them.

After the gate there was the short last lap up the steep hillside to the gibbet: and the final hundred yards down the sheer incline on the other side to the winning-post. So the race was nearly over. Lola was tired, but had reserves of energy. She increased her speed, enjoying the gentle downward slope of the field.

All too soon the gate was before her. Jump or vault? Having made her decision definitely to vault, it suddenly left her. The silly shouts of the spectators confused her. She sprang on to the top bar, swung her legs over her head — a perfect vault. But, regaining her feet, she saw that Rose was now ahead. The cheering had been for *her*; even as she concentrated on leaping the gate herself, Lola had been conscious of a perfect high jump by Rose over the other gate. Oh God, now there was fear. The sharp pull of the hill began almost at once, cruel to tired calf-muscles. Lola felt a fresh shower of sweat spray from her pores, soaking her clothes. She heard herself panting, saw Rose's muddy bottom pumping easily up the hill.

She, Lola, then, was to be the friend.

Rose the wife.

Rose the winner.

Not possible, really. The sky was crumbling, the steep earth a blur. Glancing briefly at the summit of the Down, Lola saw the deathly arms of the black gibbet, the only unmoving things before her desperate eyes. With a strangled cry she called upon the last of the energy coiling in her blood. Maybe there was still a chance. Just in case, she could not give up trying.

Dazed, Gerald watched the two small, dirty white back views struggling up the hill. Lola was catching up, but only slightly. From this distance, Rose seemed to have more bounce in her stride. Although Lola's long loping gait was suddenly consuming the hillside amazingly fast.

Gerald allowed himself a quick look at the gibbet, its rigor-mortis arms embracing the sky. Then he hurried back to his car to drive round the foot of the hill to the winning-post. He wished he had chosen another part of the Downs to end the race. There was something macabre, perhaps. . . . But, then, he had always been puzzled by his own black humour. At this very moment it brought tears to his eyes.

He stood at one end of his shabby old red silk tie lying on the grass. The large crowd of spectators kept a respectful distance behind him. This side of the hill, the gibbet was no less menacing.

Moments. Eternal moments. Brief seconds — Gerald had no idea which they were. Then they appeared on the summit, his girls — two small dots, neck and neck. Lola had made a remarkable recovery. As if by some private agreement the two of them ran simultaneously beneath the gibbet's high arms — Rose tiny on the left, Lola very tall on the right. They glanced at each other. Gerald could have sworn they smiled.

Through his binoculars he recognised the automatic movements of four tired legs out of control. As they sped down the slope, Rose seemed entirely pink, only her mouth a deeper pink hole. Lola resembled a runaway Arab horse — great mane of hair free from its ribbon now, flying loose behind her — beautiful nostrils widely flared. Both made their final effort, and Lola of the longer legs was just ahead again.

His heart blasting his chest, Gerald concentrated on the last moments of the race, the magnificent way in which Lola was to win him. In his excitement his binoculars slipped. It was with his naked eye he saw the large stone embedded in the ground ahead of her. He tried to shout, to warn. But no sound came from his throat. He heard the cheering behind him, muttered some kind of prayer. Lola increased her lead with a leap of triumph. Behind her, Rose let out a terrible cry.

Then Lola fell. Her body flung out on the ground like a length of pale material let down by the wind. Rose, unable to stop, flashed past her and over the winning-ribbon.

Gerald saw the crowd rush towards Lola before he was able to move. He was aware that Rose sat on the ground some yards behind him, shoulders heaving, moaning slightly, head bowed into crossed arms. Rose the winner.

Ignoring her, Gerald moved up the slope towards Lola. Someone was running towards a parked car, face serious.

The crowd made way for Gerald.

'She fell over a bloody stone.'

'Someone should have checked the slope was clear.'

Lola lay head down, face turned to one side. Eyes shut. Deadly pale. Mud streaking the whiteness of her. Beautiful hair tangled with sweat. A small trickle of blood, to match the winning-post ribbon made from Gerald's tie, trickling from her temple.

'Unconscious'.

'Probably something broken.'

'Someone's gone for an ambulance.'

'Bloody good sports, both of them.'

Gerald, on the ground beside her, laid his hand on her warm temple. He listened to the voices, said nothing.

'How is she?'

He looked up to see Rose on the grass beside him. Rose, warm and smelling of sweat and leaves and mud and life. Tears running silently from her eyes.

'Who knows?' said Gerald, and turned his attention back to Lola.

The ambulance came. It had difficulty negotiating the steep slope. Two men with impenetrable faces and red blankets lifted

Lola gently on to a stretcher. Gerald wanted to ask if she was alive — he had not dared put his hand on her heart. He said nothing.

One of Lola's arms trailed down the side of the stretcher, unconscious fingers feeling the ground, whose frosty sparkle had now melted. The ambulance left, its tyres cutting deeply into the mud.

'Quick,' said Gerald. He took Rose's hand, familiar and warm, in his, and hurried her to his car before the spectators could begin to question. They followed the ambulance to the hospital in silence. Passing The Bear he could not help wondering what would now happen to the lunch he had ordered for the three of them. He recognised the weakness. Always, in a crisis, his mind flew unbidden to trivial matters as if for protection from the gravity of real circumstances.

In the Casualty waiting-room, beside Rose on a plastic chair, he noticed the pinkness of her skin had quite gone. She was pale. Trembling. He felt in his pocket for his flask of brandy. They both took large gulps, both managed small smiles.

'Here's to the winner, then,' said Gerald, roughly patting her muddy knee. 'It was a magnificent race . . . a lot of fun. As for Lola. . . .'

'She'll be all right,' said Rose. 'Honestly. I know Lola. She's had plenty of falls in her time.'

Lola never regained consciousness. She died from an internal haemorrhage two days later. Some months after her death, Rose and Gerald were married: a very minor ceremony, little celebration. To begin with, events did not impair Rose's love for her husband, though after marriage he became in many ways a stranger. It was as if he was haunted constantly by the thought of Lola — which, of course, Rose understood. It was a feeling shared. But after a year or so Rose's patience with her husband's melancholy broodings began to fade, and regret at having won the race consumed her life. She imagined what might have been: Lola the happy wife, herself the brave and — eventually — contented friend. She stared at what was life with a trophy she had thought she wanted — a balding querulous man, old before his time, his charm quite flown. As she walked with him through the grave-yard of stiff white stones, Rose knew that he was empty of all thoughts of her, and only Lola, long bones in her grave, was alive in his mind.

In the Garden of the North American Martyrs

Tobias Wolff

WHEN she was young, Mary saw a brilliant and original man lose his job because he had expressed ideas that were offensive to the trustees of the college where they both taught. She shared his views, but did not sign the protest petition. She was, after all, on trial herself — as a teacher, as a woman, as an interpreter of history.

Mary watched herself. Before giving a lecture she wrote it out in full, using the arguments and often the words of other, approved writers, so that she would not by chance say something scandalous. Her own thoughts she kept to herself, and the words for them grew faint as time went on; without quite disappearing, they shrank to remote, nervous points, like birds flying away.

When the department turned into a hive of cliques, Mary went about her business and pretended not to know that people hated each other. To avoid seeming bland she let herself become eccentric in harmless ways. She took up bowling, which she learned to love, and founded the Brandon College chapter of a society dedicated to restoring the good name of Richard III. She memorised comedy routines from records and jokes from books; people groaned when she rattled them off, but she did not let that stop her, and after a time the groans became the point of the jokes. They were a kind of tribute to Mary's willingness to expose herself.

In fact no one at the College was safer than Mary, for she was making herself into something institutional, like a custom, or a mascot — part of the College's idea of itself.

Now and then she wondered whether she had been too careful. The things she said and wrote seemed flat to her, pulpy, as though someone else had squeezed the juice out of them. And once, while talking with a senior professor, Mary saw herself reflected in a window: she was leaning towards him and had her head turned so that her ear was right in front of his moving mouth. The sight disgusted her. Years later, when she had to get a hearing-aid, Mary suspected that her deafness was a result of always trying to catch everything everyone said.

In the second half of Mary's fifteenth year at Brandon the Provost called a meeting of all faculty and students to announce that the College was bankrupt and would not open its gates again. He was every bit as surprised as they; the report from the trustees had reached his desk only that morning. It seemed that Brandon's financial manager had speculated in some kind of futures and lost everything. The Provost wanted to deliver the news in person before it reached the papers. He wept openly, and so did the students and teachers, with only a few exceptions – some cynical upperclassmen who claimed to despise the education they had received.

Mary could not rid her mind of the word 'speculate'. It meant to guess; in terms of money, to gamble. How could a man gamble a college? Why should he want to do that, and how could it be that no one stopped him? To Mary, it seemed to belong to another time; she thought of a drunken plantation-owner gaming away his slaves.

She applied for jobs and got an offer from a new experimental college in Oregon. It was her only offer, so she took it.

The college was in one building. Bells rang all the time, lockers lined the hallways, and at every corner stood a buzzing water-fountain. The student newspaper came out twice a month on wet mimeograph paper. The library, which was next to the band room, had no librarian and no books to speak of.

The countryside was beautiful, though, and Mary might have enjoyed it if the rain had not caused her so much trouble. There was something wrong with her lungs that the doctors couldn't agree on, and couldn't cure; whatever it was, the dampness made it worse. On rainy days condensation formed in Mary's hearing-aid and shorted it out. She began to dread talking with people, never knowing when she would have to take out her control-box and slap it against her leg.

It rained nearly every day. When it was not raining it was getting ready to rain, or clearing. The ground glinted under the grass, and the light had a yellow undertone that flared up during storms.

There was water in Mary's basement. Her walls sweated, and she had found toadstools growing behind the refrigerator. She felt as though she were rusting out, like one of those old cars people thereabouts kept in their front yards on pieces of wood. Mary knew that everyone was dying, but it did seem to her that she was dying faster than most.

She continued to look for another job, without success. Then, in the autumn of her third year in Oregon, she got a letter from a woman named Louise who'd taught at Brandon. Louise had scored a great success with a book on Benedict Arnold, and was now on the faculty of a famous college in upstate New York. She said that one of her colleagues would be retiring at the end of the year, and asked whether Mary would be interested in the position.

The letter surprised Mary. Louise thought of herself as a great historian and of almost everyone else as useless; Mary had not known that she felt differently about her. Moreover, enthusiasm for other people's causes did not come easily to Louise, who had a way of sucking in her breath when familiar names were mentioned, as though she knew things that friendship kept her from disclosing.

Mary expected nothing, but sent a résumé and copies of her two books. Shortly after that Louise called to say that the search committee, of which she was chairwoman, had decided to grant Mary an interview in early November. 'Now, don't get your hopes *too* high,' said Louise.

'Oh, no,' said Mary, but thought: Why shouldn't I hope? They would not go to the bother and expense of bringing her to the college if they weren't serious. And she was certain that the interview would go well. She would make them like her, or at least give them no cause to dislike her.

She read about the area with a strange sense of familiarity, as if the land and its history were already known to her. And when her plane left Portland and climbed easterly into the clouds Mary felt like she was going home. The feeling stayed with her, growing stronger when they landed. She tried to describe it to Louise as they left the airport at Syracuse and drove towards the college, an hour or so away. 'It's like *déjà vu*,' she said.

'*Déjà vu* is a hoax,' said Louise. 'It's just a chemical imbalance of some kind.'

'Maybe so,' said Mary, 'But I still have this sensation.'

'Don't get serious on me,' said Louise. 'That's not your long suit. Just be your funny wisecracking old self. Tell me, now — honestly — how do I look?'

It was night, too dark to see Louise's face well, but in the airport she had seemed gaunt and pale and intense. She reminded Mary of a description in the book she'd been reading, of how Iroquois warriors gave themselves visions by fasting. She had that kind of look about her. But she wouldn't want to hear that. 'You look wonderful,' said Mary.

'There's a reason,' said Louise. 'I've taken a lover. My concentration has improved, my energy level is up, and I've lost ten pounds. I'm also getting some colour in my cheeks, though that could be the weather. I recommend the experience highly. But you probably disapprove.'

Mary didn't know what to say. She said that she was sure Louise knew best, but that didn't seem to be enough. 'Marriage is a great institution,' she added, 'but who wants to live in an institution?'

Louise groaned. 'I know you,' she said, 'and I know that right now you're thinking: But what about Ted? What about the children? The fact is, Mary, they aren't taking it well at all. Ted has become a nag.' She handed Mary her handbag. 'Be a good girl and light me a cigarette, will you? I know I told you I quit, but this whole thing has been very hard on me, very hard, and I'm afraid I've started again.'

They were in the hills now, heading north on a narrow road. Tall trees arched above them. As they topped a rise Mary saw the forest all around, deep black under the plum-coloured sky. There were a few lights and these made the darkness seem even greater.

'Ted has succeeded in completely alienating the children from me,' Louise was saying. 'There is no reasoning with any of them. In fact they refuse to discuss the matter at all, which is very ironical because over the years I have tried to instil in them a willingness to see things from the other person's point of view. If they could just *meet* Jonathan I know they would feel differently. But they won't hear of it. Jonathan', she said, 'is my lover.'

'I see,' said Mary, and nodded.

Coming around a curve they caught two deer in the headlights. The creatures' eyes lit up and their hindquarters tensed; Mary could see them shaking as the car went by. 'Deer,' she said.

'I don't know,' said Louise, 'I just don't know. I do my best and it never seems to be enough. But that's enough about me — let's talk about you. What did you think of my latest book?' She squawked and beat her palms on the steering-wheel. 'God, I love that joke,' she said. 'Seriously, though, what about you? It must have been a real shockeroo when good old Brandon folded.'

'It was hard. Things haven't been good, but they'll be a lot better if I get this job.'

'At least you have work,' said Louise. 'You should look at it from the bright side.'

'I try.'

'You seem so gloomy. I hope you're not worrying about the interview, or the class. Worrying won't do you a bit of good. Be happy.'

'Class? What class?'

'The class you're supposed to give tomorrow, after the interview. Didn't I tell you? *Mea culpa,* hon, *mea maxima culpa.* I've been uncharacteristically forgetful lately.'

'But what will I do?'

'Relax,' said Louise. 'Just pick a subject and wing it.'

'Wing it?'

'You know, open your mouth and see what comes out. Extemporise.'

'But I always work from a prepared lecture.'

Louise sighed. 'All right, I'll tell you what. Last year I wrote an article on the Marshall Plan that I got bored with and never published. You can read that.'

Parroting what Louise had written seemed wrong to Mary, at first; then it occurred to her that she had been doing the same kind of thing for many years, and that this was not the time to get scruples. 'Thanks,' she said. 'I appreciate it.'

'Here we are,' said Louise, and pulled into a circular drive with several cabins grouped around it. In two of the cabins lights were on; smoke drifted straight up from the chimneys. 'This is the visitors' centre. The college is another two miles thataway.' Louise pointed down the road. 'I'd invite you to stay at my house, but I'm spending the night with Jonathan and Ted is not good company these days. You would hardly recognise him.'

She took Mary's bags from the boot and carried them up the steps of a darkened cabin. 'Look,' she said, 'they've laid a fire for you. All you have to do is light it.' She stood in the middle of the room with her arms crossed and watched as Mary held a match under the kindling. 'There,' she said. 'You'll be snugeroo in no time. I'd love to stay and chew the fat but I can't. You just get a good night's sleep and I'll see you in the morning.'

Mary stood in the doorway and waved as Louise pulled out of the drive, spraying gravel. She filled her lungs, to taste the air: it was tart and clear. She could see the stars in their figurations, and the vague streams of light that ran among the stars.

She still felt uneasy about reading Louise's work as her own. It would be her first complete act of plagiarism. It would change her. It would make her less — how much less, she did not know. But what else could she do? She certainly couldn't 'wing' it. Words might fail her, and then what? Mary had a dread of silence. When she thought of silence she thought of drowning, as if it were a kind of water she could not swim in.

'I want this job,' she said, and settled deep into her coat. It was cashmere, and Mary had not worn it since moving to Oregon, because people thought you were pretentious if you had on anything but a Pendleton shirt or, of course, raingear. She rubbed her cheek against the upturned collar and thought of a silver moon shining through bare black branches, a white house with green shutters, red leaves falling in a hard blue sky.

Louise woke her a few hours later. She was sitting on the edge of the bed, pushing at Mary's shoulder and snuffling loudly. When Mary asked her what was wrong she said, 'I want your opinion on something. It's very important. Do you think I'm womanly?'

Mary sat up. 'Louise, can this wait?'

'No.'

'Womanly?'

Louise nodded.

'You are very beautiful,' said Mary, 'and you know how to present yourself.'

Louise stood and paced the room. 'That sonofabitch,' she said. She came back and stood over Mary. 'Let's suppose someone said I have no sense of humour. Would you agree or disagree?'

'In some things you do. I mean, yes, you have a good sense of humour.'

'What do you mean, "in some things"? What kind of things?'

'Well, if you heard that someone had been killed in an unusual way, like by an exploding cigar, you would think that was funny.'

Louise laughed.

'That's what I mean,' said Mary.

Louise went on laughing. 'Oh, Lordy,' she said. 'Now it's my turn to say something about you.' She sat down beside Mary.

'Please,' said Mary.

'Just one thing,' said Louise.

Mary waited.

'You're trembling,' said Louise. 'I was just going to say – oh, forget it. Listen, do you mind if I sleep on the couch. I'm all in.'

'Go ahead.'

'Sure it's OK? You've got a big day tomorrow.' She fell back on the sofa and kicked off her shoes. 'I was just going to say, you should use some liner on those eyebrows of yours. They sort of disappear and the effect is disconcerting.'

Neither of them slept. Louise chain-smoked cigarettes and Mary watched the coals burn down. When it was light enough that they could see each other Louise got up. 'I'll send a student for you,' she said. 'Good luck.'

The college looked the way colleges are supposed to look. Roger, the student assigned to show Mary around, explained that it was an exact copy of a college in England, right down to the gargoyles and stained-glass windows. It looked so much like a college that moviemakers sometimes used it as a set. *Andy Hardy Goes To College* had been filmed there, and every autumn they had an Andy Hardy Goes To College Day, with raccoon coats and gold-fish swallowing contests.

Above the door of the Founder's Building was a Latin motto which, roughly translated, meant 'God helps those who help themselves'. As Roger recited the names of illustrious graduates Mary was struck by the extent to which they had taken this precept to heart. They had helped themselves to railroads, mines, armies, states; to empires of finance with outposts all over the world.

Roger took Mary to the chapel and showed her a plaque bearing the names of alumni who had been killed in various wars, all the way back to the Civil War. There were not many names. Here, too, apparently, the graduates had helped themselves. 'Oh, yes,' said Roger as they were leaving, 'I forgot to tell you. The communion-rail comes from some church in Europe where Charlemagne used to go.'

They went to the gymnasium, and the three hockey rinks, and the library, where Mary inspected the card catalogue, as though she would turn down the job if they didn't have the right books. 'We have a little more time,' said Roger as they went outside. 'Would you like to see the power plant?'

Mary wanted to keep busy until the last minute, so she agreed.

Roger led her into the depths of the service building, explaining things about the machine, which was the most advanced in the country. 'People think the college is really old-fashioned,' he said, 'but it isn't. They let girls come here now, and some of the teachers are women. In fact, there's a statute that says they have to interview at least one woman for each opening. There it is.'

They were standing on an iron catwalk above the biggest machine Mary had ever beheld. Roger, who was majoring in Earth Sciences, said that it had been built from a design pioneered by a professor in his department. Where before he had been gabby Roger now became reverent. It was clear that to him this machine was the soul of the college, that indeed the purpose of the college was to provide outlets for the machine. Together they leaned against the railing and watched it hum.

Mary arrived at the committee room exactly on time for her interview, but it was empty. Her two books were on the table, along with a water-pitcher and some glasses. She sat down and picked up one of the books. The binding cracked as she opened it. The pages were smooth, clean, unread. Mary turned to the first chapter, which began 'It is generally believed that. . . .' How dull, she thought.

Nearly half an hour later Louise came in with several men. 'Sorry we're late,' she said. 'We don't have much time, so we'd better get started.' She introduced Mary to the men, but with one exception the names and faces did not stay together. The exception was Dr Howells, the department chairman, who had a porous blue nose and terrible teeth.

A shiny-faced man to Dr Howells' right spoke first. 'So,' he said, 'I understand you once taught at Brandon College.'

'It was a shame that Brandon had to close,' said a young man with a pipe in his mouth. 'There is a place for schools like Brandon.' As he talked the pipe wagged up and down.

'Now you're in Oregon,' said Dr Howells. 'I've never been there. How do you like it?'

'Not very much,' said Mary.

'Is that right?' Dr Howells leaned towards her. 'I thought everyone liked Oregon. I hear it's very green.'

'That's true,' said Mary.

'I suppose it rains a lot,' he said.

'Nearly every day.'

'I wouldn't like that,' he said, shaking his head. 'I like it dry. Of course it snows here, and you have your rain now and then, but it's a *dry* rain. Have you ever been to Utah? There's a state for you. Bryce Canyon. The Mormon Tabernacle Choir.'

'Dr Howells was brought up in Utah,' said the young man with the pipe.

'It was a different place altogether in those days,' said Dr Howells. 'Mrs Howells and I have always talked about going back when I retire, but now I'm not so sure.'

'We're a little short on time,' said Louise.

'And here I've been going on and on,' said Dr Howells. 'Before we wind things up, is there anything you want to tell us?'

'Yes. I think you should give me the job.' Mary laughed when she said this, but no one laughed back, or even looked at her. They all looked away. Mary understood then that they were not really considering her for the position. She had been brought here to satisfy a rule. She had no hope.

The men gathered their paper and shook hands with Mary and told her how much they were looking forward to her class. 'I can't get enough of the Marshall Plan,' said Dr Howells.

'Sorry about that,' said Louise when they were alone. 'I didn't think it would be so bad. That was a real bitcheroo.'

'Tell me something,' said Mary. 'You already know who you're to hire, don't you?'

Louise nodded.

'Then why did you bring me here?'

Louise began to explain about the statute and Mary interrupted. 'I know all that. But why me? Why did you pick *me*?'

Louise walked to the window. She spoke with her back to Mary. 'Things haven't been going very well for old Louise,' she said. 'I've been unhappy and I thought you might cheer me up. You used to be so funny, and I was sure you would enjoy the trip — it didn't cost you anything, and it's pretty this time of year with the leaves and everything. Mary, you don't know the things my parents did to me. And Ted is no barrel of laughs, either. Or Jonathan, the sonofabitch. I deserve some love and friendship but I don't get any.' She turned and looked at her watch.

'It's almost time for your class. We'd better go.'

'I would rather not give it. After all, there's not much point, is there?'

'But you *have* to give it. That's part of the interview.' Louise handed Mary a folder. 'All you have to do is read this. It isn't much, considering all the money we've laid out to get you here.'

Mary followed Louise down the hall to the lecture-room. The professors were sitting in the front row with their legs crossed. They smiled and nodded at Mary. Behind them the room was full

of students, some of whom had spilled over into the aisles. One of
the professors adjusted the microphone to Mary's height, crouching down as he went to the podium and back as though he would
prefer not to be seen.

Louise called the room to order. She introduced Mary and
gave the subject of the lecture, not knowing that Mary had decided
to wing it after all. Mary came to the podium unsure of what she
would say; sure only that she would rather die than read Louise's
article. The sun poured through the stained glass upon the people
around her, painting their faces. Thick streams of smoke from the
young professor's pipe drifted through a circle of red light at
Mary's feet, turning crimson and twisting like flames.

'I wonder how many of you know', she began, 'that we are in
the Long House, the ancient domain of the Five Nations of the
Iroquois.'

Two professors looked at each other.

'The Iroquois were without pity,' said Mary. 'They hunted
people down with clubs and arrows and spears and nets, and blow-
guns made from elder-stalks. They tortured their captives, sparing
no one, not even the little children. They took scalps and practised
cannibalism and slavery. Because they had no pity they became
powerful, so powerful that no other tribe dared to oppose them.
They made the other tribes pay tribute, and when they had
nothing to pay the Iroquois attacked them.'

Several of the professors began to whisper. Dr Howells was
saying something to Louise, and Louise was shaking her head.

'In one of their attacks,' said Mary, 'they captured two Jesuit
priests, Jean de Brébeuf and Gabriel Lalement. They covered
Lalement with pitch and set him on fire in front of Brébeuf.
When Brébeuf rebuked them they cut off his lips and put a
burning iron down his throat. They hung a collar of red-hot
hatchets around his neck, and poured boiling water over his head.
When he continued to preach to them they cut strips of flesh
from his body and ate them before his eyes. While he was still
alive they scalped him and cut open his breast and drank his blood.
Later, their chief tore out Brébeuf's heart and ate it, but just
before he did this Brébeuf spoke to them one last time. He said—'

'That's enough!' yelled Dr Howells, jumping to his feet.

Louise stopped shaking her head. Her eyes were perfectly round.

Mary had come to the end of her facts. She did not know what Brébeuf had said. Silence rose up around her; just when she thought she would go under and be lost in it she heard someone whistling in the hallway outside, trilling the notes like a bird, like many birds.

'Mend your lives,' she said. 'You have deceived yourselves in the pride of your hearts, and the strength of your arms. Though you soar aloft like the eagle, though your nest is set among the stars, thence I will bring you down, says the Lord. Turn from power to love. Be kind. Do justice. Walk humbly.'

Louise was waving her arms. 'Mary!' she shouted.

But Mary had more to say, much more; she waved back at Louise, then turned off her hearing-aid so that she would not be distracted again.

Kin

Edna O'Brien

I LOVED my mother, but yet I was glad when the time came to go to her mother's house each summer. It was a little house in the mountains, and it commanded a fine view of the valley and the great lake below. From the front door, glimpsed through a pair of very old binoculars, one could see the entire Shannon Lake studded with various islands. On a summer's day this was a thrill. I would be put standing on a kitchen chair, while someone held the binoculars; and sometimes I marvelled, though I could not see at all as the lenses had not been focused properly. The sunshine made everything better and, though we were not down by the lake, we imagined dipping our feet in it, or seeing people in boats fishing and then stopping to have a picnic. We imagined lake water lapping.

I felt safer in that house. It was different from our house, not so imposing, a cottage really, with no indoor water or water-closet. We went for buckets of water to the well, and there was a different well each summer. These were a source of miracle to me, these deep cold wells, sunk into the ground, in a kitchen garden, or a paddock or even a long distance away, wells that had been divined since I was last there. There was always a tin scoop near-by so that one could fill the bucket to the very brim. Then of course the full bucket was an occasion of trepidation because one was supposed not to spill. One often brought the bucket to the very threshold of the kitchen, and then out of excitement or clumsiness some would get splashed on to the concrete floor and there would be admonishments, but it was not like the admonishments in our own house; it was not momentous.

My grandfather was old and thin and hoary when I first saw him. He was the colour of a clay pipe. After the market days he would come home in the pony and trap drunk, and then as soon as he stepped out of the trap he would stagger and fall into a drain or whatever. Then he would roar for help and his grandson, who was in his twenties, would pick him up or, rather, drag him along the ground and through the house, and up the stairs to his feather bed where he moaned and groaned. The bedroom was above the kitchen, and in the night we would be below around the fire eating warm soda bread and drinking cocoa. There was nothing like it. The fresh bread would only be an hour out of the pot, and cut in thick pieces and dolloped with butter and green-gage jam. The greengage jam was a present from the postmistress, who gave it in return for the grazing of a bullock. She gave marma-lade at a different time of year and a barm-brack at Hallowe'en. He moaned upstairs, but no one was frightened of him, not even his own wife who chewed and chewed and said, 'Bad cess to them that give him the drink.' She meant the publicans. She was a minute woman with a minute face, and her thin hair was pinned up tightly. Her little face, though old, was like a bud, and when she was young she had been beautiful. There was a photo of her to prove it.

Sitting with them at night I thought that maybe I would not go home at all. Maybe I would never again lie in bed next to my mother, the two of us shivering with expectancy and with terror. Maybe I would forsake my mother.

'Maybe you'll stay here,' my aunt said, as if she had guessed my thoughts.

'I couldn't do that,' I said, not knowing why I declined because indeed the place had definite advantages. I stayed up as late as they did. I ate soda bread and jam to my heart's content. I rambled around the fields all day, admiring sally-trees, elder-bushes and the fluttering flowers. I played 'shop' to my heart's content, or I played teaching in the little dark plantation, and no one interfered or told me to stop doing it. The plantation was where I played secrets, and yet I knew the grown-ups were within shouting distance if a stranger or a tinker should surprise me there. It was pitch dark and full of young fir-trees. The ground was a carpet of bronzed fallen fir-needles. I used to kneel on them for punishment, after the playing. Then when that ritual was done I went into the flower garden, which was a mass of begonias and lupins and so a mass of bright brilliant colours. Each area had its own colour as my aunt planned it that way. I can see them now, those bright reds like lipsticks, and those yellows like the cloth of a summer dress, and those pale blues like old people's eyes, with the bees and the wasps luxuriating in each petal, or each little bell, or each flute, and the warmth of the place, and the drone of the bees, and my eyes lighting on tea-towels and flannel drawers and the various things spread out on the hedge to dry. The sun garden they called it. My aunt got the seeds and just sprinkled them around, and these various and marvellous blooms just sprang up. They even had tulips, whereas at home we had only a distressed rambling rose on a silvered arch and two clumps of devil's pokers. Our garden was sad and windy. The wind had made holes and indentations in the hedges, and the dogs had made further holes where they slept and burrowed. Our house was larger, and there was better linoleum on the floor, there were brass rods on the stairs, and there was a flush lavatory, but it did not have the same cheeriness and it was full of doom. Still, I knew that I would not stay at my grandmother's for ever. I knew it for certain when I got into bed and then desperately missed my mother, and missed the little whispering we did, and the chocolate we ate, and I missed the smell of our kind of bedclothes. Theirs were grey flannel that tickled the skin, as did the loose feathers and their pointed ends that kept irking one. There was a gaudy red quilt that I thought would come to life and turn into a sinister Santa Claus. Except that they had told me that there was no Santa Claus. My aunt told me that, she insisted. There was my aunt and her two sons Donal and Joe, and my grandmother and grandfather. Donal had gone away to England to be near a girl. My aunt and Joe would tease me each night, say that there was no Santa Claus, until I got up and stamped the floor and in contradicting them welled up with tears, and then at last when on the point of breaking down they would say that there was. Then one night they went too far. They said that my mother was not my real mother. My real mother, they said, was in Australia and that I was adopted. I could not be told that word. I began to hit the wall, and screech, and the more they insisted the more obstreperous I became. My aunt went into the parlour in search of a box of snaps to find a photo of my real mother and came out triumphant at having found it. She showed me a woman in knicker-bockers with a big floppy hat. I could have thrown it in the fire, so violent was I. They watched for each new moment of panic, and furious disbelief, and then they got the wind up when they saw I was getting out of control. I began to shake like the weather conductor on the chapel chimney, and my teeth chattered, and before long I was just this shaking creature, unable to let out any sound and seeing the room in a swoon. I felt their alarm almost as I felt my own. My aunt took hold of my wrist to feel my pulse, and my grandmother held a spoonful of tonic to my lips but I spilt it. It was called Parish's Food and was the colour of cooked beetroot. My eyes were roaming. My aunt put a big towel around me, and sat me on her knee, and as the terror lessened my tears began to flow and I cried so much that they thought I would choke because of the tears going back down the throat. They said I must never tell anyone and I must never tell my mother.

'She is my mother,' I said, and they said, 'Yes, darling,' but I knew that they were appalled at what had happened.

That night, I fell out of bed twice and my aunt had to put chairs to it to keep me in. She slept in the same room, and often I used to hear her crying for her dead husband and begging to be reunited with him in heaven. She used to talk to him and say, 'Is that you, Michael, is that you?' I often heard her body striking against the headboard, or her heavy movements when she got up to relieve herself. In the daytime we used the fields, but at night we did not go out for fear of ghosts. There was a gutter in the back kitchen that served as a channel, and twice a week she put disinfectant in it. The crux in the daytime was finding a private place and not being found or spied on by anyone. It entailed much walking and then much scouting so as not to be seen.

The morning after the fright they pampered me, scrambled me an egg and sprinkled nutmeg over it. It was heaven. Then along with these dainties my aunt announced a surprise. Our workman had sent word by the mail-car man that he was coming to see me on the Sunday, and the postman had delivered the message. Oh, what a glut of happiness. Our workman was called 'Carnero' and I loved him, too. I loved his rotting teeth, and his curly hair, and his strong hands, and his big stomach that people referred to as his corporation. He was nicknamed Carnero after a boxer. I knew that when he came he would have bars of chocolate, and maybe a letter or a silk hankie from my mother, and that he would lift me up in his arms and swing me around and say 'Sugarbush'. How many hours were there till Sunday? I asked. Yet that day, which was a Friday, did not pass without event. We had a visitor — a man. I will never know why, but my grandfather called him Tim, whereas his real name was Pat, but my grandfather was not to be told that. Tim, it seems, had died and my grandfather was not to know, because if any of the locals died it brought his own death to his mind and he dreaded death as strenuously as did all the others. Death was some weird journey that you made alone, and unbefriended, once you had snuffed it. When my aunt's husband had died — in fact had been shot by the Black and Tans — my aunt had to conceal the death from her own parents, so irrational were they about the subject. She had to stay up at home the evening her husband's remains were brought to the chapel, and when the chapel bell rung out intermittently, as it does for a death, and they asked who it was, again and again, my poor aunt had to conceal her own grief, be silent about her own tragedy, and pretend that she did not know. Next day she went to the funeral on the excuse that it was some forester whom her husband knew. Her husband was supposed to be transferred to a barracks a long way off, and meanwhile she was going to live with her parents and bring her infant sons until her husband found accommodation. She invented a name for the district where her husband was supposed to be; it was in the north of Ireland, and she invented letters that she had received from him, and the news of the 'Troubles' up there. Eventually, I expect, she told them, and I expect they collapsed and broke down. In fact the man who brought these imaginary letters would have been Tim, since he had been the postman, and it was of his death my grandfather must not be told. So there in the porch, in a worn suit, was a man called Pat answering to the name of Tim, and the news that a Tim would have, such as how were his family, and what crops had he put in, and what cattle fairs had he been to. I thought that it was peculiar that he could answer for another but I expect that everyone's news was identical.

Sunday after Mass I was down by the little green gate skipping and waiting for Carnero. As often happens, the expected one arrives just when we look away. The cuckoo called and, though I knew I would not see her, I looked in a tree where there was a shambling bird's nest, and at that moment heard Carnero's whistle. I ran down the road, and at once he hefted me up on to the crossbar of his bicycle. 'Oh, Carnero,' I cried and there was both joy and sadness in the reunion. He brought me a bag of tinned sweets, and the most beautiful present. As we got off the bicycle near the little gate he put it on me. It was a toy watch. It was the most beautiful red and each bit of the bracelet was the shape and colour of a raspberry. It had hands and though they did not move that did not matter. One could pull the bracelet part by its elastic thread and cause it to snap in or out. The hands were black and frail like an eyelash. He would not say where he had got it. I had only one craving: to stay down there by the gate with him and admire the watch and talk about home news. I could not talk to him in front of them because a child was not supposed to talk or have any wants. He was puffing from having cycled uphill and began to open his tie, and taking it off he said, 'This bloody thing.' I wondered who he had put it on for. He was in his Sunday suit and had a fishing-feather in his hat.

'Oh, Carnero, turn the bike around and bring me home with you.'

Such were my unuttered and unutterable hopes. Later my grandfather teased me and said was it in his backside I saw Carnero's looks and I said no, in every particle of him.

That night as we were saying the rosary my grandfather let out a shout, slouched forward, knocking the wooden chair and hitting himself on the rungs of it, then hitting the cement of the floor. He died delirious. He died calling on his Maker. It was ghastly. Joe was out, and only my grandmother and aunt were there to assist. They picked him up. His skin was purple, and the exact colour of my tonic, and his eyes rolled so that they were seeing every bit of the room from the ceiling, to the whitewashed wall, to the cement floor, to the settlebed, to the cans of milk, and bulging. He bucked like an animal and then let out a most beseeching howl and that was it. At that moment my aunt remembered I was there, and told me to go into the parlour and wait. It was worse in there, pitch dark and I in a place where I did not know my footing, or my way around. I'd only been in there once to fetch a tea-pot and sugar-tongs when the visitor Tim came. Had it been in our own house I would have known what to cling to — the back of a chair, the tassle of a blind, the girth of a plaster statue — but in there I held on to nothing and thought how the thing he dreaded had come to pass and now he was finding out those dire things that all his life his mind had barely kept at bay.

'May he rest in peace, may the souls of the faithful departed rest in peace.'

It was that for two days, along with litanies, and mourners smoking clay pipes, plates of cake being passed around and glasses filled. My mother and father were there, among the mourners. I was praised for growing, as if it was something I myself had caused to happen. My mother looked older in black, and I wished she had worn a georgette scarf, something to give her a bit of brightness around the throat. She did not like when I said that, and sent me off to say the Confiteor and three Hail Marys. Her sister and dry. She did not love her own father. Neither did I. Her sister and she would go down into the far room and discuss whether to bring out another bottle of whiskey or another porter cake, or whether it was time to offer the jelly. They were reluctant. The reason being that some provisions had to be held over for the next day, when the special mourners would come up after the funeral. Whereas that night half the parish was there. My grandfather was laid out upstairs in a brown habit. He had stubble on his chin and looked like a frosted plank lying there, grey-white and inanimate. As soon as they had paid their respects, the people hurried down to the kitchen, and the parlour, for the eats and the chat. No one wanted to be with the dead man, not even his wife, who had gone a bit funny and was asking my aunt annoying questions about the food and the fire, and how many priests were going to serve at the High Mass.

'Leave that to us,' my mother would say, and then my grandmother would retell the world what a palace my mother's house was, and how it was the nicest house in the countryside, and my mother would say, 'Shhhh,' as if she was being disgraced. My father said, 'Well, Missy,' to me twice, and a strange man gave me sixpence. It was a very thin old sixpence and I thought it would disappear. I called his Father out of reverence, because he looked like a priest, but he was in fact a boatman.

The funeral was on an island on the Shannon. Most of the people stayed on the quay, but we, the family, piled into two row-boats and followed the boat that carried the coffin. It was a jolty ride with big waves coming in over us and our feet getting drenched. The island itself was full of cows. The sudden arrivals made them bawl and race about, and I thought it was quite improper to see that happening, while the remains were being lowered and buried. It was totally desolate, and though my aunt sniffed a bit, and my grandmother let out ejaculations, there was no real grief, and that was the saddest thing. Next day they burned his working-clothes and threw his muddy boots on to the manure heap. Then my aunt sewed black diamonds of cloth on her clothes, on my grand-mother's and on Joe's. She wrote a long letter to her son in England, and enclosed black diamonds of cloth for him to stitch on to his effects. He worked in Liverpool in a motor-car factory. Whenever they said 'Liverpool' I thought of a whole mound of bloody liver, but then I would look down at my watch and be happy again and pretend to tell the time. The house was gloomy. I went off with Joe, who was mowing hay, and sat with him on the mowing machine and fell slightly in love. Indoors was dismal, what with my grandmother sighing, and recalling old times, such as when her husband tried to kill her with a carving-knife, and then she would snivel and miss him and say, 'The poor old creature.' My aunt was sullen, too, and asked where would the money for the funeral, and the money for the High Mass, come from. Six priests had to be paid a pound each and that was no laughing matter.

Out in the fields Joe tickled my knee and asked was I ticklish. He had a lovely long face and a beautiful whistle. He was probably about twenty-four, but he seemed old, especially because of a slouchy hat and because of a pair of trousers that were several times too big for him. When the mare passed water he nudged me

and said, 'Want lemonade?' and when she broke wind he made
disgraceful plopping sounds with his lips. He and I ate lunch on
the headland and lolled for a bit. We had bread and butter, milk
from a flask, and some ginger cake that was left over since the
funeral. It had gone damp. He sang, 'You'll be lonely, little sweet-
heart, in the spring,' and smiled a lot at me, and I felt very
important. I knew that all he would do was tickle my knee, and
the backs of my knees, because at heart he was shy, and not like
some of the local men who would want to throw you to the
ground, and press themselves over you so that you would have to
ask God to allow you to vanish. When he lifted me on to the
machine he said that we would bring out a nice little cushion on
the morrow so that I would have a soft seat. But on the morrow
it rained and he went off to the sawmill to get shelving, and my
aunt moaned about the hay getting wet and perhaps getting
ruined and there being no fodder for the cattle next winter.

That day I got into dire disaster. I was out in the fields playing,
talking, and enjoying the rainbows in the puddles, when all of a
sudden I decided to run helter skelter towards the house in case
they were cross with me. Coming through a stile that led to the
yard I decided to do a big jump and landed head over heels into
the manure heap. I fell so heavily on to it that every bit of
clothing got wet and smeared. It was a very massive manure heap,
and very squelchy. Each day the cow-house was cleaned out and
the contents shovelled there, and each week the straw and old
nesting from the hen-house was dumped there, and so was the
pigs' bedding. So it was not like falling into a sack of hay. It was
not dry and clean. It was a foul spot I fell into, and soon as I got
my bearings I decided it was wise to undress. The pleated skirt
was ruined, and so was my blouse and my navy cardigan. Damp
had gone through to my bodice, and the smell was dreadful. I was
trying to wash it off under an outside tap, using a fist of grass as a
cloth, when my aunt came out and exclaimed, 'Jesus, Mary and
Joseph, glory be to the great God today and tonight but what
have you done to yourself!' I was afraid to tell her that I fell, so I
said I was doing washing and she said in the name of God what
washing, and then she saw the ruin on the garments. She picked
up the skirt and said why on earth had she let me wear it that day,

and wasn't it the demons that came with me the day I arrived with my attaché case. I was still trying to wash and not answer this barrage of questions, all beginning with the word 'why'. As if I knew why! She got a rag and some pumice stone, plus a can of water, and I stripped to the skin and was washed out of doors and reprimanded. Then my clothes were put to soak in the can, all except for the skirt which had to be brought in to dry, and then cleaned with a clothes-brush. Mercifully my grandmother was not told.

My aunt forgave me two nights later when she was in the dairy churning and singing. I asked if I could turn the churn handle for a jiff. It was changing from liquid to solid, and the handle was becoming stiff. I tried with all my might but I was not strong enough.

'You will, when you're big,' she said and sang to me. She sang 'Far Away in Australia' and then asked what I would like to do when I grew up. I said I would like to marry Carnero, and she laughed and said what a lovely thing it was to be young and carefree. She let me look into the churn to see the mound of yellow butter that had formed. There were drops of water all over its surface, it was like some big bulk that had bathed, but not dried off. She got two sets of wooden pats, and together we began to fashion the butter into dainty shapes. She was quicker at it than I. She made little round balls of butter with prickly surfaces, then she said wouldn't it be lovely if the Curate came up for tea. He was a new curate and had rimless spectacles.

The next day she went to the town to sell the butter, and I was left to mind the house along with my grandmother. My aunt had promised to bring back a shop cake, and said that depending on the price it would either be a sponge cake or an Oxford Lunch, which was a type of fruit cake wrapped in beautiful shiny silver paper. My grandmother donned a big straw hat with a chin strap and looked very distracted. She kept thinking that there was a car or a cart coming into the back yard and had me looking out windows on the alert. Then she got a flush and I had to conduct her to the plantation, and sit on the bench next to her, and we were scarcely there when three huge fellows walked in, and we

knew at once that they were tinkers. The fear is indescribable. I
knew that tinkers took one off in their cart, hid one under shawls,
and did dire things to one. I knew that they beat their wives and
children, got drunk, had fights amongst themselves and spent
many a night cooling off in the barracks. I jumped up as they
came through the gate. My grandmother's mouth fell wide open
with shock. One of them carried shears and the other had a
weighing-pan in his hand. They asked if we had any sheep's wool
and we both said no, no sheep, only cattle. They had evil eyes
and gamey looks. There was no knowing what they would do to us.
Then they asked if we had any feathers for pillows or mattresses.
She was so crazed with fear that she said yes and led the way to
the house. As we walked along I expected a strong hand to be
clamped on my shoulder. They were dreadfully silent. Only one
had spoken and he had a shocking accent – what my mother
would call 'a gurriers's'. My grandmother sent me upstairs to get
the two bags of feathers out of the wardrobe, and she stayed
below so that they would not steal a cake of bread, or crockery
or any other thing. She was agreeing a price when I came down
or, rather, requesting a price. The talking member said it was a
barter job. We would get a lace cloth in return. She asked how
big this cloth was, and he said very big, while his companion put
his hand into the bag of feathers to make sure that there was not
anything else in there, that we were not trying to fob them off
with grass or sawdust or something. She asked where was the
cloth. They laughed. They said it was down in the caravan, at the
crossroads, ma'am. She knew then she was being cheated, but she
tried to stand her ground. She grabbed one end of the bag and
said, 'You'll not have these.'

'D'you think we're mugs?' one of them said, and gestured to
the others to pick up the two bags, which they did. Then they
looked at us as if they might mutilate us, and I prayed to St Jude
and St Antony to keep us from harm. Before going, they insisted
on being given new milk. They drank in great slugs.

'Are you afraid of me?' one of the men said to her. He was the
tallest of the three and his shirt was open. I could see the hair on
his chest, and he had a very funny look in his eyes as if he was
not thinking, like as if thinking was beyond him. His eyes had a

thickness in them. For some reason he reminded me of meat.

'Why should I be afraid of you?' she said and I would have clapped her, but for the tight corner we were in.

She blessed herself several times when they'd gone, and decided that what we did had been the practical thing to do, and in fact our only recourse. But when my aunt came back and began an intensive cross-examination the main contention was how they learned in the first place that there were feathers in the house. My aunt reasoned that they could not have known unless they had been told; they were not fortune tellers. Each time I was asked, I would seal my lips as I did not want to betray my grandmother. Each time she was asked, she described them in detail, the holes in their clothes, the safety pins instead of buttons, their villainous looks, and then she mentioned the child, me, and hinted about the things they might have done and was it not the blessing of God that we had got rid of them peaceably! My aunt's son joked about the lace cloth for weeks. He used to affect to admire it, by picking up one end of the black oilcloth on the table and saying, 'Is it Brussels lace or is it Carrickmuckross?'

Sunday came and my mother was expected to visit. My aunt had washed me the night before in an aluminium pan. I had to sit into it, and was terrified lest my cousin should peep in. He was in the back kitchen shaving and whistling. It was a question of a 'Saturday splash or Sunday's dash'. My aunt poured a can of water over my head and down my back. It was scalding hot. Then she poured rainwater over me, and by contrast it was freezing. She was not a thorough washer like my mother, but all the time she kept saying that I would be like a new pin.

My mother was not expected until the afternoon. We had washed up the dinner things and given the dogs the potato skins and milk when I started in earnest to look out for her. I went to the gate where I had waited for Carnero and, seeing no sign of her, I sauntered off down the road. I was at the crossroads when I realised how dangerous it was, as I was approaching the spot where the tinkers said their caravan was pitched. So it was back at full speed. The fuchsia was out and so were the elderberries. The fuchsia was like dangling earrings and the riper elderberries were in maroon smidges on the road. I waited in hiding the better to surprise her. She never came. It was five, and then half past five, and then it was six. I would go back to the kitchen and lift the clock that was face down on the dresser and then hurry out to my watch-post. By seven it was certain that she would not come, although I still held out hope. They hated to see me sniffle and hated even more when I refused a slice of cake. I could not bear to eat. She would still come. They said there was no point in my being so spoilt. I was imprisoned at the kitchen table in front of this slice of seed cake. In my mind I lifted the gate hasp a thousand times, and saw my mother pass by the kitchen window, as fleeting as a ghost, and by the time we all knelt down to say the rosary my imagination had run amuck. I conceived of the worst things, such as she had died, or that my father had killed her, or that she had met a man and eloped. All three were unbearable. In bed I sobbed, and chewed on the blanket so as not to be heard, and between tears, and with my aunt enjoining me to dry up, I hatched a plan. On the morrow there was no word or no letter so I decided that I would have to run away. I packed a little satchel with bread, my comb, and daftly a spare pair of ankle-socks. I told my aunt that I was going on a picnic and affected to be very happy by humming and doing little reels.

It was a dry day and the dust rose in whirls under my feet. The dogs followed and I had immense trouble getting them to go back. There were no tinkers' caravans at the crossroads, and because of that I was jubilant. I walked and then ran, and then I would have to slow down, and always when I slowed down I looked back in case they were following me. While I was running I felt I could elude them, but there was no eluding the loose stones, and the bits of rock that were wedged into the dirt road. Twice I tripped. If, coming towards me, I saw two people together then I felt safe, but if I saw one person it boded ill, as that one person could be mad, or drunk, or ready to accost me. On three occasions I had to climb into a field and hide until that one ominous person went by. Fortunately it was a quiet road as not many souls lived in that region.

When I came off the dirt road on to the main road I felt safer, and very soon a man came by in a pony and trap and offered me a lift. He looked a harmless enough person, in a frieze coat and a cloth cap. When I stepped into the trap I was surprised to find two hens clucking and agitating under a seat.

'Would you be one of the Clearys?' he asked, referring to my grandmother's family.

I said no and gave an assumed name. He plied me with questions. To get the most out of me he even got the pony to slow down, so as to lengthen the journey. We dawdled. The seat of black leather was held down with black buttons. He had a tartan rug over him. He spread it out over us both. Quickly I edged out from under it complaining about heat and midges, neither of which there were. It was a desperately lonely road with only a house here and there, a graveyard, and sometimes an orchard. The apples looked tempting on the trees. To see each ripening apple was to see a miracle. He asked if I believed in ghosts and told me that he had seen the riderless horse, on the moors.

'If you're a Minnogue,' he said, 'you should be getting out here,' and he pulled on the reins.

I had called myself Mary Minnogue because I knew a girl of that name who lived with her mother and was separated from her father. I would have liked to be her.

'I'm not,' I said, and tried to be as innocent as possible. I then had to say who I was and ask if he would drop me in the village.

'I'm passing your gate,' he said, and I was terrified that I would have to ask him up as my mother dreaded strangers, even dreaded visitors, since these diversions usually gave my father the inclination to drink and once he drank he was on a drinking bout that would last for weeks and that was notorious. Therefore I had to conjure up another lie. It was that my parents were both staying with my grandmother and that I had been despatched home to get a change of clothing for us all. He grumbled at not coming up to our house but I jumped out of the trap and said we would ask him for a card party for sure.

There was no one at home. The door was locked and the big key in its customary place under the pantry window. The kitchen bore signs of her having gone out in a hurry as the dishes were on the table and on the table, too, was her powder-puff, a near-empty powder-box, and a papier-mâché holder in which her toiletries were kept. Had she gone to the city? My heart was wild with envy. Why had she gone without me? I called upstairs and then, hearing no reply, I went up with a mind that was buzzing with fear, rage, suspicion and envy. The beds were made. The rooms seemed vast and awesome compared with the little crammed rooms of my grandmother's. I heard someone in the kitchen and hurried down with renewed palpitations. It was my mother. She had been to the shop and got some chocolate. It was rationed because of its being war-time, but she used to coax the shopkeeper to give her some. He was a bachelor. He liked her. Maybe that was why she had put powder on.

'Who brought you home, my lady?' she said stiffly. She hadn't come on Sunday. I blurted that out. She said did anyone ever hear such nonsense. She said did I know that I was to stay there until the end of August till school began. She was even more irate when she heard that I had run away. What would they now be thinking, but that I was in a bog-hole or something. She said had I no consideration and how in heaven's name was she going to get word to them, an SOS?

'Where's my father?' I asked.

'Saving hay,' she said.

I gathered the cups off the table so as to make myself useful in her eyes. Seeing the state of my canvas shoes and the marks on the ankle-socks she asked had I come through a bog or what. All I wanted to know was why she had not come on Sunday since she had promised. The bicycle got punctured, she said, and then asked did I think that with bunions, corns and welts she would walk six miles after doing a day's work. All I thought was that the homecoming was not nearly as tender as I hoped it would be, and there was no embrace and no reunion. She filled the kettle and I laid clean cups. I tried to be civil, to contain the pique and the misery that were welling up in me. I told her how many trams of hay they had made in her mother's house, and she said it was a sight more than we had done. She hauled some scones from a colander in the cupboard and told me I had better eat. She did not heat them on the top of the oven and that meant she was not melting. But I knew that before nightfall she would. But where is the use of a thing that comes too late?

I sat at the far end of the table watching the lines on her brow, watching the puckering, as she wrote a letter to my aunt explaining that I had come home. I would have to give it to the mail-car man the following morning and ask the postman to deliver it by hand. She said, 'God only knows what commotion there would be all that day and into the night looking for me.' The ink in her pen gave out and I held the near-empty ink-bottle sideways while she refilled it.

'Go back to your place,' she said and I went back to the far end of the table like someone glued to her post. I thought of the fields around my grandmother's house and the various smooth stones that I had put on the windowsill. I thought of the sun garden, of the night my grandfather had died and my vigil in the cold parlour. I thought of many things. Sitting there I wanted both to be in our house and to be back in my grandmother's missing my mother. It was as if I could taste my pain better away from her, the excruciating pain that told me how much I loved her. In her company now all was in hazard. I thought how much I needed to be without her so that I could think of her, dwell on her, and fashion her into the perfect person that she clearly was not. I resolved that for certain I would grow up and one day go away. It was a sweet thought and it was packed with punishment.

Descent from Ararat

Christopher Burney

WHEN I returned to consciousness my head seemed quite clear but curiously empty, like a smoke-room freshly aired. My senses were functioning, and I could see and hear clearly, but the impressions they made were unusually distinct and direct, like raindrops falling on a window-pane instead of on grass. Their impact was not muffled by being absorbed into the sponge of memory, where they would be fused and muddled with all the other impressions of the years. I did not think I had lost my memory, only that it seemed to be isolated from the present. I seemed, on reflection, to know a great deal: that I was lying rather precariously on the side of a mountain, that a man was standing over me, that he was dressed in what I thought of as grey tweed and shod in what I knew to be shepherd's boots. But of myself, my name, my past, I could recall nothing – or, rather, *did* recall nothing, because I was not even moved to make the effort. I had escaped from my memory. If I had lost it, I could not have thought with words or understood the man when he spoke, and in this I had no difficulty. It was just that my memory was no longer about *me*.

I had been looking about me for a minute or two, though without moving, when the man spoke.

'We shall have to spend the night out here,' he said. 'I am pretty sure your ankle's not broken, but it's quite badly sprained, and I should never be able to get you down before nightfall.'

Involuntarily, I wriggled my feet and realised for the first time that, indeed, my left ankle was hurting badly.

'Even if I went down alone,' he went on, 'I couldn't get back with help till early morning. You were so careful not to be noticed this morning when you were coming up the valley that no one will think of sending a party out to look for you. And no one will miss me in the time. So we'd better make the best of it. It's going to rain, but there's a little cave I noticed on the way up. It's only about three hundred feet below us and we should be all right there for one night. I'll see you down in the morning.'

It was cold already. We were high up, on a narrow shelf about fifty feet from the top of a precipice which formed one face of the summit and dropped sheer below us for some hundreds of feet. In front of us lay a whole mountain kingdom of green and brown and grey and white; behind us, the summit which ruled it, and beyond that again, presumably, the valley to the lowlands.

I was preoccupied with relating this scene and, above all, the man's words to myself. I could see where I was plainly enough, and the name of the mountain or even the country had not enough importance to become a question. I could understand his plan, but only in the sense that I took it for granted that what he said was right and would happen. But when he spoke about following *me*, or about *my* having done this or that, I felt rather as one does towards old men who tell you stories of their childhood, to which you have no relevance at all. I said to myself in a distinctly formal way that I should say something back to him, but he appeared not to want me to speak.

'I might not have noticed you myself,' he went on, sitting down beside me, 'but something about you told me that you were going to kill yourself. I suppose I recognised it instinctively, because, after all, I couldn't really know anything about you. Anyway, I followed you.

'I kept well behind you, as far as I could, until you were nearly on the top. I don't know whether it was out of respect for your privacy, or out of curiosity, or because I thought that if you felt like that it would be better for you in the long run actually to see the brink. I didn't let you out of sight, though. Sometimes you went very fast, as if you were determined to get there at all costs, pushing yourself along, and at others you seemed almost to stop, as if you had driven yourself beyond the limits. It was difficult not to run into you on the corners when you did that. But when you got to the top there I wished I had stopped you earlier. I didn't know what to do. I was terrified that if you saw me or if I shouted to you you might throw yourself over in sheer panic. Then I saw this shelf underneath you, so I crawled out on to it and shouted for help.'

This stirred memory of a sort in me. I could picture the cliff-top and a call for help and the body of a man lying just below. But it seemed to me that the body was mine. Of course, it was mine at this moment, but I could not remember getting there. I paid careful but disinterested attention to what the man said as he went on.

'I thought that if you saw me here it might shock you out of whatever you were thinking about. Perhaps you would instinct-ively go to help someone in distress, but more likely I thought that you would feel, so to speak, ridiculed if you found that someone else had apparently done what you intended to do and had only ended up squealing for help. Bathos is a great help to realism. Anyway, you came. You slipped and fell just as you got here and that's what sprained your ankle. Then you passed out. We've been here nearly two hours, but I couldn't possibly have got you off here alone.'

It is a very curious sensation to have someone describe the actions of someone else to you as if he were talking about you. There was no possible connection in my mind between a person who had recently wanted to throw himself off the cliff and me. All I could see was that I was indeed here with a bad ankle. I looked over the edge to where, far below, the precipice eased off into a slope of scree, and quickly drew back so that I pressed against the rock behind me. I had never liked steep drops, I knew, and the thought of willingly looking, let alone launching myself, over this one was empty and cold and impossible. At the bottom of the scree there was a dark place where the light did not reach, and as I glimpsed it my brain seemed to become like it, black and empty.

At last I managed to speak, but even my voice came out strangely and I could not positively say it was my own.

'I'm afraid I've lost my memory,' I said, and could manage no more.

'Good Heavens!' he said. 'Don't worry about that. You're not concussed, since you didn't hit your head on anything, so you've just stopped remembering about yourself. Probably it had become too unpleasant. Brains are very efficient and on the whole co-operative. So don't be in too much of a hurry to start remembering again. I rather envy you.'

'But you tell me that I was going to commit suicide. You even seem absolutely sure of it. But it doesn't mean anything to me at all. I can't even bear the thought of falling over the edge. But since I can't remember even coming here I can't say it's not true, either.'

It was curious talking like this, hunched up on a ledge so narrow that we hardly dared turn to look at each other.

'You must not worry about me,' he said. 'After I leave you in the morning we are not likely to meet again, and I am not in the least curious about what brought you up here. I know you aren't a maniac, because if you had been you would not have paused when you got to the top of the precipice. You wouldn't even have heard me call. I should have been sorry about that, but there would have been nothing I could do.

'Were you trying to make a gesture? No, I don't think so. People who do that choose public places as a rule. They are not really trying to commit suicide. They dramatise themselves and their misfortunes and, so to speak, write one scene too many. I think they hope that a rescuer will appear in it and then all their injustices will be recognised and they can have a new life in which they will be appreciated and cherished. But the rescuer doesn't always come along. Poor people! When they die, as they so often do, we should call it accidental death rather than suicide. After all, the word is used terribly loosely. All sorts of perfectly happy people, especially in war, are said to do something *suicidal*, when all they've done is to sacrifice their own lives in order to save other people's. Captain Oates wasn't lost or bewildered or unhappy. He wasn't trying to solve any internal problem of his own by going off into the blizzard. He was simply making it possible for his friends to survive when he knew that he hadn't much chance anyway.'

He paused for quite a long time and, although I could not see his face, I felt he was frowning in reflection. Eventually he went on:

'Ordinary lunatics sometimes kill themselves, too, but I think that's mostly by accident. You stay sane as long as your brain makes something comprehensible out of what it takes in. If it tried to deal with everything it would make nonsense of it, so it has its own built-in system with which it either rejects what it can't make out or simply waves it aside, as it were, and invents an excuse for things being as they are. You'd be surprised, if you thought about it, how much so-called philosophy is really inventing plausible excuses.

'In a way, your brain behaves like your ears. When the noise gets too bad, then you go mad by degrees. The safety-valves go wrong and the whole system blows up. I think a lot of what we call lunatics are people whose logical system has changed so as to make the intake of information tolerable. Maybe it will go so haywire that you'll think a lake is a cup of tea, and then you'll drown, but surely that must be an accident rather than deliberate self-destruction.'

'So you don't think I'm mad, either?' I asked.

'No,' he said, 'I'd be very surprised if you were.'

'Then why do you feel so sure I was going to commit suicide? I'll grant you it may be looked on as an accident in a lot of cases, but if you exclude maniacs and self-dramatists and plain lunatics what's left?'

'I'll tell you in a moment,' he said, 'but I think we ought to move to our cave. It will be easier to talk and we must make sure of getting to it while the sun is still up. The first few yards are going to be difficult, but if you give me your left hand and let me go first we ought to be all right. But try not to let your bad foot give way or we'll not be able to discuss anything any more.'

He stood up carefully and I did the same, only more carefully, feeling up the rock-face with my fingers. We had to face to our left, which made my right foot, the one on which I had to put my weight, the one nearest the edge. I tried and retried it before I straightened the leg, afraid that the edge would crumble. And I made my neck almost stiff by concentrating on looking upward.

I stumbled where the shelf petered out to a bare foothold, just before it reached the shoulder which marked the end of the precipice. I tried to regain my balance with my right foot, but there was no room for it, and I felt my arm jerked almost out of my shoulder as my guide, who was himself still a good yard from safety, gripped my wrist and threw himself forward. For a fraction of a second I was in mid-air and felt all the blood leave my head, but then my sprained ankle gave in to necessity and took hold again, and with a final heave we found ourselves lying on the comparatively easy slope.

He said nothing, but watched me carefully as I got to my feet again, and we went slowly across and down the slope until we came to a little hollow under an overhang. 'Cave' seemed to me a big word for what we had, which was little more than an eyrie sheltered from above, scarcely deeper than a saucer and with only a few small rocks to keep off the wind which had now risen considerably and was scouring the mountain-side. He arranged these as best he could and we sat in their small lee.

I watched him as he arranged himself into a hump, so that he exposed the least possible surface to the wind, but what I saw told me almost nothing. Physically, apart from his obvious hardiness, he was indeterminate. As to age, height, build I have been unable to manufacture a description which satisfies me. They were all middling, but there was nothing middling or indeed on any scale about the total. Simplicity seemed to have been carried so far in everything about him, in dress and voice and movement, as to defy the complications of comparison. He looked at me simply, too, neither kindly nor with authority, neither shyly nor keenly, making me an object of regard rather than of inspection.

'I wonder why we regard lunatics with such horror,' he said, 'as if they were some sort of living dead. I can't think we're right. Max Picard, who was a Swiss of all surprising things, said that they were a legitimate part of the human race and that there was never so much madness in the world as when Hitler put them all to death. It's not exactly logical, but I'm sure he was right. They look miserable to us because we put ourselves in their place and think how terrible we would feel if we were like them. But we're *not* like them, so how can we tell? Some of them may be unhappy, but we can't know enough about them to be able to judge the value of their lives to themselves. Mostly I think we are worried by the implication that our wonderful brains are not as absolutely infallible as we would like to think.'

'But still', I said a little impatiently, 'you haven't told me why you think I was going to commit suicide. I still can think of no reason myself.'

'There wouldn't be a reason,' he replied, 'at least not a direct one. One of the mistakes people make is to regard suicide as a logical solution to a problem. You worry about your health or your job or your moral bankruptcy, whatever it is, and you say, "Suicide is the only answer", as if you were an adulterous ensign. But this isn't logical or rational. It's merely traditional. It's a word commonly thought of as a solution. If a child has to write an equation and can't work out the second half, he is apt to put " = o" because he knows a lot of equations do end like that. It has a conventional look, and so does an overdose of sleeping-pills, but neither is more logical than putting out your eyes to stop reading Dickens.'

He bent his forehead forward to rest on his knees, then looked up again as if he were trying to come to a conclusion. Finally he said:

'I know what went wrong with you, but I don't know whether I can explain it to you. Let me try putting it this way.

'People not only have to be able to account for their surroundings and all the things that happen to them; they also have to be able to account for themselves. I don't mean they have to be self-conscious: on the contrary, self-consciousness is an inverted anxiety about outside things. But, apart from being this or that in relation to everything else, one is also just oneself, or, rather, one just *is*. You're not aware of it very often – at least, most people aren't – but it's nevertheless true, and also fairly obvious if you think of it. When we were crossing that last bit of the shelf just now I knew that if either of us slipped we'd be likely to go all the way, and I thought that if I saw you lying there dead it would mean a great many things to me – what to do, what to feel and so forth – but if I imagined myself instead it meant exactly nothing at all. "Me dead" in my own mind is an irrational phrase and can only make sense if I bring you or somebody else into it, like "When I'm dead don't bury me alone". Do you follow me so far?'

'Yes,' I said, 'but I'm not sure where we're going.'

'All right,' he continued, 'if there were a third person here I could point to you and say, "He is alive, human, male, presumably mortal", and so forth and this would make sense between us. But if I say to you "I am" it doesn't mean any more to you than if I said "Ooh" or "Ah". It's just an expletive, and yet it is true for me, and if you think a little you'll see that it's true for you, too.'

'Do you mean the fact that all the bits and pieces that make up the me that you know happen to be put together in this one particular whole?'

'No,' he replied, 'that's a good individualistic thought, but it's not the same as the simple fact that you are aware you are. It's knowledge, but it's entirely private and irrational. But to get on with the point: when a person's awareness of his own being is put in doubt he is in a much worse position than one who finds outside things too much for him, because there is no possible defence mechanism. And if the doubt goes on too long, then, as I say, he can no longer account for himself. He gets privately lost, and because he no longer has any reason to avoid danger or silly ideas he may easily kill himself. In a way this, too, is accidental, even though it looks planned, but it's different from the other cases because in fact he always destroys the last remnant of his own being before he actually dies. He denies himself.'

He laughed gently.

'I've never tried to put this into words before,' he said, 'and trying to communicate what is essentially irrational is extremely difficult, but I think that's the nearest I can get to it. I think that for some reason your hold on your own being had been weakened and you were not far short of saying "Oh well, that's done for", but unconsciously. This odd loss of memory about yourself bears me out. You haven't forgotten things outside yourself.'

He stretched his legs and then stiffly got to his feet.

'Before the sun goes', he said, 'I think I will see if I can find some heather or bracken. There should be some about a thousand feet down, and we are going to be very cold like this. But if I don't find any in about twenty minutes I'll come back. I can't afford to miss the way, and it will get dark fairly quickly to-night.'

He stepped over the rocks and disappeared round the shoulder of the mountain.

Our eyrie faced about west. The wind seemed to be coming from there, though it was difficult to be sure because it broke up on the mountain face and went blustering round the rock until it could find its proper way again. Clouds were piling up over towards where I was facing, high cumulus far off, dark at the base and furred with wisps of white above, and closer at hand rippled blankets of grey creeping forward between the hills and mountains lower down. The sun was setting, not in glory but in bright defiance, driving yellow shafts through every gap between the clouds. Somewhere far beyond the storm it would soon be violet, red, and peaceful, telling the shepherds they could sleep at ease; but we were to watch the night warily.

'I am,' I said tentatively as I gazed. 'I am . . . I am. . . .'

At first I knew what I was saying, repeating the sounds consciously as an experiment, like a baby toying with a new name. But soon I became aware that I was, and stopped saying anything. I just was. The hills and the clouds and the frustrated sun were no longer steep or grey or bright; they were a moving quietness, and what was quiet was me.

At last a flare of sunlight pierced low through the cloud and lit up, as it were in a frame, a small green patch far, far below me and away, with three white cottages and a dark line like a stream. People, I thought, and was half aware that the word was a disturbance, but the peace was undisturbed. Some other memory struggled for a hearing, but the sun was gone for ever before I could recall it:

> And did the Countenance Divine
> Shine forth upon our clouded hills?
> And was Jerusalem builded here . . .?

The spell went as the words came. Everything was darkening again in the west, and the cottages were invisible. I tried to recapture that sudden glimpse but could do no more than reaffirm that the lines I had remembered, surely out of a disused drawer, exactly conveyed it. Even they could not bring it back to life.

It was nearly night when he came back and put a clump of heather and bracken down beside me. He was a little out of breath.

'We want to get some of the heather under us,' he said, 'to keep us off the rock itself, and then we can use the rest for covering. It's not much, but it's better than nothing. I had to go further for it than I had expected. Have you been all right?'

We both set about making our beds and adding to the wind-break.

'Yes,' I said, 'I've been trying to see what you meant about being. I said "I am" a few times, and after a while I found that I was. But I've still no idea *who* I am.'

'Good Heavens!' he said, almost impatiently. 'What on earth do you want to know that for? *I'm* not interested. You'll spoil the whole thing if you go on worrying about second-hand things like that. It's for other people to fuss about what they call you and how they label and identify you. The only important thing for you is to be absolutely sure that you are. Don't even try to see yourself *as* anything. Just be.'

It was almost as if he were trying to save me from electrocuting myself, calling urgently, 'Don't touch it!' Then he relaxed and looked at me more mildly.

'Your memory will come back sooner or later, quite suddenly. Then you'll remember who you are and what role you have played in the world, that you can only recall now without yourself in it. But this doesn't matter. Whatever happened it obviously went wrong, and I hope that when it does come back it will be like a flat map and not real country, something you can recognise but not feel. Then, if only you can get some protection from the sort of attack that beat you last time, you'll be able to start again fresh and really live. But you haven't much time. You might remember tonight or tomorrow or any time.'

He chuckled.

'Come to think of it, a mountain isn't a bad place for making fresh starts. If we're to believe the story about Noah — and why shouldn't we? — the whole of life had to begin again from the top of Mount Ararat. It's a better story than the Greek one of Deucalion on Parnassus, which isn't much of a mountain. But think of Noah, six hundred and one years old and sitting eighteen thousand feet up on Ararat in charge of everything. He must have felt pretty strange, in spite of the promise he had from God. Once he got down everything was in good order again. Not perfect, because that was a word which hadn't been invented yet, but manageable — which, for some reason we're not told, it hadn't been before. And it still is manageable as long as you take it slowly and don't make mysteries where there are none. Anyway, Noah was so pleased with it that he planted a vineyard as quick as he could and got drunk. You'll be able to do the same with a clear conscience. You can do what you like once the anarchy has left your mind.'

That's as maybe, I thought, but the fact was that I had only been listening to him with half an ear. I had been wondering how to describe the scene of the sun shining on the cottages, the impression of which was still with me. Rather lamely I said:

'After you had gone for the heather there was a most extraordinary scene. The very last ray of sun hit a little group of cottages over there' — I pointed uselessly in the dark — 'and for some reason it put me in mind of Blake's 'Jerusalem'. It was just as if a spot-light had picked out that one little place for special attention. My memory really must be quite good if I can remember poetry.'

He was quite still for a moment, but I thought I heard him draw in his breath sharply. Then he said:

'I suspect Blake had something rather larger in mind than a cottage or two, but I suppose one never knows. Blake had a remarkable ability to make up unreal pictures that nevertheless rang true. Being and creation are like the opposite sides of the same coin, and poets have this gift of being able to turn the coin over a little so that they can get a glimpse at the other side. To some extent we are all poets if we try to be. We can, so to speak, disembody what we see, just as we can disembody ourselves for fractions of a second. But the real poet has the ability to take away his glimpses and re-embody them so that other people can see them, too.'

'But doesn't that apply to all artists?' I asked.

'I suppose so. But I like the word "poet" better. It has a more generous sound and it has been less damaged by abuse. Also I like to think of it in Greek, in its original sense. To them the poet was just the "maker", and their delicate minds stopped them from making him the maker of this or that. He wasn't limited or defined, like a cobbler or an actor, he was the purest kind of maker, composing harmonies of words which reminded them of the beauties they fleetingly descried but never tamed. He moulded the quicksilver of splendour into songs they could sing. It just happened that the Greeks were better at words than anything else, despite their being the best sculptors. But it doesn't matter what medium you use if you can capture beauty.' I heard him chuckle in the dark. 'What a thing it is! We all look for it like children look for the rainbow's end. It's useless, elusive, valueless, meaningless, and when we find it we're apt to treat it like a forbidden pet mouse and stuff it down into the corner of our minds. But we have to keep after it. Even poets can't capture it, but they snatch threads as it passes and use them to remind us.'

I said that I thought I saw what he meant, but he went on as if he had not heard me.

'Yes, these meaningless words, "being", "beauty", "poetry", are all very close to each other. Where one is the others are sure to be. We were talking about the vulnerability of people's being. How do they become disintegrated? Abstraction, guilt, brutality. I think those are the right words.

' "Brutality" is fairly obvious. I don't mean cruelty or barbarity, but absolute insensitivity, which, oddly enough, seems to be a mark of high rather than low intelligence. Very simple people make up for their ignorance by a certain amount of what we call intuition; and they are intellectually humble, which really means that they leave what they don't understand to chance. Chance is very wise. They may be crude, but they're not often vicious. Jackals are always supposed to be very inferior animals, but in fact they only scrape their livelihood as best they can. But take the fox, who has been living next to civilisation. He really is vicious. He kills for fun. Compare the Germans and the Dyaks, and I only use the Germans as an obvious example. This is a difficult championship to judge.'

Another long pause, and then:

'I shall have to take all that back, or most of it, to make my real point. Brutality is in fact only a form of abstraction, and as a matter of fact guilt is only one of its results. Do you remember anything about the war?'

I thought for a moment and then replied:

'Yes, but rather in the same way as I remember anything else. I can remember a lot of scenes and facts, but without myself being anywhere in them. I can remember London being bombed in September 1940, and Bayeux, and a place where there were a lot of Germans and cows all caught in the same enfilade from a naval pom-pom, and, I suppose, a lot of other things. But I'm always hidden somewhere behind the viewfinder. It's really as if I'd read about it, except that I have a feeling I was there.'

'You remember the mass raids on Germany?'

'Yes, but not at first hand. Not even behind the viewfinder.'

'Well, think of this. If you were a bomber pilot, you went over and dropped your bombs, and you didn't think you were dropping them on marshalling-yards. As far as you were concerned this was the enemy and this was the best way of stopping him fighting. Look at the "the enemy" and the "him". If you thought about it afterwards, you might think that you, personally, had killed perhaps a thousand or more individual people, none of whom you could have identified as the enemy. You just wiped them out *en masse*. The same applies to the Germans who did the Coventry and Exeter raids. Now, I think that if you could go off and kill all those people at a distance, not knowing who they were and just thinking of them as "the enemy", you were being abstract. You were disposing of them as if they had no personal existence, and in fact whether you killed them or not was almost irrelevant.'

'But how can you wage war if people don't do that?' I asked. 'And surely a defensive war is justified?'

'You miss my point,' he said. 'I wish war didn't happen, at least on that scale. What I want you to see is that the pilot who said to himself: "I know there are a lot of miserable people who are going to suffer, and I hate to do it, but we've got to win and this is how we're told to do it" — that pilot is perhaps to be pitied because he has tried to recognise his victims. Certainly as a man he has nothing to blame himself for. But anyone who can say "This is war, and they're the enemy" deserves a quick death himself. He doesn't want to admit that people are people.'

I must have made some sound of incipient protest, because he immediately went on:

'No, don't think I'm a pacifist. I might be an objector, but in fact I have never seen a satisfactory answer to this particular problem. Not a general one, anyway. Take the other side of the picture. After the war it was popular to think that the Russians were a particularly nice people. They had done this and that on the credit side and therefore they were to be looked on as specifically nice. And this, if you know anything at all about Russia, is patent nonsense.

'Nowadays it's fashionable to be called a humanist, which as often as not means giving yourself an aura of virtue by affecting to love everyone. Generally it involves making pious statements about people of whom you know nothing at all. In any case, I think impersonal treatment of people, whether for good or for bad, is a dangerous abstraction. It's conceited and condescending. In war you should at least see the whites of their eyes, and in other times you should start your charity at home. You won't have enough of it to go far afield.'

The clouds I had been watching earlier in the distance had moved up to us, and the wind blew a sudden squall of rain which quite ignored the barriers which my companion had thought worthy the name of cave. We both flinched a little from it.

'We won't be able to do much more talking tonight,' he said, 'but to stop you getting the wrong impression from what I've been saying let me say this. I don't believe I am advocating any form of selfishness when I say that the most important thing is your own being. I do believe that "Thou shalt love thy neighbour as thyself", but I think this means that you have to start by loving yourself — valuing is perhaps better.'

The squall became an unremitting storm. Heather, bracken, wool and skin yielded successively before it, and in a brief lull after the first deep soaking my companion said:

'Face inwards and keep your back rounded, but if you have to move make sure I'm awake first, otherwise I might forget where I am and fall off. If you get very cold, try to think about your heart and all the warm blood pumping through it. Or try to think of nothing at all.'

For a while I lay curled up in a ball watching the storm envelop us through the back of my head. I wriggled so that my clothes stood a little away from my skin in as many places as possible and said to myself, 'Ha, ha, it's pouring down but it won't get through.' And for a while it didn't get through but made my clothes feel warm and steamy like a hot towel such as barbers put very lightly round your face before they shave you. But I had been cold from the beginning. Lying out on the shelf in the afternoon had chilled me and I had done nothing since hard enough to restore my circulation. So the towel grew clammy and I had to shrink my skin further and further inwards to keep it clear. The wind dropped for a moment, and I felt a light pressure on the back of my neck.

'Wet wool is wind-proof,' said my companion, and as the rain came lashing in again I felt extraordinarily comforted.

But the comfort faded as the weather grew worse and worse. There must have been rank upon rank of those high grey clouds. I pictured them following each other smoothly across the sea and land, tall and frowning and wide about the hips like a procession of ill-tempered Queens from Wonderland shuffling toe to heel around the world. But I felt quite friendly towards them and did not blame them for my being cold.

Thinking about your heart really is quite effective if you can concentrate on it. You see a great red bellows pumping safely away at a temperature of 98.4 degrees Fahrenheit and after a while there are moments when you think you are looking into a fire-box. But it is difficult to concentrate for long.

I also tried to think about what my companion had been saying. At the time I had thought he was probably right, though it needed some reflection, but I found that I could not piece it all together again. I thought I had seen what he meant when he used the word "being", and the notion that beauty was useless gave me a little thrill of pleasure, but I could not reconstruct more and eventually I fell asleep.

Although the cold and rain constantly woke me and made me try to wriggle myself free of my sodden clothes and to keep still at all costs and not shiver, I was hardly aware of having been conscious for much of the night when my companion nudged me. The wind had dropped and changed, and our side of the mountain was nearly still. The first light had just managed to prevail over the storm-laden eastern sky, and I could make out that rain was still falling. But our overhang was protecting us now that we had survived without it. It would not have been possible to be wetter if we had been pulled out of a river, and for the first time I felt extremely hungry.

'We'd better start as soon as we can see where we're going,' he said. 'That'll be in about twenty minutes, I hope. Take your boots and stockings right off and I'll try and rub some circulation back into your legs. You can do mine. If we don't, we'll fall at the first bad foot-hold. How's your ankle?'

I felt it. I had loosened the laces of my boots before we settled down and my stockings had been soaked right through, and this seemed to have had the effect of a cold compress, because although the ankle was still sore it was not nearly as swollen as it had been. I told him it seemed to be better.

'Good,' he said as he finished taking off his own boots. 'It's going to be an interesting journey for you, and it would be a pity if it were spoilt by having to think about a mere ankle. Pain is useful enough as a reminder or a warning, but it's an awful nuisance as a distraction. Have you remembered who you are yet?'

'No,' I said, 'I haven't really thought about it any more.'

I suddenly realised that, indeed, I hadn't even wondered.

'Good again,' he said. 'I told you already your memory would come back all too soon.'

'It's odd', I said, 'to have a part of you that goes on and off work when it chooses.'

'No more odd that your memory should do that than the rest of your brain when you go to sleep. Or for that matter a muscle that's over-tired.'

'I suppose it's subconscious.'

'If you like. You're not aware of it at the time, so I suppose it's true to say it's subconscious. But don't for pity's sake imagine that there's some sort of independent force in you called *the* Subconscious. For that matter, it's also involuntary, but that doesn't mean there's a piece of you called your Will that actually decides to do things. There are just varying degrees and patterns of consciousness. All these mystical nouns made by putting a definite article in front of an adjective or a verb and imagining that that necessarily creates a Thing are the most dangerous form of abstraction. Learn to be content that you are; that is the first truth. Remind yourself always that the intangibles that you perceive when you are most conscious of being are the first realities. God, wonder, beauty, love, generosity — a mixed bag, but that's the fault of the language they are put into. They are still the elements of life. Everything else can be coped with more or less mechanically through your nervous system, and you can be sure of that to the extent that you can be sure of the system. But it's just as difficult to be as sure of it as of being. Shun the abstract bogeys like the plague. Good, Evil, Perfection, Sin and all the rest. They're the only excuse I know for believing in devils.'

'But surely', I said, 'conversation would be difficult without them?'

'Oh, yes,' he replied calmly, 'conversation certainly would be difficult, and I have no objection to people inventing all the words they need. All the fun in talking and speculation comes from seeing whether you can fit words in to fill gaps in your knowledge. But people get into bad habits. They turn words into things; they pretend they're sticks and beat people with them; and when a word has acquired enough status it actually has the power to hurt.

'A long time ago someone looked at a volcano and said, "Because fire is coming out of that mountain there must be something inside." Someone else then said, "The thing inside is called a dragon", and everyone agreed that this was a delightful way of filling the unknown. So now the English revere a Thracian who killed some dragon that had presumably grown tired of its mountain, while millions of others are geninely terrified by a creature that doesn't exist.'

He laughed.

'Still,' he went on, 'dragons are almost beneficent compared with the really miasmic words. Good and Evil are my pet aversions because so many of the others stem from them. Originally, people said things were good when they pleased them and bad when they didn't. It was a matter of individual taste. The fact that some things called pain displease nearly everyone doesn't make *a thing* of pain. If there is some substance called the Good in chocolate, which pleases a lot of people, why doesn't it please everyone? If you agree that God is good, how can there be an opposite, and what can any of those millions of people down there tell us about God or Good? Has someone poked his head down the volcano and pulled out a dragon? Give me a poet any day, who can put me in mind of God and beauty without trying to persuade me of a lot of abstract horrors.

'Come on. We'd better be on our way. It will take us quite a while to get down.'

As we were getting to our feet I asked him:

'But isn't "beauty" an abstract word?'

'Technically, I suppose it is,' he replied, 'but in fact it's really another expletive. It doesn't have much of a dictionary meaning that tells you anything about it. Men are all pretty alike, you know, and over the ages a good deal of our conversation has been devoted to trying to share our intangible enjoyments. So a few words have crept in among the practical ones which are simply our best attempt at expressing the inexpressible. But they've been badly battered by those who think Man lives by words alone provided they have meanings.'

We started slowly along a sheep-track that followed the contour, barely three hundred feet below the summit, which now appeared at intervals through rifts in the cloud. I realised that the things he was saying were still largely escaping me. The words were all right; I could understand them well enough; but I found it difficult to keep continuity, so that the whole somewhat resembled a melody played staccato very slowly. It was difficult to remember the beginning by the time I had got to the end. In the ordinary way, talk of this kind impinges on thousands of wishes, needs, prejudices and habits of thought which have been collected as by-products of things suffered and enjoyed, of questions asked and answered. There is a further layer of vicarious or generalised knowledge, but on the whole new ideas must pass through the test of what is directly known. A word like 'sin' is first referred to actual guilts and accusations; 'good' is referred to an immediately recent pleasure. But I had nothing of my own to refer to. I knew what he was talking about in that I knew the meanings of the sentences, but I could not connect them with my own experience and they therefore failed to hold my attention. Moral philosophy hardly takes root where fear is absent and the conscience clear. Mine was empty, which came to the same thing.

We had gone barely a hundred yards when I realised that he had been right in forecasting slow progress. Already my ankle had started to swell again, and I asked him to stop so that I could loosen the laces. He sat down beside me as if we had all day for our descent — which, indeed, I supposed we had.

'You remember the story of the Garden of Eden?' he asked me.

'Yes.'

'And the famous tree?'

'Yes.'

'Can you explain to me why people always seem to think that it was the tree of good and evil, when it was actually the tree of the *knowledge* of good and evil?'

'I don't remember ever having thought much about it. Surely it's one of those fables that one's taught when young and then forgets.'

'Oh, I think it's probably a fable all right, though it's difficult to be dogmatic at such a distance. Giving two different accounts of the Creation doesn't inspire one to take either literally. But so much has been made of that tree. We are supposed because of it to believe that an absolute power of evil exists, which has led to the Devil and Hell and all the other paraphernalia that have been used for burning witches and intimidating and blackmailing the young and the ignorant. But I like to suppose that it meant roughly what it said: that when people start *knowing about* Good and Evil instead of saying that this or that for them is good or evil, then they are cut off from the tree of life, which is what happened to Adam. I think it was a warning against being dogmatic about ultimate values, and particularly against judging people as if one were God.'

'But surely', I ventured, 'you are going against rather a long and respectable line of thought, aren't you?'

'I'm afraid so,' he answered equably, 'but I'm not the first and, anyway, lineage is not always the best criterion. As for respectability, the Devil has been believed in by some people in the best of faith, but he's also been used for the nastiest crimes. Tyrants have always liked to have theological backing, and a lot of them have become tyrants by being too fanatical about some dogma. Believe me, philosophers and theologians have been among the greatest enemies of truth because they so often try to get too far in order simply to be right. It is difficult to be pure in heart if you have a lot of dogmatic axes to grind.'

The cloud was gradually lifting and, although from time to time a low-hanging wisp would blot us out from the world below, we could watch the weak light gradually creep down the hills opposite until they were all grey and the valleys black chasms running through them. A little life was astir, too, which I had not seen in the evening. Some wild duck flew fast to the west to some water I could not see; a pair of swans went past so far below us that we could hardly see them, but making with their wings the first live noise we had heard other than our voices; a pair of hooded crows alighted wickedly on the hillside opposite. I did not feel quite the tranquillity of the previous evening, when the world had been withdrawing against the rainy night, but a warmth like love, and a wondering expectancy such as one has on opening a well-packed parcel. Look at it all, I said to myself; and here I am. Where can I begin? And because I could not take my eyes off it I suffered more than I need have done as we walked the next stretch.

When we sat down again my companion said:

'I'm a bit warmer now. I hope you are, too. Have you realised what an extraordinary day you're starting?'

'No,' I said, 'I hadn't thought about it.'

He looked at me quizzically.

'Well, do so,' he said with a laugh, 'or you'll miss a very rare experience.'

'I suppose it is going to be a bit strange getting down among people again and not having the remotest idea who I am or who I know or where I live. But up here it doesn't seem to matter too much.'

'Nor does it matter, but that's not the point I have in mind. I expect a great many people recover a lost memory every day. There's nothing very unusual in that. You've done something quite different. Yesterday you were in despair, you were lost. You probably hadn't decided to do away with yourself, but you'd been done away with. We don't know how, but that doesn't matter. But today, lost memory and all, you look at the world you'd given up as if it was your most precious possession. And that after as wet a night as I've ever experienced.'

'But', I said, suddenly feeling hollow in my diaphragm, 'when my memory comes back – and you say it will – presumably all the things which you say drove me to suicide will come back again. So I might as well turn right round now.'

I felt as I said it that the last sentence was stupid and even in rather bad taste, but he seemed to ignore it. At least there was no trace of displeasure in his voice when he replied; rather, it seemed as if his eagerness was mounting.

'No,' he said, 'I don't think that is likely to happen. You have to see yourself like a citadel besieged by demons. Demons aren't true, but all the bad intelligence you have been given leads you to think they are. In the end you get to the point where you will blow yourself up rather than surrender alive to the horrors which you can now practically see outside your walls. Do you follow me?'

I nodded, although he was not looking at me.

'Well, I believe that this night out on the mountain will have shown you that demons aren't true, and, if that's so, there's nothing to worry about. That's what made me think of Noah last night. But he had to wait a hundred and ninety days while the world was washed and rinsed and dried out again so that it was fit to live in. You've only had to wait a night.'

'What makes you so sure that my demons aren't real?'

'Because they only exist in your brain. They are the way you have learned to look at things, the associations you have built up and had built up for you. You know white is white, but if you are told too often and too compellingly that it's black you'll end up with your brain reacting to it as if it *was* black. You will abdicate. People call this brain-washing nowadays, because a certain form of it has been popularised, but in a subtler way it goes on the whole time. People try to persuade you that this or that is right or wrong, or that such and such is true or false. Generally it's harmless enough, but very often the reason behind it is this terrible insufficiency that drives people to boss each other about. It's to my mind a worse form of outrage than straightforward killing.'

'It would be a bit difficult to teach anyone anything at all if one were to take you literally. Someone has to do some telling.'

'I agree it's difficult to know where to draw the line, but I think there is a good test. Does the persuader hold his victim in contempt or not? Does he despise him, does he think him inferior, or even that he has no right to exist? Does he even know he exists? Of course it by no means goes without saying that he's bound to succeed. Some people have such a strong foundation in their own being that they can resist. But it doesn't alter the offence.

'I've often wondered how it came about that nearly all the poets in Russia committed suicide sooner or later after the Revolution. Pasternak was the chief exception, but he must have been an exceptionally strong character and a few centuries of the ghetto breed toughness. Most of them were more or less on the side of the Revolution, and if its savagery shocked them its hardship was not likely to do so. Even the stupidity of all the big and little tyrants who sprang up was hardly a cause for suicide. And yet they did it.

'Remember they were poets, some of them even good ones. They woke up to the fact that the new czars were Marxists and that for Marxists people have the same kind of value as cows. They're economic units. Personal units are dangerous, and poets are contemptible and subversive. All this is the opposite to what they have thought. But in course of time, if you live in a really well-run tyranny like that, you begin to have doubts about yourself. Because you can't say what you think, your power to think gets rusty. And the more the material success and the torrents of words overwhelm you the more your little self becomes weakened, until at last it turns at bay and puts an end to its own integrity.'

He kicked angrily at a small rock.

'Why did the Russians of all people get caught by Marxism?'

he asked. 'They used to have more poetic sense than most, and they had that eccentricity which is always a sign that persons are conceded to be persons. If I was taken back sixty years or so and asked to prophesy who would be Christian and who Marxist, I should have said that the Russians would be Christian, the English, Swedes and Swiss Marxist and the Americans half and half. Perhaps I'm only wrong on my timing after all. Certainly the sombre pharisaical certainties of Marx and Lenin seem to be better suited to industrialists and bankers and the humble liberalities of Jesus to the prodigals who made Russian literature. It's one of history's perversities. '

With that he stood up again and made off downhill with me stumbling in his wake. I had still hardly looked at his face, and even now I think of him in terms of his back view if I try to visualise him. For that matter, he hardly looked at me, staring at his toes or off into the distance most of the time and only suddenly turning to me if he had a new idea or if he wanted to emphasise something. And then he looked at me quite without curiosity, as if he had known me all my life. At one point I even found myself wondering whether he was an old friend, but from the way he talked this seemed impossible, and so he remained for me an indeterminate man seen from the back, dressed in indeterminate tweed made even more so by its wetness.

We had gone perhaps another five hundred yards, and I was beginning to feel that I had done as much as I could, when a hanging cloud enveloped us and my companion called a halt.

'It's not worth missing the easy way,' he said. 'You wouldn't thank me if we had to go further than we need, and still less if we started having to walk like goats.'

'You may think it funny,' I said, 'but it hadn't occurred to me to thank you. I suppose it should, but it didn't. But you can be sure I shan't blame you.'

'That's good,' he said cheerfully. 'Blaming is only a way of making oneself feel better by making someone else feel worse. But people are always doing it.'

'Wouldn't you blame me if I tried to kill you?' I asked.

'What a question!' he laughed. 'But I don't think I would. I'd try to stop you, and I might even think it was necessary for you to be locked up so that you couldn't try again. But I wouldn't blame you in the sense of making a definitive and unfavourable judgement on your entire person. I already think you are wrong in one respect: you are trying to use a purely hypothetical situation in order to form a principle. At least, I hope it's hypothetical.'

'Oh, I think I'm safe enough,' I said, though I thought to myself that perhaps I wasn't if the truth were known. 'But I don't follow you.'

'People who are always imagining situations tend to look for abstract principles. They come out with statements like "Anyone who can do that ought to be shot", or they read cases in the paper and form judgements which are not their business. They even kill on principle. I can understand someone committing murder out of temper or exasperation or in self-defence, but I could never sit on a jury and sentence a man to death simply because the principle of the law says so. The smugness of juries is something I imagine myself, and that is why I just said what I did, but in fact I don't know what I could do and I don't intend to worry about it until I have to. But if I had to give an answer one way or the other in the abstract, that would be it.'

'But how would laws ever be made if people didn't suppose situations? I thought it was one's duty as a citizen to argue about these things.'

'Good laws are based on facts, not on principles. Life would be much easier and freer if there weren't so many so-called good citizens minding other people's business, or even fictitious business, and making them vote for laws they can't possibly understand.'

He said this rather shortly and apparently regretted it.

'What I really mean', he went on less vehemently, 'is that laws are purely social things. You have to have them or you couldn't maintain society. But they have no importance in relation to the ultimate value of a person. A criminal may go to prison, but no one can have the right to consider him, as it were, a non-person. It's the sanctimoniousness of good citizens that annoys me. They try to make absolute morality out of what is just practical politics. But to get back to hypotheses, don't they tend to substitute the possible for the actual?'

'Surely you must reckon with possibilities?'

'With probabilities up to a point, I agree, but possibilities are only those things which either didn't happen or might not happen. They're too vague to worry about.'

'What about our own choice in the matter?'

'What choice?' He looked up as if genuinely astonished. 'I don't see that we have any choice in what happens. Mind you, I don't believe in hopeless predestination, either. We do more than just be happened to, and I've no use for the supposedly oriental idea that you should just sit there and take it. I wonder if in fact orientals believe quite that. But the notion that everything is just ready to happen and then something called our free-will gives us a little shove this way or that seems to me quite gratuitous. I even suspect it's demonstrably not so. Of course, as long as you believe in absolute Evil you have to invent free-will so that you can blame people for preferring the Devil and so put yourself in the right with God. It's just arrogance and narrow-mindedness, and I doubt whether it's greatly appreciated. Do you think people actually say "Now I know your plans I'll think them over, but if they don't suit me I'll go my own way"? It's almost blasphemous to suggest it. And if they don't believe in God all they can have is the conceit that they are doing what they want, which is a tautology.'

'Do you believe in God?' I asked, wishing I hadn't.

'No,' he answered in a matter-of-fact way. 'I think I know him a little. I used the word "believe" because it's the usual one, but I think it gives rise to terrible misunderstanding. To me it's something I know – that's the wrong word, too – something I am aware of like I'm aware of being, stronger than knowing. It's a question of poetry again, nothing that I can explain rationally. So-called proofs of God and all the talk and writing that goes on are really self-contradictory, though the best of it has a certain poetry that I understand. In the long run, though, I have just to sit quietly and stop arguing, as you sit under a summer sky. Then I can consent to everything without any violence to my reason.'

He turned and gave me a quick glance, and there was a certain gaiety in his eyes that told me that this was an idea which pleased him.

'Yes,' he went on emphatically as he gazed out into space again, 'that's the best word I can find: consent. I don't mean it in the permissive sense. I don't feel "if that's the way things are I'd better agree to it". I feel that I can live along with everything else. "There's the world," I say, "and there's me in the middle of it, and the more I can know about it and the more I can be myself at the same time the happier I am." Do you see what I mean?'

'I think so,' I said. 'You mean you take part in it all.'

'That's it. What I know about that's outside me I accept inside. I go along with it. But this has nothing to do with passiveness or withdrawal; on the contrary, it implies a conscious act of being aware – as aware as possible. I think that sometimes this is what is meant when people talk about free-will. "Thy will be done" is desire, not resignation. And of course there is an alternative attitude: that of not being aware and not accepting, of hustling events or complaining about them. But I still don't think that anyone has an option between the two. Everyone in fact does a little of each.'

'It certainly sounds like a doctrine of perfection,' I said.

'It's not a doctrine,' he retorted. 'It's just the way I happen to see things. A doctrine of perfection is bound to lead to grief, because no one can imitate God. As long as we have this dualism about us there's bound to be conflict between the excitable electro-chemical device on the one hand and the unique being on the other, and between the soloist and the second from the left in the back row of the choir. The great thing is to make the best of it both ways. Why science and religion must always be at logger-heads is quite beyond me. Jealousy, aided by moral rectitude and nourished on the fruit of that awful tree.'

The cloud was beginning to thin. It drifted across us in patches, and each dark patch became successively smaller and the light ones lighter. My companion sighed and said wistfully:

'It's funny that I should be so certain that what I've been telling you is true and yet I cannot let my own life follow it. I suppose my brain has been too cluttered up with other people's views. It's like having your eyesight but being kept in a dark room. But perhaps you could manage better, starting from the beginning again. If you remember that the most important thing about you is that you are, that it is your own being that sees beauty and the reflection of God, you'll be able to live with life instead of arguing with it. But don't let people bribe and blackmail you into parting with yourself. They'll try. They'll put smoke into your fresh air and they'll try to put a ceiling over you instead of the sky. Don't let them. There will always be enough who'll leave you in peace.'

The last of the cloud blew away and, like a veil removed, revealed that the dull world we had last looked at was now an array of colour under a cloudless sky made golden by the morning sun. The storm had rolled away behind us, out of sight on the other side of the mountain. The view filled me with a new zest. I wanted to play with the world, to walk about it and handle it. There it was below me, limitless fields and mountains and beyond them seas and deserts, rivers and forests, villages and cities. I had no sense of possession, no wish to own them or rule them or change them. I wanted to walk all over the world unnoticed, observing and enjoying but not interfering. But first I must get down.

I got to my feet with something of a scramble as my companion did the same more composedly. I found him looking at me with a warmth that he had not shown before.

'Yes, we'd better move,' he said, and then, as if he had been reading my thoughts: 'It's a wonderful sight, isn't it? Don't you feel you would like it all for your private garden, to come and go in as you like? The rain has washed it clean and the sun has warmed it, and you could stroll in it for the rest of your life.'

Until now he had walked ahead of me, but now he waited for me to come up with him and walked beside me.

'But I'm afraid you can't,' he said. 'Even Noah had to remember that the world is a practical affair, full of laws and problems and the need to be busy. Once you get down there you'll be more strolled upon than strolling.'

I must have unconsciously shown disappointment or disbelief, for he went on:

'You can't get away from the fact that you've got to eat and keep warm and get on with other people in order to survive. It's no use thinking of the hermit's life. That's just running away. Most of the mystical ways involve diminishing life as far as possible, which means getting as near death as you can, and I think you've had enough of that. You'll die in due course, and meanwhile the problem is to live. You'll find you have a past, which will tie you down somewhat; and you'll start again at one particular time and place, which will also limit your freedom. Don't, incidentally imagine you have any freedom apart from your partial detachment from reason; it's a word that's generally used as a protest against the obvious fact that it's at best a very relative affair. Imagine all the things that will happen to you without any by-your-leave, yet you'll have to respond to them somehow or other. That's what life is, and it's into life that you are very shortly going to be decanted. But remember that it is *you* who have been inserted into this enormous mechanism. And the mechanism works. Most of the fun is in finding out how it works, but don't worry about why it works or complain that it does work in that particular way. There's nothing you can do to change it.'

'It can't be improved?'

'No, it can't,' he answered with some vehemence. 'It changes the whole time, and some people think they can see an improvement, but it's only from their limited point of view. You'll find plenty of zealous reformers, but beware of them. You may even think one day that you've made an improvement. Put it aside. You may be an agent of some change but never either an innovator or an improver. If there is ever Paradise on earth, which I don't anticipate, it won't be due to local reforms. The only paradise I can imagine is one where everyone lives quietly, paying no more heed than they have to the works of Man and as much as they can to those of God, and, above all, respecting each other's idiocy.'

He glanced around, then stopped in his tracks and pointed eagerly to a rainbow curved over the summit we had left.

'I don't seem to be able to get away from Noah,' he said. 'In fact I'm no longer inclined to believe he was only a legend. Do you remember that the sign God gave him that there would not be another flood was a rainbow? I particularly like that part of the story. The token was beautiful and intangible. Men were licensed to be poets by it as well as to live on dry land.'

We watched the rainbow for a while and then resumed our march downward.

'Always look at rainbows,' he said after we had gone some way. 'Don't analyse them into light and raindrops. That was interesting when it was first realised, but it isn't now. Just look and realise how beautiful they are, especially the ones that are made by little clouds passing over the moon just before dawn.'

We continued downwards in silence until after a few minutes we had to climb again to cross an intermediary ridge which lay between our mountain and the valley. We went slowly and often halted, because my ankle was only just able to support me, but we said no more until we reached the top of the ridge. There we let ourselves drop in a clump of heather. I took my left boot off and uselessly fingered the swelling, feeling that I had gone as far as I could. My companion lay with his chin cupped in his hands and scanned the long easy slope ahead which led straight to the valley and the road.

Soon he said:

'Look down there. That must be a search-party. Somebody must have noticed you yesterday after all, though they seem to have taken their time worrying about you.'

Far away on the brown beginning of the hill-side could be seen a line of five men. I could just see that they swayed slightly from side to side, and this showed that they were climbing towards us. They had nearly two miles to come.

'In that case there's no need for me to stay,' he went on. 'I've a long way to go, and in the opposite direction. If I were you, I'd wait here. They'll be able to help you down between them and save that ankle of yours. You won't think I'm deserting you?'

I was so taken aback that I could not answer at once. His presence was the only furniture I had in my new condition, and the patient persistent voice had become for me what the sound of the breakers is to a dweller on the seashore. Even when he was not talking there was an undertone of suspended words, like the faint swishing of the lapping wavelets on a calm day. If he went, the whole of my experience would go with him. It is difficult to recall this predicament fully in retrospect, but it was as if I was destined to lose my memory again and with it my existence in the world.

My first reasonable thought was that he had said 'in the

opposite direction' and that this held only a little glen which led to the top of the next ridge to the west and over that to the endless sea of hills I had been looking at last night. The only sign of human dwelling I had seen there was the little group of buildings that had been lit up briefly as the sun went down, and that must have been nearly ten miles away by foot. If he were going there, surely there would be a road skirting nearer to the south? It struck me for a moment that he might be a fugitive, but it was obvious that in that case he would not have risked his safety for so long escorting a lame man back to what would be the opposite of safety to him. Besides, it was impossible to attribute anything so devious and turbulent to someone who in every way conveyed simplicity and calm. Yet I could not bring myself to ask him where he was going. The way in which he had said, 'I've a long way to go, and in the opposite direction', with a little pause for clarity where I have put the comma, made it clear that this was sufficient information for my needs and an adequate explanation.

'I don't really know,' I said at last. 'It seems odd, after all these hours, that you should suddenly fade away, here and now, in the middle of nowhere. After all, you're the only thing I remember about myself.'

He smiled and said:

'I don't think that will last long, and the fact is I cannot be of any use to you now. You've got to get down again' — he hesitated and smiled — 'to plant your vineyard and drink your wine, and those people will manage very well without me. I've nothing particular to say to them and I must go as soon as I can.'

He was on his feet, and I noticed that he took care to stand just below the sky-line, out of sight of the approaching searchers. Again I wondered whether he was afraid of them and again I saw how absurd the thought was. More probably he was anxious to avoid embarrassment.

'At least I should say thank you,' I said, 'though it sounds rather weak.'

'No, don't on any account do that,' he said sharply. 'To say thank you is a civility which is useful to bridge the gulf between people, to reassure them. But I don't need reassuring, and we haven't built any gulf between us. Perhaps that's because I've done all the talking and we haven't been able to argue. Do not try to feel gratitude, which has all the vices of a promisory note. Just accept everyone for what he is, and when he does you good be glad, and when he does you harm be sorry. But neither tie yourself to him with gratitude nor make yourself responsible for him by judgement.'

He held out his hand, but as if he neither wanted nor had the habit of it. I did the same, as awkwardly, and our handshake was perfunctory and uncommunicative.

'Anyway,' he said, 'I hope you remember to look at rainbows.'

And he walked quickly away.

He was out of sight at once round a shoulder, and I turned my attention to the distant search-party. The air was quite clear, as it often is in the hills after rain, and after I had been looking for a while I thought that I could make out that one of the men was in blue police uniform. Certainly his clothes were darker than the others, and he had a squared-off line to the top of his head which made a marked contrast to the blurred finish of his neighbours. Again I thought: Can it be true that he's on the run? And this time I slipped backwards down the slope and round the corner where he had gone. But he was already far away. I called as loudly as I dared and he heard me, but he only turned, waved, and continued on his way, moving fast. There was nothing I could do to warn or reassure him, so I climbed back to the ridge and resolved that I would not say I had seen him.

I've always wondered who he was, but I've never found out. He just appeared and disappeared.